Love on the Night Shift

Acclaim for Radclyffe's Fiction

"*Dangerous Waters* is a bumpy ride through a devastating time with powerful events and resolute characters. Radclyffe gives us the strong, dedicated women we love to read in a story that keeps us turning pages until the end."—*Lambda Literary Review*

"Radclyffe's *Dangerous Waters* has the feel of a tense television drama, as the narrative interchanges between hurricane trackers and first responders. Sawyer and Dara butt heads in the beginning as each moves for some level of control during the storm's approach, and the interference of a lovely television reporter adds an engaging love triangle threat to the sexual tension brewing between them."—*RT Book Reviews*

"*Love After Hours*, the fourth in Radclyffe's Rivers Community series, evokes the sense of a continuing drama as Gina and Carrie's slow-burning romance intertwines with details of other Rivers residents. They become part of a greater picture where friends and family support each other in personal and recreational endeavors. Vivid settings and characters draw in the reader…"—*RT Book Reviews*

Secret Hearts "delivers exactly what it says on the tin: poignant story, sweet romance, great characters, chemistry and hot sex scenes. Radclyffe knows how to pen a good lesbian romance."—*LezReviewBooks Blog*

Wild Shores "will hook you early. Radclyffe weaves a chance encounter into all-out steamy romance. These strong, dynamic women have great conversations, and fantastic chemistry."—*The Romantic Reader Blog*

In **2016 RWA/OCC Book Buyers Best award winner for suspense and mystery with romantic elements** *Price of Honor* "Radclyffe is master of the action-thriller series…The old familiar characters are there, but enough new blood is introduced to give it a fresh feel and open new avenues for intrigue."—*Curve Magazine*

In *Prescription for Love* "Radclyffe populates her small town with colorful characters, among the most memorable being Flann's little sister, Margie, and Abby's 15-year-old trans son, Blake…This romantic drama has plenty of heart and soul."—*Publishers Weekly*

2013 RWA/New England Bean Pot award winner for contemporary romance *Crossroads* "will draw the reader in and make her heart ache, willing the two main characters to find love and a life together. It's a story that lingers long after coming to 'the end.'"—*Lambda Literary*

In **2012 RWA/FTHRW Lories and RWA HODRW Aspen Gold award winner** *Firestorm* "Radclyffe brings another hot lesbian romance for her readers."—*The Lesbrary*

Foreword Review Book of the Year finalist and IPPY silver medalist *Trauma Alert* "is hard to put down and it will sizzle in the reader's hands. The characters are hot, the sex scenes explicit and explosive, and the book is moved along by an interesting plot with well drawn secondary characters. The real star of this show is the attraction between the two characters, both of whom resist and then fall head over heels."—*Lambda Literary Reviews*

Lambda Literary Award Finalist *Best Lesbian Romance 2010* features "stories [that] are diverse in tone, style, and subject, making for more variety than in many, similar anthologies…well written, each containing a satisfying, surprising twist. Best Lesbian Romance series editor Radclyffe has assembled a respectable crop of 17 authors for this year's offering."—*Curve Magazine*

2010 Prism award winner and ForeWord Review Book of the Year Award finalist *Secrets in the Stone* is "so powerfully [written] that the worlds of these three women shimmer between reality and dreams…A strong, must read novel that will linger in the minds of readers long after the last page is turned."—*Just About Write*

In **Benjamin Franklin Award finalist** *Desire by Starlight* "Radclyffe writes romance with such heart and her down-to-earth characters not only come to life but leap off the page until you feel like you know them. What Jenna and Gard feel for each other is not only a spark but an inferno and, as a reader, you will be washed away in this tumultuous romance until you can do nothing but succumb to it."—*Queer Magazine Online*

Lambda Literary Award winner *Stolen Moments* "is a collection of steamy stories about women who just couldn't wait. It's sex when desire overrides reason, and it's incredibly hot!"—*On Our Backs*

Lambda Literary Award winner *Distant Shores, Silent Thunder* "weaves an intricate tapestry about passion and commitment between lovers. The story explores the fragile nature of trust and the sanctuary provided by loving relationships."—*Sapphic Reader*

Lambda Literary Award Finalist *Justice Served* delivers a "crisply written, fast-paced story with twists and turns and keeps us guessing until the final explosive ending."—*Independent Gay Writer*

Lambda Literary Award finalist *Turn Back Time* "is filled with wonderful love scenes, which are both tender and hot."—*MegaScene*

Applause for L.L. Raand's Midnight Hunters Series

The Midnight Hunt
RWA 2012 VCRW Laurel Wreath winner *Blood Hunt*
Night Hunt
The Lone Hunt

"Raand has built a complex world inhabited by werewolves, vampires, and other paranormal beings…Raand has given her readers a complex plot filled with wonderful characters as well as insight into the hierarchy of Sylvan's pack and vampire clans. There are many plot twists and turns, as well as erotic sex scenes in this riveting novel that keep the pages flying until its satisfying conclusion."—*Just About Write*

"Once again, I am amazed at the storytelling ability of L.L. Raand aka Radclyffe. In *Blood Hunt*, she mixes high levels of sheer eroticism that will leave you squirming in your seat with an impeccable multi-character storyline all streaming together to form one great read." —*Queer Magazine Online*

"*The Midnight Hunt* has a gripping story to tell, and while there are also some truly erotic sex scenes, the story always takes precedence. This is a great read which is not easily put down nor easily forgotten."—*Just About Write*

"Are you sick of the same old hetero vampire/werewolf story plastered in every bookstore and at every movie theater? Well, I've got the cure to your werewolf fever. *The Midnight Hunt* is first in, what I hope is, a long-running series of fantasy erotica for L.L. Raand (aka Radclyffe)."—*Queer Magazine Online*

"Any reader familiar with Radclyffe's writing will recognize the author's style within *The Midnight Hunt*, yet at the same time it is most definitely a new direction. The author delivers an excellent story here, one that is engrossing from the very beginning. Raand has pieced together an intricate world, and provided just enough details for the reader to become enmeshed in the new world. The action moves quickly throughout the book and it's hard to put down."—*Three Dollar Bill Reviews*

By Radclyffe

The Provincetown Tales

Safe Harbor

Beyond the Breakwater

Distant Shores, Silent Thunder

Storms of Change

Winds of Fortune

Returning Tides

Sheltering Dunes

PMC Hospitals Romances

Passion's Bright Fury (prequel)

Fated Love

Night Call

Crossroads

Passionate Rivals

Rivers Community Romances

Against Doctor's Orders

Prescription for Love

Love on Call

Love After Hours

Love to the Rescue

Love on the Night Shift

Honor Series

Above All, Honor

Honor Bound

Love & Honor

Honor Guards

Honor Reclaimed

Honor Under Siege

Word of Honor

Oath of Honor

(First Responders)

Code of Honor

Price of Honor

Cost of Honor

Justice Series

A Matter of Trust (prequel)

Shield of Justice

In Pursuit of Justice

Justice in the Shadows

Justice Served

Justice for All

First Responders Novels

Trauma Alert	Wild Shores
Firestorm	Heart Stop
Taking Fire	Dangerous Waters

Romances

Innocent Hearts	When Dreams Tremble
Promising Hearts	The Lonely Hearts Club
Love's Melody Lost	Secrets in the Stone
Love's Tender Warriors	Desire by Starlight
Tomorrow's Promise	Homestead
Love's Masquerade	The Color of Love
shadowland	Secret Hearts
Turn Back Time	

Short Fiction

Collected Stories by Radclyffe
Erotic Interludes: *Change Of Pace*
Radical Encounters

Stacia Seaman and Radclyffe, eds.:
Erotic Interludes Vol. 2–5
Romantic Interludes Vol. 1–2
Breathless: *Tales of Celebration*
Women of the Dark Streets
Amor and More: Love Everafter
Myth & Magic: Queer Fairy Tales

Writing As L.L. Raand
Midnight Hunters

The Midnight Hunt	The Lone Hunt
Blood Hunt	The Magic Hunt
Night Hunt	Shadow Hunt

Visit us at www.boldstrokesbooks.com

LOVE ON THE NIGHT SHIFT

by

RADCLY*f*FE

2020

LOVE ON THE NIGHT SHIFT

ISBN 13: 978-1-63555-668-1

This Trade Paperback Original Is Published By
Bold Strokes Books, Inc.
P.O. Box 249
Valley Falls, NY 12185

First Edition: May 2020

Credits

Editors: Ruth Sternglantz and Stacia Seaman
Production Design: Stacia Seaman
Cover Design by Tammy Seidick

Acknowledgments

Anyone who's ever worked in a hospital recognizes the sense of community created in the face of life-and-death crises, human suffering and survival, loss and triumph. Rivalries, loyalties, and yes, romances are all part of the small-town atmosphere that emerges in this often-indescribable world inside a hospital. My intention in this series has always been to show the Rivers (hospital) as a community within a community. There's not much difference between a rural hospital and a big-city tertiary care center when you're the one alone in the middle of the night with a decision to make. *Love on the Night Shift* holds a special place for me in my medical romance series, as I always found night call one of the hardest parts of being on call. The camaraderie and support of one's colleagues is often what gets you through the dark.

I hope you all enjoy this little glimpse of the ER after hours.

Many thanks go to: senior editor Sandy Lowe for too many things to name—professionally and personally; my longtime, hopefully not long-suffering, editor Ruth Sternglantz for making each book a better read; editor Stacia Seaman for consummate skill and hard work; and my good friends and first readers Paula and Eva for encouragement, insights, and suggestions that always improve the final story.

And as always, thanks to Lee for the dream. *Amo te.*

Radclyffe, 2020

To Lee

CHAPTER ONE

Blaise juggled her shoulder bag, her navy blue windbreaker with *Coach* in yellow script on the chest, and a take-out cup of coffee—thank God the café stayed open until eleven p.m. on Friday and Saturday nights—while she worked the combination lock on her locker with her free hand. If she hurried, she might still have time for a sandwich and, okay, yes, a piece of pie, before shift change. Of course, she missed the second digit while trying to steady the stupid thing and turn it at the same time and had to put everything down on the bench behind her and start over again.

Haste makes waste. Her mother's voice chided her with one of the fifty million sayings she'd heard at least that many times growing up. Her mother had had one for just about every occasion, including the one she'd uttered the last time they'd spoken.

You've made your bed, now you'll have to lie in it.

Thank you, Mom, for stating the obvious. Again.

She hadn't actually said that. By then even trying to have a conversation was pointless. She'd just grabbed her backpack and carried it across the village from the south side to the north side and into the big white hotel on the corner of Main and Union.

And now was *so* not the time to replay old, old news. If she hadn't just come from her own mother-daughter encounter—which she prayed to all that was holy she'd handled better than *her* mother had—she wouldn't be resurrecting memories long gone and buried. She blew an errant strand of hair out of her eyes, told herself it would be a long night if she planned on being aggravated for the next ten hours, and swiftly dialed in the combination. She tossed the bag and jacket on the hook inside her locker, grabbed her stethoscope from the top shelf, and slid her phone into the back pocket of her scrubs.

Time check: 10:40 p.m.

Nope. Too late. She squelched the frustration, hunger pangs, and visions of pie. Maybe later if things were quiet. Ha. Like Friday nights were ever quiet.

The door from the corridor thudded open, and Blaise glanced over her shoulder. She expected another member of the night shift, but Abby Remy dropped down on the bench next to her instead.

"It's never a good sign when you're here at this hour," Blaise said.

"I hadn't planned on being here either," Abby said, running both hands through her blond hair and shaking out some of the crimps in the shoulder length waves, "but Davis called in at the last minute. Penny is in labor, and it's their first, so he's way too distracted to work until she's closer to delivery."

"Good for them. First times ought to be extra-special," Blaise said, even knowing that wasn't always true. She leaned back against the wall of narrow gray lockers and sipped her coffee. "I'm surprised you didn't get one of the day shift people to stay on. Hardly seems right for the chief to pick up the slack."

"You know, I spend so much time behind my desk these days that I don't actually mind grabbing a few charts," Abby said with a shrug.

"Don't let that get around or you'll be filling in more often," Blaise teased. Abby never appeared stressed, fatigued, or out of sorts. Even in the midst of an ER crisis, Abby was the coolest doctor Blaise had ever worked with—well, at least *one* of the coolest. Abby's wife Flann might give Abby a run for her money in that area, except Flann was a surgeon, and like all her breed, tended to be edgy and impatient with lesser mortals. Only her natural charm and stellar skills made Flann a favorite to everyone in the ER.

"I'll remember that." Abby laughed. "You're running a little behind, aren't you? I thought you usually had an early dinner—or late lunch, I suppose it would be for you night owls—before you started."

"I do." Blaise patted the protein bar she'd stuck in the top pocket of her scrub top on her way out of the kitchen earlier. "But tonight I'll have to make do with this until I get a break. Taylor decided to negotiate her weekend activities right before I was ready to leave the house."

Abby grinned. "Smart tactic. She probably figured you'd be rushed and cave quickly."

"No doubt." Blaise sighed. "I have regretted more than once teaching her the very word *negotiate*, which seemed innocent enough when we were discussing eating peas. Now it comes back to haunt me on a regular basis when it comes to teen activities after dark."

"Let me guess," Abby said. "This would have to do with the party at the Homestead following the night game tomorrow."

"Is every kid in the school going to this thing?" Blaise said.

"Well, to hear Blake talk, absolutely. Since Bill is home from Afghanistan for good now and assistant coaching again, it's kind of a double celebration."

"At least we know if they're at the Homestead, they won't be getting into trouble," Blaise said.

"It's after the after-after-party I'm worried about," Abby muttered. "You know how these things morph and spread out like an amoeba."

Blaise grimaced. "Nice image, but yes. I'm sure you said what I said—straight home when the party at the Riverses' breaks up. No changing locations."

"I did better than that—I'm going."

Blaise snorted. "I bet that went over well."

Abby gave her a look. "Well, someone has to help out with half the junior and senior classes showing up. I volunteered me and Flann."

"Did you get around to who's driving the kids?" Blaise asked.

"Absolutely, and it isn't going to be Mark Chavez."

"We made it that far too," Blaise said. "Mark drives just like his brother Phil did, and I'm afraid we're going to have him in here some night too. Taylor knows she's never to ride with him. Day or night."

Abby's expression turned grim. "I'm not sure Mark doesn't drive that way just to prove that he's as big a man as his older brother, who was probably trying to prove he was every bit as tough as their father."

"How about we divide and conquer," Blaise said. "I'm off tomorrow night—I can drive them to the game. You've got party detail."

"Sounds fair to me. Although you might want to swing by the party yourself—Ida's baking."

"That's all I needed to hear," Blaise said as she and Abby walked down the hall toward the ER. "Although Taylor will die of mortification if she sees me there."

"Gotta love teenagers." Abby rolled her eyes.

"How's Blake doing? He's made so many friends this summer—it's hard to remember this is a new school for him."

Abby was silent for a moment, but Blaise wasn't worried that she'd offended her—they'd gotten to be good friends since Abby had taken over as chief in the ER, being about the same age and with teenagers who they'd raised alone for a long time. Of course Abby wasn't alone now, and Blaise…well, her life was the way she wanted it.

She got that Abby was protective of Blake, as any parent would be whose child had to struggle against prejudice and ignorance. Even so, Abby let Blake make his own way in the quagmire of drama and angst and shifting friendships that seemed to typify teen life, which took more courage than Blaise believed she might have in the same circumstances. She'd thought about gender identity issues when Taylor started growing up, in a sort of theoretical way, letting Taylor know it was okay to talk about how she was feeling if she ever had questions or uncertainty. She'd been clear—she hoped—that no matter how Taylor identified, she would be loved. But she'd never before seriously considered what it might be like if one day Taylor told her she identified as trans. Since Abby and Blake had become part of the community, and Abby had become a friend, Blaise thought about gender in a much more personal way.

Blaise touched Abby's arm. "You don't have to tell me if it's private."

"No, it's not that," Abby said. "He hasn't said anything. He might not, of course, unless something really serious comes up. Having friends like Margie and Taylor and Dave will really help him if…" She sighed. "He's always been strong. I wasn't certain moving up here would be the right thing to do, taking him out of Manhattan to…here."

Blaise laughed at Abby's tone. "You mean *here*, as in the middle of nowhere?"

Abby smiled and pushed the big square button on the wall that opened the automatic doors to the ER-Trauma wing. "It isn't, you know. The middle of nowhere. In a lot of ways it's the middle of everywhere. Big cities are more the anonymous places that could be anywhere. This—this land, this life—has history. People can sink roots."

"Oh my God," Blaise said, "you've been converted. Next thing you know, you'll be living on a farm and raising goats."

Abby smiled. "Well, you know, we will have fifteen acres, and there's a nice big barn already there. And look who's talking—you're a local, right?"

Blaise nodded. "True enough. But I live in the village and I don't have any livestock."

"I don't think you've ever mentioned it," Abby said as they reached the central nurses' station. "Ever lived anywhere else?"

"Not really," Blaise said. Six months in New York City hardly counted and weren't worth mentioning—or remembering. "It's almost eleven, Abby. You should go home."

"I will. I just want to be sure there's no loose ends before Mari takes over."

Blaise glanced at the intake board on the wall which had until recently been a whiteboard that the charge nurses updated with colored markers, but which, following the new expansion, had morphed into a digital display. She hadn't liked it at first, and after one of the PAs rightly dubbed it the train station board, she realized why. The modern ER-Trauma wing was state of the art but had lost some of the charm inherent in the original Rivers hospital building. Still, she couldn't argue with having everything she needed when a critical case arrived. At the moment, only four patients occupied the board, listed by cubicle number, name, provisional diagnosis, and pending tests or consults. She scanned the list on autopilot until she reached the last entry, and for just a second, her brain stuttered to a standstill.

The last patient, whose name she recognized—a common occurrence in their small community—was waiting for a surgical consult. The name of the surgeon she recognized too, and the jolt of shock sent her heart racing. "Who's that up there on the board for room eleven?"

Abby gave her a quizzical expression. "Wilbur Hopkins? He's a sixty-two-year-old white male complaining of a cold foot. We're waiting—"

"No, not Wilbur. I know Wilbur—I went to high school with his youngest." Hearing the edge in her voice, Blaise took a breath to dispel some of the tightness in her chest. "The surgeon. McClure. We don't have a McClure."

"Oh," Abby said. "We do now. McClure just started this afternoon and, of course, like all newbies, got first call."

"I didn't know there were new residents starting this time of year," Blaise said, because that's what it had to be, right? Just a coincidence. Coincidences happened all the time.

"Oh, sorry, I wasn't clear. No, Grady's staff, not a resident. The state took since July to process all the paperwork."

"Grady McClure." The tangle of nerves in Blaise's midsection unknotted but left her slightly nauseous. "Where's he from?"

"She—not he. Flann knew her from training in Baltimore. She was really happy to snag her."

"I can just imagine." Blaise turned away from the board as if that might magically make the *McClure* in red block letters disappear too. She was way past being rattled by ghosts. "I better let Sean know I'm here."

"I hear you!" Sean Durkee, the evening charge nurse, came around the corner. Tall, ginger-haired, and still as fit at forty as he had been when he'd been the star center who'd led the high school basketball team to the state championships, he sported his usual good-natured grin. "Hey, Blaise, let me know when you're ready for report."

"You two go ahead," Abby said. "I'll go find Mari and let her know what's happening."

"I just saw her headed to the conference room," Sean said.

Blaise forced a smile and grabbed the chart on the patient in one and motioned to Sean. "Ready when you are."

"Not all that much doing tonight."

Blaise kept her smile in place. If only that was true.

Grady ran the ultrasound probe over the top of Wilbur Hopkins's right foot for the third time, trying to convince herself she heard a pulse. There might've been a whisper of something running through the posterior tibial vessel, but his cold dusky foot was a pretty good indicator that not much blood was getting down there. She moved up and listened again around the back of his knee and then the inner aspect of his thigh. Certain, she straightened and rested the probe back on top of the portable ultrasound machine. "Mr. Hopkins—"

"You can call me Wilbur, Doc," the bewhiskered man said with a smile that had probably turned a lot of hearts in his younger days. Maybe still did despite the slight sagging of his cheeks and the hint of a belly beneath the faded green T-shirt. The square outline of a cigarette pack in the chest pocket of his T-shirt accounted for the huskiness in his voice, and almost certainly for the lack of blood flow to his leg.

"Okay, Wilbur," Grady said. "You've got a blockage in the artery to your leg and it needs to get opened up."

"You can do it with one of those balloon things, right?"

Grady waggled her hand. "Maybe. It depends on where the blockage is, how old it is, what the vessels look like—"

"That's a whole lotta maybes and depends." He didn't sound angry, just resigned. "What's your best guess?"

"I'd rather not have to guess. That's why we need some special X-rays. I'm going to make some calls so we can do that and get a better look at things. We'll call in another surgeon too, depending on what the X-rays show."

"I guess I better call my wife," Wilbur said good-naturedly.

"One of us can do that if you want," Grady said, "but let's wait just a bit until I get a good look at what's going on inside."

"Well then, let's do it. Tomorrow?"

"Tonight."

Wilbur pressed his lips together, his smile disappearing. "I don't suppose I could step outside for a while. While, you know, you get everything ready."

Grady narrowed her eyes. "Step outside to look at the moon or to have a smoke?"

His sweet grin flashed again. "I never *have* been much of a stargazer."

"I can't let you do it," Grady said. "It could make things worse, and I don't want you to lose your foot."

"That could happen?"

"It might."

"I can't drive a truck without my foot." Wilbur sucked in a breath. "If I can't drive, I can't make a living."

"That's why we're not going to take any chances, and we're not waiting until tomorrow."

"All right then," he said, letting out a long breath. "I guess you ought to get to it."

Grady laughed. "Good idea."

She turned, grabbed the white, yellow, and green striped curtain, and whipped it aside. The woman standing an inch away was about her height and flinched as their eyes met.

"Whoa! Sorry," Grady blurted. The startled eyes staring back at her were an unusual hue of gray-blue that reminded her of the Pacific in winter. Not cold, the way you might expect, but depthless, as if all the secrets in the world were hiding below the surface.

"Who—" The blonde with the storm-blue eyes continued to stare at her. "Are you the surgeon?"

"That's me." Grady grinned and held out a hand. "I'm Grady McClure."

When she got no response from the woman wearing navy blue scrub pants and a scrub shirt with tiny iridescent fish all over it, she tapped the plastic name tag pinned to the lab coat she'd been given after her nickel tour of the hospital eight hours earlier. "Dr. Grady McClure. Says so right here."

Still no smile. Grady tilted her head, trying to determine if the fish were all going in one direction or not. "That is one seriously strange scrub shirt."

"I'm Blaise Richelieu," the woman said abruptly, as if she'd just now noticed Grady and wasn't all that happy to see her. "Charge nurse on the night shift. What do you need?"

Grady felt her eyebrows rise. Something about the cold shoulder turned in her direction for no good reason irritated her more than it should have. "Well, that's a loaded question."

Richelieu's lips pressed together. No-nonsense attitude. No sense of humor, either.

"I was referring to your patient, Doctor," Blaise said in a voice as icy as her now chilly expression.

"Okay." All business it would be, then, since friendly was definitely off the table. Grady strode toward the nurses' station. Blaise kept pace with her. "I need to know how to reach someone in interventional radiology. I need an arteriogram."

"Tonight?" Blaise asked.

"Yes, tonight." Grady leaned against the counter. "Is that going to be a problem?"

Blaise swallowed back the retort forming on her lips. Grady McClure, all tousled black hair and unholy blue eyes and angular planes in a face too damn handsome for words, came on strong and was probably used to getting what she wanted on the basis of sexy good looks alone. Not very generous of her, Blaise admitted, but she wasn't used to being so off-balance. And *that* was not acceptable. She had a patient to think about. "No, of course not. Well, it might be a bit of a problem if Mary Anne Okonsky's on call. Because she does not like getting out of bed in the middle of the night."

"Who does?" McClure said with a devil's smile.

Blaise gritted her teeth. Was everything that came out of her mouth innuendo? She probably got a lot of mileage out of her sexy, teasing grin. That wasn't. Sexy *or* charming. Most definitely not. Not as far as Blaise was concerned.

"Some people choose specialties so they won't have to get out of bed in the middle of the night," Blaise said. "So I understand."

"Well, tonight is not that night," Grady said with a careless shrug. "You want me to deliver the bad news? I just need to know who to call."

"No, I'll handle it. You can take care of the chart…or whatever." Blaise turned away and slowed when she sensed Grady right behind her. "Something else?"

"I need a cup of coffee. Can I get you one?" Grady asked.

Blaise schooled her expression to hide her surprise. Doctors and nurses didn't have the kind of hierarchical division that had existed even ten years before, but they weren't always easy colleagues, either. "I just had one, thanks."

"Well," Grady said, "I'll be in the…" She shrugged, grinned again. "I'm not exactly sure where I'll be. Where do you hide the coffee down here?"

Blaise blew out a breath and pointed down the hallway to her right. "Break room is down there. I can't vouch for how old the coffee is."

"Coffee is never too old, kind of like women that way."

Blaise spun on her heel. Way, way too charming to be anything but trouble. Luckily, she'd been cured of susceptibility to sexy and charming a long time ago.

Chapter Two

The ER break room was nicer than a lot Grady had seen. The furniture wasn't twenty years old, the floor had yet to acquire layers of scuff marks and ground-in particles of indeterminate origin, and the appliances didn't look like they'd been pilfered from a rummage sale. But then, the whole ER-Trauma complex was new. State of the art. Somebody had put a lot of bucks into it. That's part of the reason she'd come. That and the fact she wasn't likely to be the *other* McClure here, the way she might be in a lot of places. The coffee, though, looked a little more lethal than she wanted to chance. She looked in the usual places and found the premeasured packets of generic coffee and filters and, after running hot water in the pot to dislodge the sludge, put a fresh batch on to brew. While she went through the motions on autopilot, she considered Blaise Richelieu.

Blaise bugged her, or rather, the clear No Trespassing sign planted firmly in Blaise's metaphorical front yard bugged her. Grady wasn't used to keep-off messages. She usually had no trouble connecting with people, male or female. Maybe she put a little extra effort into the women—that just came naturally—but she hadn't even had a chance to open her mouth before Richelieu froze her out. Now, if she'd been meeting someone new in a different ER six months ago, she might suspect her reputation—deserved or not—had preceded her, but hell, no one here knew her. No one had a chance to form any kind of impression…yet. But the icy blonde sure acted like she had a grudge going. The disdain in Blaise Richelieu's eyes bugged the bejesus out of her. What the hell had she done to put the storm clouds in Blaise's eyes?

She'd just finished pouring a cup and was rummaging in the refrigerator for those little take-out containers of half-and-half when someone said over her shoulder, "They're in the bottom drawer on the right."

"Thanks." Grady grabbed a couple and turned around. The dark-haired, dark-eyed woman in the flight suit held out a hand.

"Brody Clark. You must be the new guy."

"Grady McClure." Grady grinned. "It shows, does it?"

"Well, I don't know you and you're on call, which usually spells new guy, and you made a pot of coffee. Doubling down."

"That wasn't my intention. I just wanted to live through the night, and whatever was in the pot looked poisonous."

"I know what you mean. I was planning on making some new stuff myself." Brody ambled over, helped herself to a mug of coffee. "I heard you were starting. Welcome aboard."

"Thanks—it's good to finally get going. I've been cooling my heels all summer waiting for the red tape to get cleared out."

"Where you from?"

"How far back do you mean?"

"You can skip grade school." Brody grinned. "How long is the rest of the story?"

"Not all that long, really." Grady didn't mention it would be longer than either of them had time for if she picked up where the story really started. And she really didn't want to get into the McClure family saga if she didn't have to. "I grew up in Southern California, went to Stanford, came east for med school, trained in Maryland, and here I am."

"Short and sweet."

"Pretty much."

Brody narrowed her eyes. "Maryland, huh? Shock Trauma?"

Grady nodded. "That's the place."

"Huh." Brody hitched a hip against the edge of the round table that sat in the middle of the break room.

Grady's stomach tightened at Brody's speculative expression. *Here it comes.* The question she'd been waiting for—the one she always got before anyone took a good look at her. "What?"

"Maryland Shock Trauma is a big-league center. Now, we're pretty well-positioned here to see a lot of action—rural, sure, but plenty of highways nearby with north-south traffic between Canada and the capital to keep the trauma unit full. Plus, we're the biggest thing for a few hundred miles, which means lots of tertiary transfers. But still, we don't exactly have a national profile. Yet. How'd you end up here?"

"Easy," Grady said, giving the answer that was part truth and part dissemblance. Not the question she'd been expecting. The reprieve was like a chain wrapped tight around her chest suddenly snapping loose. "Flann was a surgery resident when I was a student, and we got to be friends. When I was ready to start looking for a job, I asked her for advice, and she made me an offer I couldn't refuse."

"I'll bet she did." Brody laughed.

"What about you?" Grady pointed to the wings on Brody's sleeve. "How'd *you* end up here?"

"The wings I earned in the Army, but would you believe me if I said I grew up here?"

"You know," Grady said, "I would. I bet fifty percent of the people working in this place grew up here."

"You'd be wrong."

"Really? Because—"

"Ninety percent, more like it."

"Now that I believe." Grady cocked her head. "But you left and came back, sounds like."

"Not what I was planning." Brody looked pensive. "Well, I came back—I guess you could say unexpectedly—when Abigail Remy and Presley Worth, the new CEO, decided to turn this place into a level one trauma center and wanted air evac available."

"To tell you the truth," Grady said, "I mostly came for the view."

Brody laughed. "You'll have plenty of that around here."

"I'll be happy if I'm too busy to notice," Grady said.

Brody gave her a look. "I hope you play softball."

"Huh?"

The break room door opened, interrupting Grady's attempt to decipher the non sequitur. Blaise Richelieu hurried in, her smooth, tanned forehead creased.

Grady straightened. "What?"

"I think you'd better come look at Wilbur Hopkins."

Grady dumped her coffee in the sink, strode to the door, and held it open for Blaise. "He didn't sneak outside for a smoke, did he?"

"No, but now he's complaining of pain in the opposite leg, and I think his toes are dusky."

"Crap." Grady broke into a jog. Blaise kept pace. "When did it start?"

"I checked his vitals right after you left, and he looked fine. I checked on him as soon as he called. It couldn't be more than a few minutes."

"Good thing patients around here get a lot of attention," Grady muttered. Good thing Blaise knew what she was about too. If what she thought was happening was happening, Wilbur was in trouble and even the shortest delay could kill him.

"He's lucky that we're not busy," Blaise said. "But it's Friday night, and we're likely to get hit almost anytime."

"Where's the radiologist?"

"I called her, and she's bitching, but she's on her way."

Grady raised a brow. "Why didn't you have me call? Then she could have bitched at me."

Blaise gave her a long look. "Because it didn't occur to me that you'd want to bother with something as simple as notifying a consult. Do you?"

Grady let out a breath and rounded the corner to the nurses' station. "How long have you been a charge nurse down here?"

"I've worked in the ER since I finished nursing school twelve years ago," Blaise said. "I've been charge on the night shift for seven."

"Well, in that case," Grady said, heading for Wilbur's cubicle, "I don't need you to call me for *anything* unless you think there's something I should see."

Blaise hesitated, working through her surprise and struggling with equal amounts of begrudging respect and reserve. Grady McClure seemed a lot more confident than most brand-new attendings, who pretty much all wanted to prove themselves the minute they landed. A lot of times, that translated into being authoritarian and control freaks. If anything, Grady seemed uncharacteristically laid-back. Maybe that was because she didn't know what she didn't know—or *did* and was covering it up with overconfidence. Something to bear watching. It wouldn't be the first time Blaise had run up against new personnel of all kinds who'd been in over their heads and too proud to admit it.

"Believe me, Dr. McClure, you'll be the first one to know if there's any kind of problem. Otherwise, I'm happy to do whatever is necessary to keep things moving along efficiently."

"Sounds like we're on the same page." Grady quirked a brow. "Finally."

Blaise didn't agree but had no reason to say so.

Grady pulled the curtain back and Blaise followed her to the bedside.

"What's going on, Mr. Hopkins?" Grady lifted the sheets up from the bottom of the bed to expose both lower extremities. The right foot was a deep purple from the ankle down. The left foot, which had been pale but warm a half hour ago, was mottled with patches of light blue and white.

"You're supposed to call me Wilbur, remember," Wilbur said, his voice strained and tight.

Grady rested her hand on his toes. Cold.

"Okay, Wilbur, here's the story. You've got something going on in your arteries that's blocking the blood flow to your legs. It started on the right, but now it's getting to be a problem on the left. You're going to need surgery pretty quick, and chances are we're going to need to go in your belly and replace part of the damaged artery."

"That sounds like a chore," Wilbur rasped.

"It's not simple," Grady said, "but we do it all the time. And Wilbur? It has to be done. Okay?"

"I guess you better call my wife."

"I'll take care of that, Wilbur," Blaise said. "You don't need to worry about her. We'll look after her while you're in surgery."

"It's the smoking, isn't it." He looked from Grady to Blaise. "That caused it?"

"Maybe," Grady said, "but right now that's not important. What's important is taking care of things and getting you back on your feet. Blaise will bring you some consent forms to sign. As soon as we get the X-rays, I'll go over the surgery plan with you."

"Remember, Doc," Wilbur said, "I need both my feet."

"I know that."

Grady stepped out into the hall and Blaise followed. "You're thinking abdominal aortic occlusion?"

Grady nodded. "Could be an embolus. Could be dissection— although I'd expect more pain with that. But it's progressing fast and if we don't move, he's going to have a kidney at risk next."

Blaise tensed. "I'll let the OR know."

"Is there a full team in-house for the OR, or do we need to get people in?"

"We're level one now," Blaise said. "An OR team's in-house."

"Good." Grady grimaced. "Where the hell are the surgery residents?"

"They should've been called when you were."

Grady lifted a shoulder. "When I got down here, nobody showed up."

"Let me check with the OR. In the meantime, I'll get an ER resident to help you." Blaise grabbed the wall phone and dialed the extension to the OR. After a second, one of the OR nurses answered.

"OR. Reilly."

"Patty," Blaise said, "it's Blaise Richelieu down in the ER. Are you guys running a room up there right now?"

"Yes," Patty said. "An ICU patient developed acute cholecystitis, and Flann brought her down about forty-five minutes ago. Why?"

"We've got an acute abdominal aortic occlusion down here who needs to come up as soon as we get images."

"I don't think Flann's going to be done for another hour. There's a lot of inflammation, and the bile duct looks like tissue paper. We'll need to get another team in."

"Is there anything I can do?"

"No," Patty said briskly. "We'll take care of it. Just keep us up-to-date on the timing. I'll let anesthesia know now, so they can get somebody down there to see him."

"Okay, thanks."

Blaise hung up and glanced at Grady. "The OR's running a room right now. Another team has to come in, but by the time you're ready, they'll be here."

"Advantages of not having any traffic, I guess," Grady said. "Okay—I need whoever's on call for vascular tonight, and where the hell is radiology?"

"Radiology is right here." The click of heels rapidly approaching down the hall announced the arrival of a short, middle-aged brunette in a designer sweater, pants, and low heels who looked like she'd been called away from a dinner party.

"Thought you said she'd be sleeping," Grady said out of the corner of her mouth.

Blaise smothered a laugh. She did not want to find Grady McClure amusing. Or anything else. "Hi, Dr. Okonsky. Thanks for getting here so quickly."

"Well?" Okonsky said sharply. "Where's the patient?"

"Right this way." Grady turned and headed down the hall.

"Who is that?" Okonsky glared at Blaise. "Tell me you called me in on the say-so of an ER resident."

Blaise smiled and herded the radiologist down the hall after Grady. "Grady McClure, one of the new surgeons."

"Hmpf." Okonsky gave Grady a passing glance as she drew even with her. "Do you really have something?"

"Oh, we have something," Grady said with a slow smile, clearly not perturbed by Okonsky's attitude. "Let me introduce you to Mr. Hopkins, and then you can tell me just what."

"Hmpf."

Blaise watched Grady escort Mary Anne Okonsky to the cubicle, pull back the curtain, and murmur something that made Okonsky laugh. That in and of itself was worthy of a bulletin in the local news. McClure was a bona fide charmer, all right.

Sighing, Blaise grabbed Wilbur Hopkins's chart and did what she always did when there were things she couldn't change and didn't want to think about. She worked. Working and raising Taylor were not only her greatest pleasures, they were her salvation. That at least was something she could count on.

CHAPTER THREE

This is the radiologist, Mr. Hopkins," Grady said as she showed Okonsky into cubicle eleven. "She's going to—"

Okonsky swept past her and morphed into a smiling vision of warmth and compassion as she held out her hand and grasped Wilbur's. "I'm Dr. Mary Anne Okonsky. I hear you've got a bit of problem in your arteries, Mr. Hopkins. Let me tell you what we're going to do to help you get that fixed."

"Yes, ma'am. I believe you will."

Clearly unneeded, Grady backed out of the cubicle and let the curtain fall closed. Maybe it was Okonsky's no-doubt expensive perfume—a mixture of dark plum and spice—that had the guy so spellbound, although she favored the light whiff of lemon and vanilla she caught whenever she was close to Blaise Richelieu. But then, she'd never gone for women with designer tastes. Too many of them reminded her of her mother. Although to be fair, Veronica McClure was only living the life to which she'd been raised.

Hell, if *she* hadn't grown up in Gavin's shadow with a mad passion to be as good as he was at everything, she'd probably have been sucked into the same self-centered vortex as most of her friends. She owed a lot of her drive and stubbornness to her lifelong campaign to best her brother—just once.

As she walked down to the nurses' station to make sure Wilbur was squared away for the OR, she registered the sounds of business in the ER picking up. Somewhere a baby cried. Monitors beeped, an aide trundled by pushing a rattling gurney at top speed, and a phone rang at the nurses' station.

Behind the waist-high counter, Blaise juggled her cell in one hand and grabbed the ringing phone with the other.

"Hold on, honey," Blaise said into her cell, and a second later into the other, "ER. Richelieu."

Grady frowned. *Honey?*

"Hi, Peggy. Yes. He's still here…Mary Anne just showed up… right." Blaise looked up, her gaze meeting Grady's. "She's right here. I'll tell her. Thanks."

Honey? Grady wanted to ask and couldn't figure out how. Husband, wife, lover? Damn. She should have checked things out with Brody when she'd had the chance, instead of discussing the damn coffee and where she'd trained. Man, she was slipping.

"Just a second," Blaise murmured to Grady, rubbing her eyes as if chasing away a brewing headache, and went back to her cell. To *Honey.* "Does Abby know?…Fine. All right. You're in for the night. I'll see you in the morning."

She sighed, set her cell aside, and glanced at Grady again. "Sorry. That was the OR. They'll be ready for you when you come up. Where are we with Wilbur?"

"Mary Anne is with him. You didn't mention she was going to turn into a siren."

Blaise gaped and then burst out laughing. "Oh my God, you are so right. Patients love her."

"I can see why." Grady grinned. She really liked Blaise's laugh— nothing self-conscious about it. Blaise didn't try to hide her pleasure, and Grady suddenly very much wanted to know if she responded that way to other kinds of pleasure. She cleared her throat and dragged her mind away from images of Blaise in a very different situation, looking up at her and laughing or…other things. "So, did you find me a resident to get Wilbur pre-oped?"

"I just paged the ER resident on call. The surgery residents are probably with Flann or in the ICU. I can get a PA for you too, but right now we're trying to clear out the other rooms." She nodded at the board and Grady turned to look, blinking away the last visions of Blaise Richelieu in her bed, flushed and breathless and gazing at her through pleasure-drenched eyes. She really, really wanted to be the one to put that look in Blaise's eyes. And that was a big WTF. She enjoyed sex, sure, but she didn't obsess about women. Or *a* woman.

Right. Check the board and forget the fantasies. Three more names had been added while she'd been back with Wilbur.

Grady cleared her throat. "Things are picking up. Anything surgical?"

"I don't think so," Blaise said. "It looks like something for ortho, probably a gastroenteritis that will end up going home, and a dog bite the ER resident should be able to handle."

Grady nodded, still mulling over who might have been on the phone with Blaise.

"Is there something else I can do for you?" Blaise asked as the silence stretched.

"Oh"—Grady turned back with a slow smile—"probably, but I'm good for right now."

Blaise gave Grady that thousand-yard stare that she was starting to get used to. She'd figure out a way to get through that steely barrier, sooner or later, especially with the added incentive of Blaise's sexy laugh as a reward. Getting Blaise to smile back at her was starting to feel like a personal challenge. At least, finding out why Blaise seemed determined *not* to was a worthy endeavor.

"Here's your help," Blaise said coolly.

A harried looking guy with a short high fade, a few extra pounds around the middle, and a stethoscope hanging from his neck careened around the corner. "Sorry, sorry," he said in a rush. "I just finished putting that cast on the kid with the greenstick fracture." He looked from Blaise to Grady. "You paged me, right?"

"Akeem," Blaise said, "this is Grady McClure, the surgeon on call. We've got an emergency case going down for angiography. Grab the chart on Hopkins and make sure all the labs are in order, see what we need for consents, and give transport a hand taking him down."

"Right, on it." He started down the hall, then spun on his heel. "Where?"

Blaise smiled. "Room eleven. Wilbur Hopkins."

"Right, on it." He zoomed off, the Merck Manual peeking out of the back pocket of his scrub pants.

"First year?" Grady asked, watching the ER resident hustle away.

"Mm-hmm. One of the best I've seen too."

"So," Grady said, "you run everything down here?"

She shook her head. "Hardly. But right about now, Abby and Mari—she's the PA on shift tonight—are doing sign-out. There's no point bothering them so that they can tell him exactly what I just did."

"You know, this place is an interesting combination of modern and old-school."

"What do you mean?"

"The ER is brand-new, and from what Flann told me, your new

training programs are also. And then you've got a lot of veteran people like yourself, who are probably used to doing things without the benefit of all these trainees."

Blaise pursed her lips. "And your point?"

"Some places, and a lot of staff, might have a hard time adjusting, but that doesn't seem like what's happening here. You're making the best use of the experienced people while integrating all the new ones. It's impressive."

"I hadn't thought of it quite like that, but you're right." Blaise was taken aback once again. Just when she thought Grady McClure was another typical full-of-herself charmer who might be a great doctor but was too blinded by her own image, she was surprised at how observant she was. Not many doctors—not many people, period—would have noticed so much in so short a time. "I really hope it stays that way."

"That'll probably have a lot to do with who's in charge, and from what little I've seen so far, Abby Remy doesn't seem to be the type who's going to squeeze people into rigid little boxes," Grady said.

"Thanks," Abby said, walking up behind Grady. "And if you mean I plan to use everyone to their best abilities, you've got that right." She smiled at Blaise. "Off topic for a minute—did you get the same call I did while ago?"

Blaise rolled her eyes. "You mean the binge-watching *Stranger Things* gathering at your place? Yes. Are you okay with it?"

"Sure." Abby smiled. "But we really need a bigger house."

"That should be happening soon, right?"

"That's what Gina says. Her crew is just finishing up with the floors, and we ought to be moving in in another week or so. Then Blake will have his own room, and we'll have two guest rooms. I'm thinking bunk beds at the rate we're going."

"I am so sorry that I don't have a bigger place," Blaise said. "I'd be happy to have them."

Abby waved a hand. "I'm fine with it. Believe me, I'm just happy that Blake has found his crew."

"Well, don't plan on feeding them breakfast," Blaise said. "I'll take care of that."

"You know they're not going to get up until noon."

"I'm off tomorrow. I can handle staying up. Just march them out onto the porch when they surface."

"I'll call you when they start moving around." Laughing, Abby turned to Grady. "Are you set with Wilbur Hopkins?"

"Yes," Grady said. "We'll go right to the OR after imaging."

Blaise added, "Pedro Alvarez is on his way in."

"Are you planning to scrub with him?" Abby asked Grady.

"Absolutely."

"That may leave us short for surgery coverage if you're in the OR."

"I'll handle it," Grady said.

Abby nodded. "All right then. I'm going home."

"Good night," Blaise called after her. "I owe you one."

"No, you don't," Abby called back.

Grady raised a brow. "Was that all in code?"

"It's motherspeak," Blaise said.

Grady stiffened. "Oh. Okay. I get the picture…sort of. How old is your kid?"

Blaise pulled one of the electronic charts out of the chart rack. She didn't know why, but Taylor was not a topic she wanted to discuss with Grady. Almost everyone in the ER—at least those who were part of the *old* Rivers—knew Taylor, since she'd spent a good part of her childhood in the day care center provided for staff. But Grady wasn't part of the hospital family, and Taylor was as personal as it got. Everything about Taylor was off-limits to people Blaise didn't know well enough to trust.

"Taylor is sixteen," she said. "Sorry, I need to check on this patient."

"I'll let you know how Wilbur does," Grady called as Blaise turned away.

"Thanks, I appreciate that."

Blaise made a circuit of all the occupied rooms, checked on the ER residents and PAs to make sure everyone had what they needed, and ensured that all of the patients who were waiting were stable. When she returned to the station, Wilbur's room was empty and Grady was gone. She took a deep breath.

Grady unsettled her in a way she couldn't define. Plenty of attractive—all right, damn it, *sexy*—women had entered her orbit in the ER, and most of them had been too consumed with their own success, or too inflated by it, to interest her. Grady fit the mold and should have been easy to ignore, but she kept contradicting the picture Blaise assumed for her. That was new, and disturbing. With any luck, she wouldn't run into her very often, and she wouldn't be forced to ask herself questions she didn't want to answer.

❖

Abby pulled up in front of the renovated schoolhouse that had been her pick as a place to live when she and Blake had moved into the community. Centrally located and a quick walk—and even quicker drive—to the hospital in an emergency, the place had seemed perfect when she made the decision to leave Manhattan for a smaller community and a chance for Blake to start anew in a school where everyone would meet him as the young man he knew himself to be. She let herself in through the gate in the white picket fence and strolled down the flagstone walk, enjoying the crisp September night and smiling at the memory of how bucolic it had seemed from her vantage point of a Manhattanite—the perfect picture-postcard one-room schoolhouse that had served generations of families who still inhabited much of the village and surrounding countryside. The symbolism hadn't been lost on her at the time, of how she hoped that *her* family would soon become part of the fabric of their new community.

A front porch had been added on and was wide enough for several rocking chairs, which had been one of her first purchases. Because what was a farmhouse, or any house in the country, without rocking chairs on the porch? The front door led into what had been the school's only room, now divided into a kitchen in the rear with a large counter wide enough for seating, so visitors could keep the cook company. Another room had been added at the rear to create a bedroom which, as soon as she'd seen it, she'd known was meant for her. Someone had been thoughtful enough to add bay windows, and the window seat looked out over a large rolling pasture that ended in a grove of towering pines that climbed the wooded hill where the hospital reigned over the village. A back door led to a rear deck, where she'd promptly put more chairs and a small table. A staircase opposite the kitchen ended in a loft that was perfect for Blake, at least at the time. She hadn't quite envisioned the way life would change.

Faint light emanated from the windows on either side of the front door, and she let herself in to her still charming and way too small house. The sofa separating the living area from the kitchen nook—thank goodness she'd had the good sense to purchase a large one—was presently occupied by five teens who somehow managed to arrange themselves with most of their body parts actually *on* the sofa. Various extremities dangled here and there in configurations she imagined would be painful, but having seen this tangle of youths in the same position dozens of times before, she had to assume they were at least somewhat comfortable.

Her son slouched in the center of the sofa with his feet propped on the facing barnwood coffee table. Margie, her wife's younger sister, which made Margie her sister-in-law, but she could hardly think of Margie that way, more like a daughter, which wasn't quite right either, considering how close Margie and Blake had become—but she wasn't going to think about that right now—leaned against Blake's shoulder with her legs stretched over Taylor Richelieu's lap. Dave Kincaid occupied the space on Blake's right with his arm draped around Blake's shoulders and his fingers resting on Taylor's arm. Somehow, Tim Brunel managed to squeeze himself into the left corner and nestled against Taylor with Margie's sock-clad feet in his lap. They looked like a litter of puppies.

These five were familiar denizens of her living room, having come together over the summer at the 4-H club. She doubted that any of them planned on being farmers, but the club was one of the social centers for the area youths, since lots of the local teens did live on farms. Even if farming wasn't in their future, they were all instilled with a certain love for the land and, most certainly, for the animals. It had taken Blake a hot New York minute to fall in love with everything country. He'd decided within days of arrival he was going to be a vet, and once he met Val Valentine and began to volunteer at her animal clinic, his future was set.

Blake had met other teens over the course of the summer, but these five had bonded in a special way. Margie was the spirit of the group, Blake the heart, and Taylor the brains. Dave Kincaid, the local high school quarterback, was a hero to everyone and a much sought after date possibility for quite a few of the girls and boys in the junior and senior classes. He seemed rather oblivious to his charm and fame. Tim was quiet, with a sunny indomitable disposition, which was exactly what Abby liked to see in a kid who wanted to be a peace officer. She'd given up trying to figure out if there were any romantic combinations emerging, as she wasn't completely sure she understood the new rules of teen relationships. She *did* appreciate their social dynamics were very different from what she'd grown up with and from what she had anticipated when she had looked down at Blake as a baby and imagined what Blake's future would be.

Blake had been assigned female at birth, so the pictures Abby'd made were nothing like what she'd come to realize in the last three years was the real truth. Blake had known for far longer, and when he'd told her that he was certain, all the images of her future had shifted. In addition to wanting to protect him, something she knew no parent really ever could, she wanted to remain open and supportive while she tried to learn as much as she could as quickly as possible. She was still learning, but thankfully, Blake was strong enough to follow his instincts. He led the way for all of them.

He glanced over now and gave her a little bit of a wave. She checked the television and after a few seconds recognized *Stranger Things*.

She walked behind the sofa to ruffle his hair on the way to the kitchen, smiling when he pretended to duck his head to escape. Flann probably wouldn't be home for another hour or so, and since the next day was Saturday and she was second call, she wasn't worried about being a little tired in the morning. She grabbed the bottle of red they'd opened the night before, poured herself a glass, and strolled back into the living area. She took the only open seat, an overstuffed chair next to the sofa, and half watched the television while she sipped her wine.

"Hi, Dr. Remy," Taylor whispered from her place at the corner of the sofa.

"Hi, Taylor."

"Did my mom say she was coming to get us in the morning?"

Abby smiled into her glass. "Mm-hmm."

Taylor let out a long-suffering sigh. "I knew she would."

Abby had a feeling that being a predictable parent wasn't necessarily such a bad thing, but of course she would never say so. Instead, she asked a predictable question so as not to disappoint. "Who drove you over here?"

"Dave," Taylor said. "He texted me just after my mom left for the hospital and said he and Tim were on the way over here and did I want to come."

"Sounds plausible," Abby murmured, figuring they probably all planned it, but considering that Dave was old enough to drive after dark with a senior license, and she'd ridden with him and knew he was a good driver, and they were all sitting around in her living room, she was altogether pleased.

Taylor laughed, apparently knowing their plan to meet up for the night was obvious. "Is Dr. Rivers at the hospital, still?"

"Yes, she has a case," Abby said. "She probably will be there for a while."

"I don't think I'd like that very much, having to get up in the middle of the night and work," Taylor said.

Margie poked Taylor in the stomach. "That's because you're a princess."

Taylor looked affronted. "Am not." She looked at Tim. "Are you going to say anything in my defense?"

Tim smiled his good-natured smile. "Maybe you're a little bit of a princess, but you deserve it."

Blake chuckled.

Taylor rolled her eyes and pretended to huff, but Abby sensed she didn't mind the appellation. She was a math geek on her way to being valedictorian and also had the good fortune of being one of the prettiest girls in the school. She looked like Blaise—blond hair the color of corn silk, eyes as blue as a summer sky, and a lithe athletic body. She played on the field hockey team that Blaise coached, and managed to be a star there as well. Taylor was one of the lucky ones, not because she was bright and pretty and talented, but because she'd somehow grown up with a good dose of humility and a generous spirit. And for that, everyone liked her, whereas she might have been the person everyone resented. Blaise deserved a lot of credit for that, and for the millionth time, Abby wondered just how much was nature and how much nurture really went into forming their children. She tried not to think too much about that and just appreciated how remarkable Blake had turned out to be.

"You're all staying here tonight, right?" Abby said for form, since they all knew by now they weren't going anywhere in the middle of the night.

A dutiful chorus of yeses followed.

"Good." Abby rose and drained the last of her wine. "You all know where the sleeping bags are—you can sort it out for yourselves. But if you're sleeping down here, I can't promise we won't wake you up in the morning."

"That's okay," Blake said. "Margie and I have a shift at the hospital, so we'll be up early anyhow."

The other three groaned.

Dave gave Blake a squeeze. "It might be nice if you could arrange not to work on Saturday mornings once in a while, you know."

"Well, I guess we can to talk to the ER chief about that." Blake grinned at his mother.

Abby shook her head. "I don't have anything to say about it. You have to take it up with Glenn. She handles all the PAs and interns."

"No, forget it," Margie said. "Glenn's a harda—um, particular about the rotations."

"Good point." Laughing, Abby waved and made her way to the bedroom. They'd all be up half the night with the television on, probably falling asleep in front of it, and she'd awaken to a tangle of snoring teens in the morning. She could think of worse ways to wake up. She also was happy the television would be playing, because she planned on staying awake until Flann got home. After all, it was Friday night, she had nowhere to be in the morning, and late night surgeries always left Flann with a lot of excess energy.

CHAPTER FOUR

The instant the bedroom door opened, Abby woke from her light sleep. She moved the e-reader that had been resting on her chest as she dozed onto the nightstand and pushed back the covers for Flann.

"Hi," Abby murmured.

Flann came around to Abby's side of the bed, shucking her clothes as she walked, and leaned down to kiss her. "Hi, baby. I wondered if you'd be awake or not."

"I intended to be." Abby pushed up on the pillows and scraped her hair out of her face with one hand. At least she hadn't been drooling. "And I am, mostly."

"How awake?"

"Plenty for what you're thinking." Abby surveyed Flann's form in the faint glow cast by the vanity lights in the adjacent bathroom. Despite her unpredictable schedule, Flann managed to get a run in three or four times a week, and she looked it. Lean by nature, she was nicely muscled in all the right places and gently curved in others. Abby held out her hand and waggled her fingers. "You can't stand there naked and just tease me. Come to bed."

"Let me jump in the shower first."

Abby let out a sigh. "Hurry."

Flann was an expert at getting ready at a moment's notice and was back in literally minutes. Her skin was slightly cool from the shower as she slid under the sheets next to Abby. Leaning on one elbow, she danced her fingertips down the center of Abby's chest and circled her navel. Abby shivered.

"So," Flann said, "Blake is asleep on the sofa in the living room with Dave Kincaid."

"I'm surprised they're not still watching *Stranger Things*," Abby said, slipping an arm around Flann's waist and tugging her closer. Flann's leg automatically slid between hers, a movement so practiced and automatic that still managed to be so incredibly arousing every single time. Abby sighed, her attention narrowing to the point between her thighs that throbbed against Flann's smooth soft skin.

"Yes, but Blake and Dave are sleeping together on the sofa," Flann repeated.

"Are they naked?" Abby muttered, rocking her hips to turn the teasing pleasure into something a lot more acute.

"No," Flann exclaimed.

"Well then, it's not the first time."

"All right then." Flann sighed. "Is my sister here?"

Talk first, then. Abby stopped moving but wrapped a leg around the back of Flann's to keep her right against that perfect spot. "She'd better be. That was the deal. None of them were to leave. Usually they're very good about it, so I'm sure the other three are upstairs."

"The other three?" Flann said slowly. "Who, and where are they sleeping? The loft is the size of a chicken coop. In fact, the one we built at Harp's is bigger."

Abby smiled to herself. Flann was adorable when she was being all protective and parental. "Honey, things are different now. Margie and Taylor and Tim are up there."

"In what combination?"

"That's the point. It's not a combination at all. They're all friends, and they're incredibly easy with one another, and it's not about sex."

"Bull," Flann said. "They're teenagers. It's always about sex."

Abby tapped Flann's chin. "That's because *you* always have sex on the brain, Dr. Rivers."

Flann caught Abby's wrist and nipped at her fingertip. "Look who's talking."

"True. And it will undoubtedly happen for them any day. But right now, they're all happy being part of their group. The next time you come home, it might be Margie and Taylor on the sofa or Tim and Blake, or some other combination. They're sorting it out."

"It's weird," Flann decided.

Abby pulled Flann all the way on top of her and stroked her back. "No, it's just different, and I think it's pretty healthy. If they're not sure about sex yet, they don't feel any pressure to make decisions, or even to pair off, which probably puts off a lot of drama and angst for a few years. I'm not complaining about *that*."

"Okay, I concede that." Flann kissed Abby, but before Abby could take it deeper still, she raised her head. "I still think I should have a talk with my sister."

"For what, the hundredth time?"

Flann grinned in the faint light. "It makes me feel better."

"Well, I have an idea how to make you feel better." Abby lifted her hips and turned, maneuvering Flann onto her back. She settled above her and kissed her. This time she didn't stop until she needed to breathe. "Just lie there and I'll show you."

Flann chuckled. "Anything you say."

❖

Despite Abby's determination to sleep in, she woke at her usual time of five thirty. Flann slept soundly beside her, one arm thrown around her middle. She lay there, waiting for the sun to come up and listening to a rooster who was too impatient to bother. As far as *he* was concerned, everyone should be awake. After a few minutes, she eased out from beneath Flann's arm, pulled on a tee and sweatpants, and kicked into her favorite shearling-lined slippers. She slipped out of the bedroom, closing the door carefully behind her, and instantly, miraculously, smelled coffee. Surely, she was hallucinating.

But there on the kitchen counter, clearly visible in the dim illumination from the undercounter lights, sat a pot of coffee on the coffeemaker. She tiptoed into the kitchen, pulled a mug off one of the hooks hanging under the counter, and poured herself a cup. The house was completely quiet as she padded down the hall, grabbed a sweatshirt, and carried her coffee out onto the back deck. Blake, similarly garbed in sweatpants and hoodie, lounged in an Adirondack chair with a mug in his hands. Abby sat down beside him.

"You're up awfully early," she said.

"I have to be at the hospital in an hour, and I was awake." He lifted his shoulder. "Plus, I like it out here when the sun comes up, and it's gonna be too cold to sit outside before too long."

"Maybe we'll get lucky and have an Indian summer," Abby said, sipping the coffee. It was strong, just the way she liked it. She'd taught him well.

"Something on your mind?" Abby asked when the silence stretched. Blake wasn't usually such an early riser.

"Not really," Blake said.

"Not really isn't actually no," Abby said.

Blake laughed softly. "Something on yours?"

Abby grinned. Smart-ass. "Yeah. You. How's school?"

"It's only been two weeks. I can't really be behind in anything yet."

"Okay, how were the first two weeks, then? And you're never behind in your schoolwork."

"I like most of my teachers." Another shrug. "I think the math teacher thinks we're all morons—well, except for Taylor, of course, but other than that it's okay."

"Okay is good," Abby said slowly. "And the social situation?"

Blake shifted in his chair, gave her a look. "You mean, is anybody giving me a hard time about being trans?"

"That would be the gist of it, yup."

"Only the usual dickheads—and not much at all. Probably the same thing they do to every new kid."

"Who?" Abby sipped her coffee and concentrated on the mist rising from the cornfield, keeping her anger under wraps. This was about Blake's feelings, not hers.

"Just a couple of chickenshits who make a comment now and then when I walk past. You know the ones—from the fair."

Abby sighed. "I'm sorry. Which doesn't help at all and doesn't change anything, but I am."

"I know." Blake gazed out over the pasture as the first streaks of red and orange broke in the sky. "A few other kids are curious, but they don't know what to do about it, so they don't say anything. Just a look when they think I'm not looking. But mostly, nobody cares."

"That's good, then." Probably as good as could be expected, but she still hated that he had to deal with any of it.

"It's good we came here," Blake said.

A tightness around Abby's heart she hadn't even known was there shattered as if a hammer had divided a length of chain with a single blow. "I'm glad. It seemed like a good idea…in theory. But it's a lot to handle—new school, new friends, and new dickheads."

"The dickheads are all the same." Blake grinned. "It's a lot harder for people to get used to the change when they've known you a certain way for your whole life, and then you're different."

"I think you're right. But that doesn't mean they shouldn't try. And no excuse for ignorance." She couldn't quite hide her anger.

He looked at her again, and again, she was taken by surprise by the change in his face and the maturity in his eyes. His jaw had started to get a little heavier, the way boys' faces did as they moved out of adolescence, and any day now, he'd need to shave. "You never said it was hard for you."

Abby steadied her coffee cup on the arm of her chair with one hand and reached for his hand with the other. Their fingers clasped, and she gave his hand a little shake. "It's not hard. It's scary sometimes, because I don't always know what's the best thing to do."

"Me neither."

Abby smiled. "Well, you, me, and Flann can always figure that out."

"Is Flann going to be mad if Margie and I have sex?"

"Well, okay," Abby said on a long exhalation. "That's a right-angle turn in the conversation. Are you planning to?"

"We haven't decided yet. We talked about it. But, you know, that's a big thing."

"It is," Abby said, ignoring the uncertainty swarming in her middle. "Can I ask you, are you in love with her?"

"I love her," Blake said instantly.

Abby smiled. "I know that."

"I love Dave too," Blake said.

"Are you thinking about having sex with Dave?" Abby said.

Blake lifted his shoulder. "Sometimes, yeah. I think he'd be into it, but he doesn't push. You know."

"Well, to answer your first question, no, Flann isn't going to be mad. She's probably going to be panicked because Margie's her sister, and your sister's not supposed to have sex. Plus you're her kid, and your kid is *definitely* not supposed to have sex."

"Um, you know that's crazy, right?"

Abby laughed. "Yes, I do, but as your mother, I completely understand it."

"Well, it's not happening yet. But, you know, someday."

"Well, when someday comes, or anytime before then, I'm here if you want to talk about it. And you know the drill. Safe sex, right?"

"We all know that, Mom," Blake said with a verbal eyeroll, as if Abby was hopelessly behind the times.

And maybe she was, but she was catching up fast.

❖

Shortly before seven, Blaise carried a cup of freshly brewed coffee into the ER conference room and sat down at the table. Blake Remy and Margie Rivers were already there, both looking bright-eyed and eager.

"Morning!" they announced in unison, as if being there was the most exciting thing in their universe.

"Morning," Blaise said, consciously not asking about Taylor. Taylor was fine—undoubtedly fast asleep. A morning person she was not. Where she got that trait from, Blaise couldn't fathom.

Margie, Blaise noticed, had grown a few inches over the summer, and her always pretty face had begun to show the refined bone structure of the woman she was becoming. Blake's voice had dropped further in just the last few weeks. He was turning into one of those effortlessly handsome types who were destined to break hearts. For an instant, she thought of another handsome heartbreaker and, just as quickly, put Grady McClure out of her mind.

"You two still working with Val Valentine too?" Blaise asked.

Margie rolled her eyes. "Blake is—on Sundays. *He* doesn't have to stay home and help around the house."

Blake laughed. "*My* mother doesn't make enough food on Sunday to feed an army for a week."

"Yeah—that's because Flann comes home every Sunday that you guys don't eat with us and grabs leftovers," Margie said. "Abby doesn't have to cook!"

Mari Mateo, one of the ER PAs and the fiancée of Flann Rivers's best friend, walked in on the end of Margie's sentence. "You mean Glenn could be getting in on that, and I'm just finding out? Your mother is the best cook in…anywhere."

"You guys are always welcome." Margie made a face but her eyes were shining. "We always have plenty."

Emery D'Angelo, the charge nurse for the day shift, strode in on the dot of seven. "Reinforcements have arrived," he announced as he plopped down beside Blake. Six two, brawny build, and butter-soft tenor, he ran the ER like he'd run his hospital detail in the Army. Disciplined, organized, compassionate. "Hit it."

"Okay," Mari said, tapping her tablet, "we've got six pendings who've already been worked up and are waiting for labs, X-rays, or consults." She glanced at Blaise with a silent request for an update.

They'd done this hundreds of times before and could read each other's minds. Blaise went down the list, identifying each patient by name, preliminary diagnosis, outstanding labs and X-rays, and pending consults as well as any new information that might've come in since Mari last saw them. Emery checked the information in his digital files and added whatever notes he needed.

"The ER residents on call today are Marshall and Kwan," Mari said when Blaise finished. "And you've got the other nurses, plus Blake and Margie."

Emery grunted. "Not too bad."

Blaise smothered a smile. Emery had been one of the holdouts opposed to the new emergency room training programs. He'd been a medic in Iraq and had been vocal in his opinion that civilian trainees were coddled, inexperienced, and too arrogant to learn from the people who really knew what they were talking about. Meaning, most of the time, him.

Abby had made it clear to everyone that the training program was going forward and that she expected everyone to contribute to the education of the residents. Emery hadn't seemed to have any issues with the new PA training program, perhaps because he saw those non-physician but highly trained professionals to be more like himself. Regardless, he was doing his job, and Blaise had no complaints. He'd even softened up a little bit in the last couple of weeks after having worked more closely with some of the residents. Fortunately, most of them were wise enough to take the advice of people who knew more about some things than they did. That helped a lot.

"What about Wilbur Hopkins," Mari asked. "Do we have any word on his status?"

"I checked with the OR forty-five minutes ago," Blaise said, "and they were near to finishing."

"Long case," Mari said.

"Yes, they had to put in an aortic bifurcation graft, so he clearly had a lot of damage."

"Long recovery too," Emery said.

Blaise and the other ER staff always tried to get follow-up on the patients they referred for admission or surgery. They weren't just a way station on the path to some other caretaker. They were part of a team, even if they weren't physically involved with the patient's care after they left the emergency room. They wanted to know that their part in the patient's care had been appropriate, that everything had been done that should've been done, and they often followed the critical patients during their hospital stay and updated one another informally. Abby encouraged it and, at weekly rounds, reviewed all the admissions through the emergency room and expected updates on patient care. Like Emery, some of the veteran staff had complained about the extra work at first, but not nearly as many as had complained about the training program. They'd already been doing their own follow-up, and having it formalized hadn't changed anything.

"I'm going to stop by the OR when I leave this morning," Blaise said. "His wife is waiting upstairs, and I talked to her on the telephone, so I'll check in with her."

"That's great." Mari closed her tablet. "I think that covers it, then."

"All right"—Emery stood, motioning to Blake and Margie—"let's go find the docs and get you two assigned."

"Have a good one," Mari and Blaise said together.

Blaise rinsed her cup in the sink and put it on the sideboard. "You need a ride?"

"No," Mari said, "Glenn is picking me up, and we're going out for breakfast."

"I'll see you Sunday, then."

"Okay…Wait, are you going the party at the Homestead tonight?" Mari asked.

"Is everyone in town going?" Blaise asked.

Mari grinned. "You know Glenn and I will be. Come with."

Blaise hesitated. Abby *had* invited her. Suddenly the prospect of a Saturday night doing laundry wasn't very appealing. "I just might."

Mari grinned. "Great. Because you're right. Everyone will be there."

Blaise wondered if that included newcomers, like a certain dark-haired, sexy attending. Not that she really cared, not at all.

CHAPTER FIVE

Patty, one of the OR supervisors, was at the OR desk when Blaise entered.

"Aren't you just about ready to go home?" Blaise asked.

Patty gave her a look. "Soon. I'm waiting until OR seven clears out. Once housekeeping starts on it, I'm outta here."

She glanced at the row of monitors that showed all of the individual operating rooms, and Blaise craned her neck to take a peek. She watched Grady and Pedro Alvarez, the vascular surgeon and—she squinted to make out the third surgeon—surgery resident Courtney Valentine coordinate moving Wilbur Hopkins from the operating room table into an ICU bed. The anesthesiologist guided his head during the transfer to keep the breathing tube in place and then hooked him back up to a portable ventilator. The OR nurses checked to be sure that all his lines, catheters, drainage tubes, and other essential equipment followed onto the bed with him. The ICU resident who had come to help transport, along with Grady and Courtney, pushed the bed out of the room. Within seconds, the operating room was empty except for the hampers filled with linens and surgical gowns, the stainless steel buckets holding bloody sponges, soiled dressing wrappers, and the detritus left over from starting IVs, hanging IV bags, and opening instrument packs, and random bits of trash on the floor.

Patty let out a long sigh as two housekeeping staffers moved into camera range with mops and huge wheeled trash bins filled with red bags, denoting contaminated contents for disposal. "That's it for me. What are you doing up here? Oh, are you looking for Wilbur's wife?"

"I thought I would stop by and see her. Is that okay?"

"Of course. I'm sure she'd like that. Pedro's probably going out to talk to her, soon as he changes into clean scrubs. Or else McClure will when she gets Wilbur settled in the ICU."

"How did it go?" Blaise asked, hoping she sounded nonchalant. It was an appropriate question and something Wilbur's wife would want to know. She wasn't really asking for information about Grady.

"It was a tough case, but from what I could see when I peeked my head in a few times, and what I heard from the OR nurses when they took a break, it was going fine. McClure apparently has really good hands, and Pedro is a magician, so Wilbur should do really well. But you know how it is—if the patient's got bad vessels in his belly, he's got bad vessels everywhere, so until he's out of the ICU it's never a sure thing."

"I know. I can tell his wife that everything went well and that Dr. Alvarez or Dr. McClure will be out to talk to her, right?"

"Absolutely."

Blaise was always careful to be certain that she gave the appropriate message to the patient's family and didn't relay any information that might contradict what the surgeon would tell them, or want them to know, at any certain point. She paused. "So McClure looks like a good addition."

"Flann has never missed," Patty said as they walked out into the hall. "When she hires someone new, they're always the best." She lifted a shoulder. "I don't particularly swing in McClure's direction, but if I did, she's easy to look at, a real charmer, and I think even a couple of the nurses who wouldn't ordinarily be interested were taken with her."

Blaise bit her lip to hold back a retort. She knew it was just a coincidence, because it couldn't be anything else, but Grady just reminded her far too much of things—of people—she really wanted to forget. She wished she hadn't asked.

"Well," she said briskly, "I know you want to get home, and I have to eventually collect my daughter." She laughed. "Although I doubt I'll hear from her for a few hours yet."

Patty stopped by the OR locker room. "Have a good one, and thanks for getting Wilbur up here so quickly."

"Anytime." Blaise crossed the hall to the surgical waiting room and poked her head inside. The only person there was a middle-aged woman in a red flannel shirt, navy blue pants, and calf-high muck boots. She'd probably grabbed the closest thing she could on the way out of her house in a hurry, and her barn boots would've been right by the door.

"Mrs. Hopkins?" Blaise asked.

The woman got to her feet. "Yes, I'm Cindy Hopkins. My husband, is he—"

Blaise quickly joined her. "He's on his way to the intensive care unit. His surgery is finished. The OR nurses tell me that it went very well, and one of the doctors will be out to give you more information very soon."

"Oh," Cindy said, reaching for the arm of the chair where she'd been sitting. "That's...that's good."

Blaise slipped a hand under her elbow. "Why don't you go ahead and sit down again. It's been a very long night."

"Thank you," Cindy Hopkins said.

"I'll get you something to drink. Water? Coffee?"

"Just...just some water would be good," Cindy said.

"I got it," Grady McClure said from behind Blaise. As Blaise turned to watch, she filled one of the disposable cups from the water cooler and carried it over to Cindy. "Here you go."

Cindy glanced up at her, her eyes widening slightly. "Thank you."

Grady crouched low enough to put her eyes at the same level as Cindy's. "I'm Dr. McClure," Grady said.

"My husband's surgeon," Mrs. Hopkins said.

"One of them, yes, ma'am," Grady said. "Dr. Alvarez is the vascular surgeon, and he'll be by to talk to you as well. I just wanted you to know that your husband is being made comfortable in the ICU right now, and when the nurses have him all settled, which will probably take close to half an hour, one of them will be out to let you know when you'll be able to see him for just a couple of minutes. He won't be awake yet and he may not know you're there, but he might, so if you touch his hand and talk to him, he'll know."

Cindy Hopkins's lips trembled, and she held on to Grady's gaze as if it was a lifeline. She nodded.

As Grady spoke in a low, measured tone, Blaise sensed a bubble of intimacy and empathy closing around Grady and the patient's wife, as if all that really mattered, all that *existed*, were the words that fell between the two of them. She'd seen it before, the almost magical connection that some health care providers were able to make instantaneously with patients. Something in their eyes, the way they held their bodies, the tone of their voices. She wasn't certain it was a skill that could be learned, and she knew it was a trait that carried over into other situations. She'd felt it herself with Grady from their first interaction—a level of intimacy that should have taken much longer to form but was no less intense for its brevity.

Grady seemed to have all the time in the world, and Blaise was nearly as captivated as Cindy as Grady went on, "Dr. Alvarez will explain to you what we did, and what we can expect with your husband's recovery. But right now the only thing you need to think about is that his surgery is over. He's doing very well, and we're going to be doing everything we can to make sure he continues to do well. Okay?"

"You'll be taking care of Wilbur while he's here?" Cindy asked.

"Dr. Alvarez will be in charge, but I'll be looking in on him too." Grady stood. "If you have any questions at any time, you can have the ICU nurses page one of us."

"Thank you so much," Cindy said.

"Of course." Grady said good-bye and walked with Blaise out into the hall. She stopped and slid her hands into the pockets of her lab coat. "Aren't you done with your shift?"

"Yes," Blaise said. "I just wanted to check on Wilbur's wife, and the case. Patty said it went really well."

"Really well. Pedro Alvarez is a really good surgeon."

Pedro came around the corner. "So's McClure."

Pedro was short, barrel-chested, and handsome as sin, with sparkling dark eyes, an exuberant personality, and an ego the size of North America. Everyone loved him, from staff to patients. He clapped Grady on the shoulder.

Grady looked uncomfortable but managed to smile. "I didn't have all that much to do, really."

"Well, anytime you want to scrub in, McClure, just let me know. Thanks for the assist."

"My pleasure," Grady said. As Pedro disappeared into the waiting room, she leaned toward Blaise. "Buy you breakfast?"

"Oh…no, thanks, I have to pick up my daughter."

"Didn't Abby Remy say the kids probably wouldn't even be awake until noon?"

"Yes, but…"

"And you said you weren't going to go to sleep right away because you had the day off."

Blaise narrowed her eyes. "Okay, what, do you have eidetic auditory powers, and you remember everything you hear word for word?"

Grady looked smug. "When I'm interested in who's talking."

Blaise ignored the little jolt of pleasure at Grady's shameless flirting. She should say no. She *wanted* to say no. Except she didn't. Because she was curious, and she hadn't been curious in a very long time.

"Just breakfast."

Grady held her hands palm up. "Of course. What else."

What else indeed. Blaise shook her head and marched toward the elevators.

Grady hurried to catch her. She hadn't really expected Blaise to say yes. The invitation had popped out because during the quiet times in the OR when Pedro had been suturing and she'd been assisting, or when they'd been waiting for the scrub nurses to open one of the grafts, her mind had drifted unerringly back to Blaise. Snippets of conversation, a quick glimpse of Blaise watching her when Blaise thought she wouldn't notice, an energy in the air whenever they were alone. Hormones, pheromones, maybe, but the effect was real. She was attracted, and she didn't want to spend twenty-four hours—maybe more—wondering if she was imagining the speculative look in Blaise's eye.

When Blaise finally said yes, a surge of excitement bubbled through her chest. She ought to have been tired. She'd been standing for six hours in one spot, her attention riveted on the twelve-inch-square space in front of her, which was all that was visible of Wilbur Hopkins's open abdomen. When she looked into the wound, she didn't see Wilbur. Instead, the vessels and organs formed a familiar roadmap, leading her on a journey she'd taken hundreds of times before, but one whose paths changed with every trip, whose route to the destination was subtly different, each and every time. The roadblocks, the detours, or the new highways were always a surprise. Every surgery was an adventure, filled with the consoling sense of the known and the exhilaration of anticipation.

Once the incision was closed and the drapes were removed and Wilbur appeared, everything changed again. The patient, not the surgery, became the focus, and all that mattered was getting Wilbur Hopkins safely out of the hospital. That and being assured that those in Wilbur's life were supported and informed. Usually, once she'd settled the patient in recovery and talked to the family, the high began to dissipate. But the instant she'd seen Blaise, the adrenaline had surged again. Blaise ignited the same sense of challenge and exhilarating journey as stepping into the OR did. She wanted to step onto that unknown highway, to ride out the twists and turns and obstacles, and ultimately, if she got lucky, end at a satisfying destination. She'd often felt that way when she was about to get involved with a woman, but never about one she'd just met—and never so intensely.

"Are you sure you're not too tired?" Blaise asked as they rode the elevator down in silence.

Grady's attention jerked back to the present, and she leaned her shoulder against the elevator wall to face Blaise. They were alone, and Blaise was inches away from her. The urge to kiss her was as unexpected as it was overwhelming. Something in her face might have revealed what she was thinking because Blaise took a step back.

"I'm not tired," Grady said, hearing the huskiness in her voice. She didn't bother to hide whatever was in her eyes because Blaise had already seen it. "I was just thinking…about you, actually."

Blaise held her hand up between them like a traffic cop, and Grady couldn't help but grin. "That sounds a little ominous. Should I ask what you were thinking about?"

Grady wasn't entirely certain that Blaise really wanted to know the answer. Blaise always had a little edge of defensiveness in her voice, as if she was fighting with herself as much as resisting Grady's attempts to get closer.

"It isn't anything too dangerous. I don't think so, at any rate."

Blaise huffed. She didn't believe that for a second. Grady McClure was dangerous. She'd been wary of her from the instant they'd met, and it wasn't just because of the knee-jerk response to her name. Grady, with her easy smile and insistent flirting and bursts of genuine interest and unexpected empathy, made her wary and…intrigued. That persistent urge to discover the real Grady beneath the practiced charm was even more unsettling than her instinctual uncertainty about her. Blaise liked people. She liked women. Differently than men, true, but when she met a new woman for the first time, she didn't automatically note how sexy she was—okay, sometimes she did, she was still breathing, after all—but usually attraction came slowly when she discovered who they were as people, enjoyed their sense of humor, and found out they shared common interests. She thought Abby Remy was wonderfully attractive—although, come to think of it, she never got any of the twinges she had when she looked at Grady. But then, Abby was married, and she definitely did not go there. But still, she could appreciate everything about her. And then there was Grady.

Grady was studying her. She could feel it. Actually *studying* her, as if there was something to see that she was keeping hidden. And, of course, there was. And that was enough to make her stiffen her shoulders and lift her chin. Grady McClure was not going to poke around in places she wasn't invited. In places no one was invited.

"So," Grady said, "back at you. What are you thinking?"

"You first," Blaise said.

Grady laughed. Blaise was not going to give in easily. That was challenge number one—getting Blaise to admit she was interested. Not admit it to Grady, although that would be nice, but to herself. Because she was, or she wouldn't be riding down in the elevator for a spur-of-the-moment breakfast with a woman she just met. Grady knew that as surely as she knew she didn't usually want to spend time—doing *anything*—with a woman as badly as she did with Blaise.

Blaise Richelieu was not the kind of woman who took chances. If Grady had to put words to her, they would be competent, confident, studied, certain. All of those things came from having a firm hold on her emotions and as much control as possible on her environment. That was clear from the way she handled everything in the emergency room. From her conversation on the phone with her daughter to her interactions with Abby. Blaise planned her life. No unanticipated detours for her. And that's what Grady was. An unanticipated bump in the road. She laughed again. She couldn't stop thinking about highways and unknown destinations for some reason.

Blaise raised an eyebrow.

"Okay, you win," Grady said. "I was thinking that you rarely drive above the speed limit, maybe a safe three or four miles over but not enough to get you a ticket. When you use MapQuest, you pick the most direct route, unless of course you get an alert there's heavy traffic, and then you weigh your decision considering directness versus speed. You plan your weekend meals ahead of time, and I bet you cook on Sunday afternoon. Oh, and you drive a Subaru—plenty of cargo space, environmentally efficient, and great in the snow." She stopped, watching Blaise, whose pupils widened just a little, a faint flush rising to her cheeks. "How am I doing?"

"It just so happens," Blaise said, "that I have a big not-so-fuel-efficient Suburban."

"But I got the other stuff right, didn't I?"

Blaise actually clenched her jaws. Grady could tell because a little muscle bunched at the angle of her very elegant cheek. That was very sexy, and she liked knowing that she'd gotten a response. Challenge number two. She'd have to watch very closely to discover exactly how

Blaise felt about things because she wasn't going to reveal them easily. So she studied her even more.

"Okay, four for me, one for you. Your turn."

The elevator opened, and they stepped out.

"I was thinking you're complicated."

Grady stared. "What?"

"Complicated. Contradictory."

"That sounds bad." Grady frowned. She hadn't expected her to accept the offer of breakfast, and she hadn't expected a serious answer to her question. And now she didn't know what to think of the answer. "Is it?"

Blaise slowed and searched her face, looking for something Grady was half afraid she would find—and half afraid she wouldn't.

"I don't know yet."

Challenge number three. Discover a way around the roadblocks Blaise set out to keep her away, and why they were there.

Blaise stopped at the foot of the sidewalk adjacent to the employee lot on the west side of the main hospital.

"Where are you parked?" Blaise asked.

"On Union Street."

Blaise gave her a look. Union Street was in the center of town, and nowhere near the hospital. "How did you get to work?"

"I ran."

"You ran. Up the mountain?"

Grady snorted. "It's not exactly a mountain—it's a big hill."

"Well, that's true, but I happen to know that with the twists and turns and the rise in elevation, it's pretty challenging."

"You run?"

Blaise didn't answer for a moment. Then, with obvious reluctance, she nodded. "I do."

"So you know it's not that big a deal."

"It would be for most casual runners."

Grady lifted a shoulder. "I don't have time to do much of anything else, in terms of exercise, so I run."

"I know what you mean," Blaise said. "What do you do for strength training?"

"Push-ups. It gets all the muscle groups, and I can do it at home. You?" They reached the front door of the hospital and Blaise pushed it open. Grady grabbed it and held it from behind, her arm brushing Blaise's shoulder. The heat of her body, which shouldn't have been noticeable, seared through Blaise at the slight touch. She quickly moved to the side to break the contact as Grady followed her outside.

"Planks. I hate them, but they're wonderful."

"Yeah," Grady said, "I feel that way about yoga."

Blaise laughed, that pure free sound that was so at odds with her usual restrained composure. Grady's heart gave a little thump, and the frisson of excitement that she was beginning to associate with being around Blaise returned. The sun was up, bright in a blue sky, and despite the September chill, the morning was glorious. And Blaise glowed.

"I drove," Blaise said quietly. "Come on. I'm parked back here."

Grady followed her, and at that moment, she knew with certainty she would've followed her anywhere just for the chance to hear that laughter again.

CHAPTER SIX

"This is me," Blaise said, clicking the remote to open the doors on the black Suburban.

"Nice ride. So, let me guess—when you're not running the emergency room, you're toting around the hospital VIPs."

"Actually," Blaise said, climbing into the driver's side and starting the engine, "I'm toting sports equipment and half a field hockey team."

Grady hurried to jump in beside her. "I guess your daughter plays?"

"She does," Blaise said. "I also coach."

"Play in college?"

Blaise backed out of the parking place a little faster than she'd intended, hitting the brakes hard enough to rock them both back. If Grady noticed, she didn't say anything. She had intended to play field hockey in college, but that hadn't happened when she'd gotten pregnant and college turned into something very different. "No."

Grady tilted her head. "Okay. So, let me guess. Lacrosse or—"

"That's your favorite game, isn't it? Playing at guessing until you find out what you want to know?" As soon as the words were out, Blaise immediately wanted to kick herself. She'd just opened a door she absolutely wanted to keep closed. The door marked *Let's Get Personal*. The *Tell Me About Yourself* door. Doors like that swung both ways, and she wasn't offering to reciprocate.

Grady of course walked right through and planted herself in the middle of the *I Want To Get to Know You* room. "I enjoy finding out about the women I find interesting, but I've got other games I like better. If you're interested."

Blaise gripped the wheel at ten and two, as if she was back in driver's ed a decade and a half ago, and stared straight ahead as she maneuvered the SUV down the winding road from the summit, where the Rivers presided over the valley and the village, to Main Street. The two-lane road divided the village into the north and south sides, and the one major cross street in the center neatly cut east to west.

"I walked into that one, didn't I," Blaise said.

Grady stretched, seeming to fill up the usually roomy front, and draped her arm along the top of the bench seat. Her fingers came to rest an inch or two from Blaise's shoulder, but Blaise could swear she could feel them brushing her skin. Could her imagination really make her skin tingle otherwise? Blaise cut her a look and Grady smiled, looking a lot like one of her favorite lazy cats, indolent and arrogant, with a self-satisfied smirk as if she had a secret that she knew you wanted to know. Which of course, was completely not true. There was nothing about Grady McClure that she wanted to know.

She could hear her mother's voice reminding her only a fool tells lies to themselves. If she didn't want to know more about Grady, why was she going out to breakfast with her?

She sighed. "There's nothing to tell."

"About field hockey?" Grady prompted, knowing damn well Blaise wasn't talking about field hockey. Blaise was uneasy and struggling with herself. Maybe it was Grady, or maybe she was always this uncomfortable with anyone getting close. Teasing seemed to work. She'd almost seen a smile a couple of times, and she didn't miss the flush that started on Blaise's neck and moved down to the vee of her silly scrub shirt covered with iridescent fish. How a woman could look so sexy wearing something like that was beyond her, but Blaise managed.

Grady had seen women in scrubs, dozens of them, every single day of her life for years, and no one had ever looked as good as Blaise did. So good, that every time she looked at her, she thought about what was underneath the school of fish, and right at this moment, the vision was enough to make her clit twitch. She shifted her hips and stretched out a little bit more. She'd changed into jeans and a T-shirt when she'd left the OR, and for some reason, her favorite slouch-around jeans felt a little bit too tight in vital spots. Blaise Richelieu was driving her crazy in more ways than one.

"Sports is usually one of those safe topics, you know," Grady nudged. "Like the weather."

"You know what there is to know, and it's none too illuminating," Blaise said. "My daughter plays. I played in high school, so I know the rules, and I can run up and down the field enough times to keep up for at least part of the game. End of story."

"You look like you're in shape enough to keep up with almost anything," Grady murmured, and this time, Blaise was the one who shifted a little bit in her seat. *Score.* Blaise was interested. The question was, why was she throwing up roadblocks over simple things like high school sports?

"So," Blaise said, slowing as she reached the village center. For a Saturday morning, everyone in ten counties seemed to be in town, and they were all looking for parking places. Traffic crawled. "Choices are relatively limited. We've got the Two Sisters Café, which makes a decent diner-type breakfast, anything you want, served with a side of coronary artery disease. It's usually my go-to place. There's the café—great coffee, fresh pastries, and usually a breakfast special or two. Other than that, there's the doughnut cart on Main Street—gourmet doughnuts, croissants, pastries, and other absolutely sinful concoctions."

"Are there really such things as gourmet doughnuts?" Grady asked.

"Wait until you taste one and you'll know." Blaise glanced over at Grady and their eyes caught and held.

The air left Grady's lungs, as if a tornado had swept out of nowhere and ripped the insides out of everything it touched. Blaise was beautiful. And sexy. And totally in control. Grady still couldn't figure out if Blaise even liked her or not. *Patience.* Yeah, right. Not her strong suit.

Blaise broke their eye contact and eased around a pickup that stopped to back in to the curb in front of the feed store.

Grady found her breath, but her stomach still simmered from the connection. She hadn't been so turned on from just sitting next to a woman in forever. "Actually, they all sound great. I'll choose one, and you can choose one of the other places some other time."

"Maybe we should take it one meal at a time," Blaise said.

Grady recognized that line. She'd used it herself when she'd wanted to make it clear—nicely, but definitely—that she wasn't considering a next time. But she didn't think it was a line. Blaise wasn't the type. She said what she meant. Grady put on the brakes, as much as she was capable of doing when she wanted to be hitting the gas. "Okay, I can wait until you change your mind. A while."

Blaise snorted and turned her attention back to the road. Grady McClure was as smooth as they came and was coming on to *her*, that much was clear. Grady also enjoyed the game, and that was not something Blaise wanted to join in on. She wasn't a player, not in relationships, at least. She hadn't had a chance to play in the bedroom in such a long time that she had a feeling she'd be a little rusty. But that was of no consequence because Grady McClure and the bedroom were two things that were never going to meet. And if she was totally honest with herself, which she really tried to be, she *was* enjoying Grady's interest. Women had come on to her before, and she'd enjoyed the interest as anyone would, but this was different. Grady's interest was intense, so intense it was tangible, and unrelenting. She'd be lying if she said she didn't enjoy it on some level. And *knowing* that she recognized her susceptibility to a little sexual interest was enough to ease her discomfort. She would never willingly walk into the wrong situation again.

"The café it is, then," Blaise said lightly. She had this situation in hand. No worries.

"My treat," Grady said.

Blaise shook her head. "No, I'll pay my own way."

"Because?"

Blaise glanced over at her. "Because I want to be very clear about what this is, and what it isn't."

"What is it?" Grady asked, the softness in her voice and the openness in her expression so profound, Blaise was momentarily speechless. Grady seemed almost vulnerable for a moment, as if Blaise held all the power to decide what—if anything—was happening between them. Grady showed a side of herself that Blaise didn't expect to be there. One she didn't want to be there. One she didn't want to be blinded—or blindsided—by.

Blaise kept her eyes on the road. "Not a date."

"Okay," Grady said, and added after a minute, "so does that mean there *could* be a date—in that you date women?"

Blaise continued to stare straight ahead. "Unknown but unlikely and yes."

"Wait—let me sort that out." Grady inwardly breathed a sigh of relief. Blaise was saying no date right now, but women were on her dance card. One hurdle over. "So could I ask the next obvious question?"

"No, I don't have a partner or spouse," Blaise said.

"Well, that's a good place to—"

Blaise glanced at her. "What about you?"

Grady held up both hands. "Me? Nope. No spouse, partner, girlfriend, boyfriend, or pets."

Blaise laughed.

Grady silently applauded. Score another point.

"I'm not sure where pets come into it," Blaise said, "but I suppose you ought to know. I have cats."

Grady clutched her chest. "Oh no, not cats. Not man's worst friend. Not those independent little buggers who do pretty much whatever they please and expect you to feed them anyways."

"I'm afraid so."

"Cats, plural?"

"Two to be exact, foundlings."

"Meaning they found you."

Blaise's attention was on the road again as they crawled another block and waited for sixty more pickups and SUVs to park, but her smile was obvious and Grady felt as if she just scored a home run.

"I know what you mean about cats claiming homes when they feel like it, but in this case, Taylor found them in a cardboard box behind the school."

Grady shook her head. "Oh, man. What is wrong with people sometimes?"

"I don't know. I'll never understand it. A person might not be an animal person, but to do something like that…"

"So there were only two?"

"Oh no," Blaise said with a laugh. "There were six, but I put my foot down and told her she could keep two if she found homes for everyone else."

"And how many parents of her friends gave you a phone call to complain about their new additions?"

"Believe it or not, she only had to hit up Sean—did you meet him? He's one of the nurses in the ER?"

"No, not yet."

"You'll like him. He's great. He took two. And one of the maintenance guys who was there when Taylor found the kittens asked her about them the next day and took the other two."

"That's great."

"So why no pets…" Blaise said. "There. A spot. Hold on."

She zoomed around yet another truck waiting for someone else to pull out and put on her blinker.

"What are they doing at this place," Grady said as she straight-armed the dash, "giving away food?"

"On weekend days, they make doughnuts. Cream-filled and apple cider sugar. There'll be a line out the door in another five minutes."

"Good, I like doughnuts."

Blaise pulled over to the curb half a block away from the storefront restaurant with a sign that said *Bakery and Café* above the door.

"But not cats?"

"I'm a dog person," Grady said, "and until recently I lived in an apartment. That plus my schedule…there's no way I could even keep fish."

"I know what you mean. Cats look like they're independent, but they really are upset if you leave them alone too long." Blaise shut off the engine. "I'm not really sure how I feel about someone who isn't a cat person, though."

"I can acquire the taste," Grady said instantly. She enjoyed the banter, and she particularly enjoyed making Blaise smile. She'd had to work hard to get every little tidbit of info, but she'd been smart enough to avoid asking about Taylor, even though she wondered. Was there a Taylor's Daddy in the picture or some other ex somewhere, or had Blaise wanted a child and chosen to do it as a single mom? Having a kid said so much about a person, but Blaise shut down any conversation about her daughter in a flash. She was protective, and Grady respected that. So she'd wait. She'd be doing a lot of waiting where Blaise was concerned—waiting to judge her interest, waiting to gain her trust, waiting for a date. Waiting was not one of her strong points.

Blaise was a lot more of a challenge than she usually entertained with women. She rarely had the time or the energy to put in the effort to work up to a date. She dated casually, had sex casually, *not* as often as most people seemed to think, because she didn't have a long-term to offer. She was a transient, geographically and maybe physically too. Long-term meant opening up, and that wasn't something she'd grown up doing. Quite the opposite. Her family was big on appearance and perception to the outside world, but internally even bigger on competition. Her father and brother had a big head start in the competition area, but at least she had them to thank for surgery. She might have chosen surgery to level the playing field, but she'd never regretted it. She was good at it, it fulfilled her, and it was a hell of a lot of fun. But she'd had to learn to cover her disappointment when she never quite caught up to either of them, and they let her know it, since being hurt or disappointed was a sign of weakness. And she had to hide her sadness knowing her mother was disappointed in her. Despite looking like she'd fit in with her mother's set, she never had. She'd always been more interested in *having* one of the girls than *being* one of them. While it wasn't outwardly acceptable to be anti-queer, her mother would've far preferred she'd chosen male partners, and reminded her of that fact often. So often, she'd been finding excuses to avoid the West Coast for years.

"Still hungry?" Blaise murmured.

Grady started. Hell, she'd been drifting. Maybe she was more tired than she thought. She straightened and got back in the game. "Hey, yes, totally."

"Good, because I'm starving."

Blaise climbed out of the truck, and Grady jumped out her side. She was hungrier than she'd realized just a few seconds ago and, looking at Blaise, realized it wasn't all about breakfast.

CHAPTER SEVEN

The Bakery and Café was housed in a renovated bank on the corner of Main and a narrow residential street. The white clapboard and occasional brick homes that dated back to the eighteen hundreds all featured wraparound porches and big yards. Nothing at all like the sprawling modern glass and concrete edifices perched on the hillsides in Bel Air. Grady could actually see herself living in some of these places—if she ever wanted a house, that is. Houses suggested something permanent, though, and she'd been living an itinerant lifestyle moving from one training program to another for years. Settling down wasn't a picture she could easily conjure.

The café occupied a single room that had once been the bank lobby, with fifteen-foot-high ceilings, tall narrow floor-to-ceiling windows on the street sides, a counter in the back that led to the kitchen, and a unique alcove connecting to the restrooms through what had previously been the bank vault. The large reinforced brass-plated door stood open, and its interior held shelves where the deposit boxes had once been. Now the vault showcased items from local craftspeople, along with T-shirts and the occasional mug. Hanging Edison lights and several fans that turned lazily pierced the original tin ceiling at intervals, and the place smelled like cinnamon and sugar and was packed with people of all ages seated at long tables. Half a dozen others circled looking for seats.

"Wow," Grady murmured as they joined the line leading up to the counter to place orders. "This must be where every one of the passengers in those cars we were following was headed."

"Most of them," Blaise said. "I don't usually come at this time on Saturday mornings, so it's a treat."

"It is," Grady said, thinking about the doughnuts, but imagining

Blaise with sugar dappled on her upper lip and how that might taste if she kissed it away. Heat rushed up from her center and spread through her chest, and she tugged at the collar of her T-shirt. "Hot in here."

Blaise glanced at her, one blond brow arching. "It's a bakery, and there are probably fifty people in this room. I'm sure that's above the occupancy code."

"You're right, but I don't think it's the heat from them I'm feeling."

With a shake of her head and a frown, but with a smile that belied her irritation, Blaise stepped up to the counter. "Two blackberry filled, please, and two eggs scrambled. Plus coffee."

The middle-aged guy with his gray hair pulled back and tied at the nape of his neck with a leather thong glanced at Grady. "What are you having?"

"I'll have the same, but add the breakfast sausage."

"You got it." He scribbled something on a piece of paper and turned to push it through the pass-through to the kitchen. "Help yourself to the coffee. Cups on the sideboard and refills are free."

"Thanks, Harold."

"No problem, Blaise." His gaze lingered on Grady for a moment, as if categorizing her in some way, and then he turned his attention to the next customer in line.

"I think we can grab those two seats at the end of the middle table," Blaise said as an elderly couple rose and began to collect their dishware.

"Yeah—no one seems to be waiting for them." Everyone ate family-style, it seemed, but at least at the end of the long table, they'd have a tiny bit of privacy. Grady followed Blaise over to the red-checked-oilcloth covered table, and once they'd claimed their spots, asked, "Can I get you coffee?"

"That'd be great. Black with—"

"Cream and one blue packet," Grady finished.

"How exactly did you know that?"

"I watched you pour one in the break room last night."

"You're disturbingly observant."

"Some people might consider that a plus."

Blaise leaned back in her chair and blew a small breath as she rolled her eyes. "Please. Go. Hunt and gather coffee."

Laughing, Grady threaded her way through the myriad of tables and chairs to a cabinet along the side wall that held coffee urns and cups. She filled two mugs, added the necessaries, and carefully carried them back. She'd never given much thought—as in none at all—to getting coffee for someone before, but she felt downright pleased at the moment, as if the act signaled to anyone watching that she was with Blaise. As in *with* with. She mentally threw a bucket of cold water over her head. Reality check. Like procuring a simple cup of coffee was all it would take.

"Here you go," Grady said, passing Blaise her mug as she sat opposite her.

"Thank you," Blaise said and cradled the mug. "I definitely need this."

Grady blew on her coffee and took a tentative sip. A bold French roast. "Yep. Pretty perfect. Clever of them to offer free refills too."

"It's one of those little things that people remember. That makes them feel special."

Grady tried to come up with the name of the last person who'd made her feel special, or one she'd tried to make feel that way, and couldn't. She didn't mind the first so much, but she wasn't proud of the second. Hell, some of those women she'd slept with and hadn't given them much more attention than passing conversation. True, they'd all professed, just like her, to have no interest in anything beyond mutual, casual pleasure, but that wasn't the point. She still should have *tried*. Sensing Blaise watching and waiting, she went for neutral ground. Passing conversation. "Are you coming back later with the kids?"

"They'll probably be ready for more lunch-type food. We'll try the diner."

"I heard you say you're not working tonight," Grady said. "Off the weekend?"

"No, I'm on tomorrow night. You?"

"Free until Monday. Sort of." Grady shrugged. She'd rather be at the hospital with something to occupy her mind than sitting around in her not yet furnished one-bedroom apartment with nothing to do except…think about having nothing to do. "I think I'm second call tomorrow, but I'll have to check the email from Flann. It's kind of a loose schedule, and I pretty much got the idea I should be available if needed."

Blaise said, "Probably not what you're used to. I don't think any of the Rivers docs are ever really not on call. They're always popping in and out."

"I suppose that has something to do with everyone calling the hospital the Rivers."

"Well, you know the story, don't you?"

"Vaguely," Grady said. "Flann never really talked much about it, more than to say she wasn't the only doc in the family. I understood that a lot of her family was in medicine and everyone pretty much worked here."

"Yeah, that's a bit of an understatement." Blaise laughed. "When Flann says her family works here, she means *all* her family for a hundred years or more. The hospital was founded by the Rivers family, and there's always been a Rivers to head the staff. The hospital and the family are kind of the same thing."

"A medical legacy," Grady said quietly, thinking about her own family history. Flann's story couldn't be more different from hers. There was nothing that bound her family together—if anything, their shared profession had kept them apart—a never ending source of pressure, and bars that kept getting higher and higher to surpass. "Couldn't be easy, living in the shadow of that kind of past."

"I guess that might be true," Blaise said, "though I never got that sense from any of the Riverses I know. For them, being part of the hospital is more a question of loyalty and responsibility."

Blaise was quiet for a moment, and Grady forced a smile. She wasn't used to women studying her, and she wasn't sure what she was revealing. Not that that mattered now. Her past was just that—past. She'd worked her ass off to survive her residency, and now she had the job she wanted in a new place, where she didn't have to live in anyone's shadow. She was her own person, and that was all she'd ever wanted. She cleared her throat. "I take it Flann or Harper will be the next chief of staff, then."

"Oh, that will be Harper," Blaise said. "It's always been going to be Harper. She's got the temperament for it."

Grady laughed. "You mean Flann's not diplomatic enough?"

"Yes, but not a criticism. That's part of what makes her so good," Blaise said with a shake of her head and a secret kind of a smile that had Grady bristling for some reason. "Flann and Harper are competitive, but they're so close in age, I guess that's to be expected. Flann has never seen a game she didn't want to win, though, and that's why I want her operating on me or mine if the need ever comes."

"I know what you mean," Grady said. "It was tough, the residency program, and Flann always seemed to effortlessly be the best."

"I'm not surprised—she's always been that way. Harper is the quiet and intense one, and Flann is the showy, confident one. They're both really good. I remember in high school..." Blaise flushed and grew silent.

"Oh, come on," Grady said, "you *cannot* stop there."

"Let's just say Flann was really popular with everyone."

"You had a crush on her? Did you ever go out with her?" Grady heard the edge of interrogation in her voice but the words were already out. Of course Blaise had had relationships—she had a kid, for crying out loud. Still...Grady preferred to imagine them in the far distant past in the form of shadowy, unsatisfying, forgettable lovers.

"No," Blaise said instantly. "To both."

Grady narrowed her eyes. Blaise answered so quickly, and so emphatically, her response made Grady question whether she was glossing over some kind of thing with Flann. The thought bothered her even though her rational mind knew that was crazy. Flann was married now, and from the way she talked about her wife, nuts about her, and Blaise was no way the sort of woman to get involved with someone in a relationship. But all the same, the idea of Blaise lusting after anyone, especially someone Grady had always found just a little overwhelming—not that she'd ever say that out loud—bothered her. A lot.

"So you were one of the rare ones to resist the Rivers magic?" Grady probed.

"I'm not all that susceptible to magic. Besides, I wasn't—" Blaise jumped up as Harold called their order number. "I'll get that."

She sped off before Grady had a chance to ask her for the rest of her sentence or to get their food herself. Yep, Blaise was definitely avoiding something, and Grady tried hard not to imagine her ever being attracted to Flann. Even though it was ancient history and never happened. She rubbed her forehead. She'd never been this sensitive, or even that interested, in any other woman's current or past dating history.

A few moments later Blaise slid their plates onto the table and settled across from her.

"I don't know what to eat first," Grady said, eyeing her plate of eggs, sausage, toast she hadn't ordered, and two warm doughnuts that smelled like sin.

"Well, I do," Blaise said and picked up one of the cream-filled doughnuts. She bit into it, and sure enough, a small dusting of white powder lingered on her upper lip.

Grady's stomach tightened. Her imagination had failed her on this one—Blaise was way sexier than she'd pictured with that tempting bit of sweetness on her perfectly sculpted deep rose-colored lip. And yep, she most definitely wanted to kiss that sugar away.

"Aren't you going to try one?" Blaise asked.

Grady realized she was staring at Blaise's mouth. Not real obvious much.

"Uh-huh," she said a little blankly. Maybe she was extra tired, but her fortitude failed her. She slowly extended her arm, giving Blaise a chance to draw back, and when Blaise remained perfectly still, her gaze fixed on Grady's, Grady rested her fingertips against the angle of Blaise's jaw and gently brushed her top lip with her thumb. "Sugar."

For a fraction of a second, Blaise leaned her cheek against Grady's palm, filling her hand with softness and warmth, and then, as if she hadn't meant to do that, straightened.

Blaise's cheeks flushed, and she laughed a little self-consciously. "It's hard to eat one of these without making a mess."

"That's not a mess from where I'm sitting," Grady said. "That's devastating."

"You have to stop flirting." Blaise's pupils flickered and the tiny gold specks in the deep sea-blue glittered.

"I'm not flirting."

"And if you believe that, you're fooling yourself. Eat your doughnut, Dr. McClure."

Grady took a bite and gave herself a moment to enjoy the explosion of sweet-tart dark berry flavor before returning to task. "So, you were telling me about your crush on Flann."

"We're talking high school here—what could it matter?" Blaise sounded grumpy. *Curious.*

"High school isn't that far in the past, and besides—sometimes those years say a lot about who we are."

"God, I hope not," Blaise murmured, no longer surprised that Grady had her thinking back to her not-so-happy high school days. Grady harbored a very disconcerting talent for taking her places she didn't want to go—or go back to—and an even more dangerous ability to get her to say things she didn't mean to. She didn't even want to think about how damn good Grady's hand had felt on her face for that fleeting second. She never got so personal with anyone she'd just met, and rarely with some of those closest to her. Even Abby didn't know all the story, and since Abby wasn't the type to ask—unlike her breakfast companion of the moment—she wasn't ever likely to. Time to divert the conversation. She'd been the focus for far too long. "Are you still pining for your first love?"

"Me? Hell no. I can't even remember that far back." Grady pointed a finger. "There you go again, turning the tables. *You* are an expert at that."

"Most people don't notice—they'd rather talk about themselves anyhow."

"Not me," Grady said darkly.

"And that's why you ask so many questions and love guessing games."

"I wouldn't have to guess if you'd tell me."

"All right." Blaise laughed and polished off her doughnut. Maybe a little information would stem the curiosity tide. "I did not date girls in high school. Crushes, sure—although *not* Flann Rivers. Too many other girls crushed on her already."

"Selective, were you?"

Blaise's expression shuttered closed. "More like in denial. Today I'd call it questioning, but back then I was a little slow to recognize what I was feeling. I take it that was not the case for you."

Grady polished off her doughnut and studied the second one. "I'll die a swift death if I eat that one right now, won't I?"

Blaise picked up her second and took a bite. "Depends on how tough you are."

"Ha." Grady plucked hers up and bit a chunk out of it. Blackberry filling dribbled down her chin. "Damn."

Blaise grabbed a napkin and held it out. "Here. Take this."

"I've found that thumbs work just as well for that," Grady murmured, taking the napkin.

"And I've found this to be a safer and less messy alternative."

"Do you always choose safe and less messy?"

"Whenever possible," Blaise said with total seriousness.

CHAPTER EIGHT

Grady pushed her plate away and sighed. "This place could become a very bad habit."

"As bad habits go, you could do worse."

"If I wasn't trying to make a good impression," Grady shot back, "I'd say I *have* done worse. Much worse."

"Oh," Blaise said laughing. "That's clever, you see. Most people would immediately want to know what evil you've been up to."

"Most people, but not you?"

Blaise pursed her lips. "I believe everyone is entitled to keep their secrets, if they want."

"Ah," Grady said. They weren't talking about her any longer. She was coming to recognize that pattern with Blaise. Approach and avoid. Whenever Grady circled in too close, or Blaise let something a little bit personal slip out, Blaise retreated. Grady wondered if Blaise even knew she was doing it. So many questions, so many challenges. No wonder she was fascinated.

"Nothing evil, I promise." Grady pressed her hand to her heart and was rewarded by a smile. Blaise's attention shifted abruptly and Grady looked over her shoulder. Flann Rivers, her sandy hair tousled, her brown eyes lively, wended her way between the tables toward them. In casual khakis, a red cotton button-down with the cuffs turned back, and scuffed brown loafers, Flann looked like she hadn't a care in the world. And maybe she hadn't, or at least none that threatened what mattered. Inexplicably envious, Grady wondered what that kind of contentment would feel like.

"Hey, Blaise. Hi, Grady," Flann said. "You found this place pretty fast, McClure."

"Thank Blaise for that," Grady said.

"Hi, Flann." Blaise smiled, an altogether welcoming smile that made Grady bristle internally. And wasn't that dumb.

"You two here for the doughnuts?" Flann asked.

"We've already had our share," Blaise said.

Flann frowned. "I hope you left some, because Abby has a hankering for the apple cider sugar doughnuts."

"We're not guilty if they're gone," Blaise said, laughing. "We had the cream filled. Are the kids up yet?"

"I heard stirrings when I left. Abby said you were feeding them this morning."

"I'll be over in just a few minutes," Blaise said.

"I'll buy extra doughnuts to ward off starvation, just in case."

Blaise laughed and Flann shot Grady a look. "Heard you had a big case your first night. Sorry I wasn't around to give you a hand."

"No problem," Grady said. "Blaise took care of getting him squared away for the OR. I just showed up."

"She's our secret weapon. If you need to get an emergency on the schedule, find Blaise. She'll make it happen." Flann sent her megawatt smile in Blaise's direction, and Blaise rolled her eyes. She looked pleased, though.

Flann glanced over her shoulder at the line growing toward the door. "I better go. Listen, there's a thing out at the Homestead tonight. Kind of a community gathering to celebrate…" She shrugged. "Well, anything you want. There's a big football game tonight against one of our longtime rivals, but win or lose, we'll be celebrating. You two should come."

Grady glanced at Blaise questioningly.

"Ah," Blaise said a little hesitantly, "I'm not sure I can make it. I'll pick up Taylor and anyone else who needs a ride home, though, when you all want to throw the kids out."

Flann snorted. "Huh. Margie will probably invite half the school to stay over."

"I have a feeling that's already been done."

"True. Well, hope you make it." Flann waved and headed toward the counter.

"The Homestead," Grady said after Flann was out of earshot. "That's her family's place?"

"Uh-huh. The Rivers family have had that property for—"

"I know, a hundred years?" Grady said, beginning to feel like she had nothing to offer that compared to the Riverses and their history and their superpowers.

Blaze raised a brow. "You're sounding a little testy."

Grady blew out a breath. "Sorry. Tired. It's just that—well, you know, tough act to follow."

"I wasn't aware you were following anyone," Blaise said quietly.

"Yeah, you're right, that's just me. Sometimes I'm competitive when I don't need to be."

"I imagine that comes with the territory. I've never known a surgeon who wasn't."

"Thanks for letting me off the hook. I didn't mean to be an ass."

Blaise laughed. "Really?"

"Okay, debatable."

Blaise smiled at that, taking the sting out of Grady's embarrassment, and went on, "So, yes, the Rivers family home is known as the Homestead, after a time when theirs was one of the largest holdings in the area, and the Riverses one of the founding families. Now their home is always open to everyone in the community, and they do throw super parties. Mainly because Ida Rivers is perhaps the finest cook in five states, possibly more."

"So about this thing tonight," Grady said, getting back to what really mattered. Because if Blaise was going to be there, she wanted to be there too. It beat the hell out of sitting around at home not watching bad television.

"It's supposed to be a celebration for the football team and the high school kids, but it sounds to me like it's morphing into something a whole lot bigger."

"There will be adults there, right?" Grady asked.

"From the sound of it, everyone will be there." Blaise paused. "I'm on retrieval duty, so I'm not planning on going until I pick up the kids."

"Oh. Okay."

"I'll give you the address," Blaise said, "and you can GPS it if you decide to go. It's just a few miles outside town."

"That would be great. If I had a vehicle."

Blaise stared. "You don't have a car?"

"I didn't need one in the city. Parking was too expensive, and I didn't go anywhere. If I needed to buy groceries, they have this nifty system where you can just rent a car for an hour. Pick it up at a designated spot, drive around, drop it off, and get charged. I guess you probably don't have that here."

"I guess you'll have to get used to walking a lot. Fortunately, there's a good grocery store right in town and decent cafés, but if you want anything fancier than diner food or the bakery, you're going to be in trouble."

"I don't get out much," Grady said.

"Well, now that you're not a resident, maybe that will change," Blaise said.

"Maybe a lot of things will change," Grady murmured. "So I probably won't see you tonight, then."

Blaise looked like she was going to say something and then stopped herself. "Well, as I said, I'm not planning on going."

"Right, I understand," Grady said. "Saturday nights are probably, you know, jumping around here."

"You have no idea." Blaise rose and gathered her plate and cutlery and carried everything over to the bins put out for them by the kitchen. "I'm going to drive over to Abby's. Can I give you a ride home?"

"No, thanks." Grady deposited her dishes and walked outside with Blaise. If she could think of a reasonable way to prolong their time together, she would. She was facing a long day with nothing planned but a few hours' sleep and not much else to do. Being with Blaise made an hour pass as if it was just a minute. When she was with her, she was unaware of anything else in the world, except Blaise. Reluctantly, she added, "I don't live that far—I'll just walk. But thanks. Thanks for breakfast too."

Blaise paused as if considering her words. She did that a lot. "I enjoyed it. Have a good day."

"You too," Grady called as Blaise turned and jogged over to her SUV. She would've stood and watched Blaise drive away if that wouldn't make her seem totally weird, which it would. When Blaise climbed into her vehicle without looking back, Grady finally walked off in the opposite direction. She wasn't the least bit tired. Just the opposite. Exhilarated.

If she'd been a whistling person, she might've whistled. The sun shone, the morning was proving to be a warm, early fall day, and she'd just spent an hour with a fascinating woman. She couldn't ask for a lot more. Except to do it again.

❖

Blaise pulled into the narrow drive on the side of Abby and Flann's house, parked, and got out. Taylor, her blond hair in disarray, slouched on the porch swing, her feet propped on a white wicker coffee table, in a T-shirt featuring a band from when Blaise was young and sweatpants with the school logo down the thigh. Dave Kincaid, in a football jersey and matching sweats, occupied the opposite end of the glider. They looked half asleep.

"Morning," Blaise said as she let herself in through the gate in the white picket fence. A border of marigolds on either side of the stone walk defied the cooler nights, still packed with tight yellow and orange heads. The single-room schoolhouse had been retired with the construction of a larger modern school on the east side of town long before she was born and had been empty for years before being renovated. She had always loved the place and had secretly told herself one day it would come up for sale and she'd buy it. She hadn't quite been able to manage it that spring, not with Taylor looking at colleges already and the college fund she'd started when Taylor was born looking less and less likely to cover the costs. Now Abby owned it and Taylor had made it her second home. Her plans, it seemed, would have to wait.

"Hi, Mom," Taylor called, yawning and closing her eyes again.

And there was the reason she'd never be bitter when her plans took a shape she hadn't foreseen. "Morning, honey."

Dave murmured, "Good morning, Ms. Richelieu."

"Hi, Dave." She rapped on the screen door and peered into the room beyond. She didn't see anyone in the living room. She hadn't thought about how early it still was on a Saturday. Hopefully she wasn't disturbing anything intimate. If she was, she trusted Abby to let her know. While she waited, she faced her own simmering embarrassment. What an ass. She should have offered to give Grady a ride out to the Homestead for the party. The words had been on the tip of her tongue, and then she'd swallowed them. If Grady had been anyone else, she wouldn't have hesitated. Maybe she'd held back because part of her *wanted* to offer. And wasn't that too twisted to figure out, when the last thing she wanted to be doing was thinking about Grady McClure.

"Hey," Abby said from the other side of the screen door. "You coming in?"

"Oh yes. Sorry. I was just…are you sure you're not busy? I'm early. I can just collect the kids…"

Abby glanced past her to the kids on the swing, cocked her brow, and gestured her inside. "Tim went home a while ago to babysit his younger brother. And those two aren't even awake yet." When they'd moved a few feet away into the living room, Abby continued in a low voice, "With a house full of kids, we took care of personal matters much earlier. Flann's going for a run now. I'm already bored."

Blaise laughed. "I don't see how you have time to be. I'm so sorry the kids have apparently designated this as their clubhouse."

Abby threw an arm around her shoulders and squeezed. "I told you, I really don't mind. It's easier on my nerves to have them here than wondering where they are and what they're up to. You want coffee?"

Blaise was about to say no, and then realized what she wanted as much as coffee was conversation. Taylor was clearly in no hurry to leave, and Abby was her best friend. "Half a cup. Otherwise I'll never get to sleep today."

"Great." Abby motioned her into the kitchen while she poured coffee. "You know where the cream and sugar are."

Blaise doctored her coffee. "Thanks."

"Come on, let's take them out back."

Blaise followed Abby outside and eased into the wooden Adirondack chair with a sigh. The back deck faced southeast, and the morning sun draped over her like a soothing hand, dispelling some of the ache in her tired body. She couldn't remember if she'd had a chance to sit down all night, which likely meant she hadn't. "This is nice."

"Long night?"

"Mm. Busy. It feels good to sit and talk."

"I know. We never get a chance to do much of either, especially with you on nights and me day shift half the time."

"Well, luckily, you work nights half the time too. Even when you're *not* on call."

Abby laughed. "I know. But it doesn't leave any time for real talking."

"It's true."

"So, since we're talking, Flann mentioned she ran into you and Grady McClure at the bakery this morning."

Trust Abby to get to the point. Blaise wasn't surprised or offended to have been the subject of casual discussion. That was the way of life in a small community like theirs. Just about anything was a fair topic for conversation. "Yes. I ran into her this morning just as she was finishing up with Mr. Hopkins. We ended up going to breakfast."

"Hm." Abby telegraphed more than words as she stretched her feet out onto a wicker ottoman.

"Mr. Hopkins is doing well," Blaise said, steering the conversation away from Grady, and breakfast, and Abby's unspoken comment. Maybe she didn't want all that much conversation just yet—not when she hadn't had time to process her jumbled feelings about Grady and her own out of character behavior yet.

"I know, Flann called the ICU for a rundown on the patients this morning, and they gave her report. McClure did all right last night?"

"As far as I saw, yes. And the OR nurses seemed to like her."

"Well, that's a ringing endorsement. How about you?"

"Sorry?"

Abby rolled her eyes. "Oh, come on. When's the last time you went to breakfast with anyone besides me since I've known you?"

"Well, that's only been a few months."

"Okay, before then."

"Well, Taylor and I—"

"Our children do not count."

"Mari and I go out fairly often," Blaise said archly.

"Uh-huh. Mari. Who's totally taken."

"Well, for all I know, Grady could be taken too," Blaise said just a bit grumpily. "And it wasn't like that. So it doesn't matter."

"Did you ask her?"

"About what?"

"If she was taken?"

"She isn't. She said so."

"Aha. So the two of you were doing the first-date talk."

"No," Blaise said emphatically. "Quite the opposite. We were doing the not-a-date talk."

"Who started that?"

Blaise studied her coffee.

"Not your type?" Abby asked quietly.

"Very much not my type," Blaise said.

"You know, matchmaking is not one of my interests," Abby said. "But I admit to natural curiosity and all that. What's your type?"

"If I actually knew," Blaise said, hoping not to sound bitter, "I'd probably be able to tell you. But not Grady McClure. Someone…steady and ordinary…and humble."

Abby laughed out loud. "Oh boy. You're in the wrong place to meet people like that. Between the flight crews, the first responders, and the ER staff you're pretty much surrounded by not-ordinary and not-humble."

Abby was still chuckling when Blaise said decidedly grumpily, "I never said I was looking."

"Fair enough. But just the same, you're right. That's definitely not McClure, at least from what I could see from our brief acquaintance."

"Exactly." Blaise should have felt vindicated since Abby agreed, but the memory of Grady's thumb brushing over her lip popped up out of nowhere and her breath caught. A distracting wave of warmth rose in her middle and settled deeper. Ordinary, steady women did not take such confident license. Even if Grady *had* given her a chance to avoid the touch, which she hadn't done, had she. And her emotions happily tangled themselves back into a jumble all over again.

"But she's not bad looking," Abby said offhandedly.

"Talk about understatement," Blaise muttered.

Abby's eyes glinted. "So you think she's hot?"

"Hot? Are we teenagers now?"

"Well, I think she's hot."

"Oh, really?"

Abby shrugged. "Well, I might have, ten years ago and pre-Flann. But I can certainly appreciate she is attractive."

"What do you know about her?" Blaise asked quietly.

Abby set her cup down on the arm of the chair. "Serious question?" Blaise nodded.

"Honestly, not all that much. I know that Flann was a few years ahead of her during residency. McClure was the best of her year and, according to Flann, one of the best she's seen period. Flann never really talked very much about Grady's personal life, but I gathered McClure could've gone anywhere and decided to come here. It's a bit of a mystery to me, but Flann doesn't seem bothered by it."

"You think she's using this position as a stepping-stone to something else, then," Blaise said, unaccountably disappointed at the thought that Grady would only be around a short while. Yet another very good reason to keep her distance.

"I don't know. It sort of seems unlikely. If she could've gone anywhere else, she wouldn't need to come here first. So I am inclined to go along with Flann and accept that this is what she wanted, for whatever reason. Maybe it's lifestyle. Not everyone wants bright lights, big city."

"No," Blaise said, thinking about what she'd once thought she wanted. "Not everyone does."

"So why did you go to breakfast with her?"

Blaise met Abby's gaze. "I wish I knew."

"When you find out, I want to be the second one to know."

Blaise laughed, and her confusion eased. Abby had a way of making anything feel possible. "Swear."

"So, tonight. You're coming, right?"

"Oh my God, everyone is talking about this. I'll try, okay?"

"Just picking up the kids, anyhow. Just come a little earlier. You know you won't be sorry."

Maybe she should, just a little sorry now that she hadn't offered Grady that ride. And a lot more relieved that she hadn't. What she needed was a little time to find her balance around her, and a bit of distance was just the prescription for that.

Chapter Nine

Grady woke in the midafternoon, naked beneath the plain white sheet beside an open window. Sunlight cut a swath across the bed, warming her arm where it rested outside the covers. Someone was mowing a lawn, and the scent of fresh cut grass drifted in on a lazy breeze. She turned on her side and stared outside. She should probably put up a shade or blinds, or something, but she liked the light. And the air. A huge old maple tree obscured part of her view of the adjacent house, so the next-door neighbors might not be able to see into her bedroom even if they wanted to. It was weird, looking out her window directly at the window of someone else's house just yards away, and sometimes hearing their voices coming through open windows or wafting up from front porches where they sat and talked. Nothing at all like an apartment building in the city, where dozens of people lived in even closer proximity than here, but where she might not recognize her closest neighbor in the elevator.

She'd been in the village just a couple of days, long enough to look at the list of places the Realtor Flann had put her in touch with had to show her. That had taken all of an hour. She'd decided on the first place that wasn't on Main Street because she knew it wouldn't matter where she lived, as long as it wasn't too far from the hospital. The next day she'd unpacked her few boxes and trunks and walked around, at loose ends. Once she'd gone to work, everything had settled into place. Until Blaise. Now everything was completely unsettled, in a way she liked.

Grady stretched, pulled an arm behind her head, and stared at the ceiling. Her gaze was slightly unfocused, but the image was perfectly clear. Blaise Richelieu, sitting across from her in the bakery, surrounded by townspeople, on an ordinary Saturday morning that had to be one of the most memorable of her life. She couldn't recall a time when every word resonated in the air, shimmering like a precious jewel that she wanted to capture and keep hidden, to take out and enjoy again and again. Grady laughed out loud. Talk about flight of imagination.

She was losing her mind. Blaise had definitely derailed her sanity.

The stirring in her belly was pleasant and anything but imaginary, and the thrumming slightly lower, even more so. She hadn't had sex in quite a while, but the way her pulse surged and her body clenched wasn't just physical hunger for a familiar release. This time the anticipation of pleasure held a promise of something more. The thrill of the unknown was enough to have her hand moving lower, coming to rest between her thighs, exploring the wanting that was so familiar and yet so much more intense this time. She closed her eyes as her thighs tightened, but when Blaise's face flickered behind her closed lids, she gently pushed the image away. She didn't want an orgasm with a phantom woman where Blaise was concerned. If and when, she wanted to feel her everywhere. She concentrated instead on the rising pressure and the pounding urgency beneath her fingers and, with a sharp intake of breath and a brief groan between gritted teeth, she came hard and fast.

Blowing out a breath, she rolled onto her back and opened her eyes. She had no doubt where her arousal originated. Blaise had struck a chord in her the instant she'd seen her, and that had only grown the more they'd bantered and teased and tentatively explored. Blaise was beautiful, true, and Grady enjoyed looking at her, liked the confident, graceful way she moved, and got lost in her eyes when they sparkled with amusement or flared hotter when she was annoyed. That attraction still simmered in her belly and added to the pleasure she'd just experienced—hormones and whatever other subtle chemistries were ignited by some individuals and not others. But what drew her even deeper and kept her entranced was what lay hidden beneath Blaise's cool, almost serene gaze. She was so controlled that she was barely touchable. And oh, how that made Grady want to touch. Her clit twinged again just thinking about it.

She chuckled. She hadn't been so on edge, so forthrightly horny, since she was a teenager. She had a little more restraint now than she'd had then, but if she didn't want to spend the rest of the afternoon fantasizing, she had to move. She tossed the sheet aside, grabbed clean jeans from a stack on the dresser along with a short sleeve navy polo, and carried them into the bathroom for a shower. Ten minutes later she was dressed with nowhere to go.

One thing she didn't plan on doing was spending the rest of the day in her apartment, so out was the only answer. As she hit the sidewalk, she realized she was hungry. She ambled to the intersection of her block and Main and turned right in the direction of the hospital. The place was like a homing beacon, and she the pigeon. She might travel out of sight, but she'd always come home. After walking along a row of adjoining three- and four-story buildings that had once been homes but had been converted into storefronts at street level, she crossed to a place called Clark's that advertised pizza, subs, and burgers in the window. The food was either good or all there was available, since the booths along the walls and tables in the center of the large room were packed, mostly with teenagers.

She ordered two slices at the counter and carried them, along with a bottle of water, to a table only slightly smeared with marinara sauce and settled back to enjoy her late lunch. The door opened and three kids came in, a boy and two girls. Grady watched them idly as they jostled their way up to the counter to order. She paused midbite as they turned back, searching for seats, her focus captured by one of the girls—the taller of the two who'd just come in, a blonde with blue eyes, flawless honey-gold complexion, and a natural confidence that was evident just from the way she scanned the room, her gaze passing over Grady as she pointed to a free table opposite her.

Embarrassed for no good reason, and not wanting to be caught staring, Grady averted her gaze. Something had drawn her attention, though, and she sensed she was missing something she should have recognized. Since they were clambering around a table three feet away, she could hardly avoid seeing them out of the corner of her eye. The niggling feeling didn't go away, and she couldn't put her finger on just what caused it. Annoying. And strange.

"Hey, Taylor," the boy said as the trio pulled out chairs, his voice that in-between baritone and cracking tenor a lot of boys developed in their midteens, "didn't your mom take you guys out to eat earlier?"

"Sure," the blonde said, "but that was *hours* ago. And I only had pancakes. I'm starving."

"Not a news flash!" The other girl, athletic-looking with riotous reddish blond waves and ice blue eyes, laughed and poked Taylor good-naturedly "You're always starving."

"So where's the crime?" Taylor swiped a piece of pizza off a paper plate and took a bite. "Where are we meeting up for the game?"

As the trio ate and chatted about the game and the after-party and the maybe after-after-party if they got lucky, Grady finished her pizza and gathered up the paper plates and napkins to carry to the trash. Taylor. Couldn't be anyone other than Blaise's daughter. She looked like Blaise. That must've been what struck Grady as so familiar.

Mystery solved, Grady hit the sidewalk and started toward the hospital without even really thinking about it. She wasn't on call, but that didn't matter. She knew she'd always be welcome there. Traffic on a late Saturday afternoon was still pretty brisk, the day pleasantly warm, and she was feeling energized. She strode west on Main and turned up the side street that ended in the winding, tree shrouded approach road to the hospital. Already the trip seemed familiar and evoked a sense of belonging she hadn't felt in Baltimore despite having lived there for six years. Maybe that was because this place was her choice, a place where she could *be* herself, free from expectations and the reputation for being untrustworthy in the dating arena she'd somehow garnered after an assistant vice president at Shock Trauma had read a lot more into a few encounters than she'd ever intended.

She'd never realized how much she wanted that blank slate, until she'd come here and walked in to discover no one knew her. Well, Flann did, but even then, their relationship was based on real experience. When she'd been a young resident, Flann had been a fellow, which in the hierarchy of things was second to godliness. Grady'd learned from her, not just in the operating room, but in dealing with other residents and patients. She'd had some catching up to do, maybe still did, but she was a match for Flann in confidence and, she'd heard it said, in arrogance too. Funny how being compared to Flann never bothered her, maybe because she respected her so much. If she could be as good as Flann in the OR, she'd be happy. As to the rest of the mostly good-natured comparisons, she didn't really worry too much about her standing in the bedroom department. She never had any particular difficulties there, although in the last couple of years, those activities had fallen off.

Not that she was a monk or anything. She had moments of loneliness and stress and sheer physical need, and there'd been encounters. Short-lived and pleasant and forgotten—not because they never mattered, but because they left no lasting impressions. She was very, very careful that mutual expectations were clear before things went too far.

Lasting impressions. She wasn't even sure what those would've looked like, not until that morning. Blaise Richelieu had left a lasting impression without even trying. Maybe *despite* not trying. A smile, a rare bit of laughter, a gaze that cut through every shield Grady had. And when Grady'd touched her? Unforgettable. For just the merest second, she'd touched her, and she could feel the warmth and softness of her still. She'd wanted to kiss her.

Something to think about. Or maybe best not to think too much at all. She'd usually done all right following her instincts. And her instincts all shouted Blaise's name.

She rounded the last bend in the road and the hospital rose up before her, a magnificent edifice that must've been palatial a hundred and twenty-five years ago. Massive brick façade, two-story-tall white colonnades flanking the entrance, two wings curving out from the main building. The hospital perched atop the mountain, high above the community that created and sustained it, and to which it gave back purpose and security.

Grady took a moment just to absorb its grandeur. There weren't many like it left in the entire country. Rural hospitals were falling by the dozens every month, in the changing world of medicine where cost mattered more sometimes than care. Flann had assured her that was not going to be the case with the Rivers. They'd weathered the change and, rather than give up their heritage and their mission, they'd brought in Presley Worth, the CEO and representative of an enormous medical conglomerate, against the wishes of many in the hospital who feared that Presley would destroy the heart of their community. What she had done was just the opposite. She had revitalized the medical center, bringing in new affiliations with surrounding hospitals and medical professionals, building the new ER-Trauma wing, securing appropriation for residencies, medevac capabilities, and new staff. The Rivers was a first-class primary care center now, and as Grady walked through the ER doors, she could see herself there as part of it.

A big shouldered, sandy-haired guy in plain green scrubs looked up as she strolled down to the nurses' station. His name tag read Emery D'Angelo, RN. She held out her hand. "Hi. Dr. Grady McClure. I'm new here."

"I know who you are. You took care of Mr. Hopkins last night. Good save."

"Thanks," she said. "I had plenty of help. I was just about to go upstairs to see him. Thought I'd stop in and see if you had anything going down here." She glanced over her shoulder at the board. Pretty full, and the halls bustled with staff—nurses, techs, PAs, and residents hustling in and out of cubicles and wheeling patients in chairs or on stretchers to the elevators. "Looks busy."

"The usual Saturday afternoon stuff—a few broken bones, colds, and belly pain." He shrugged. "I don't think we've got anything surgical, though."

"Well, there's always something to do, right?" She grinned. "I'll be around for a while."

He shook his head. "I don't know if I want you hanging around. You might bring us bad luck."

At that moment, the radio on his belt beeped and he hit the on button. "This is Rivers base, go ahead."

"Rivers, this is Medevac 2-1-5. We're inbound fifteen minutes with a fifty-four-year-old male, partial traumatic amputation, right hand."

Emery looked at Grady, pointed a finger, and mouthed, *See what I mean?*

He toggled the radio again. "Roger that. Do you have any amputated parts?"

"Several partial digits. Secured in an ice bath," came the reply.

"Roger that."

"So who's on call for surgery?" Grady asked when Emery signed off.

"Matt Hinkle," Emery said. "I'll give him a call."

"I'm right here—will he care if I check the patient first?"

Emory raised a shoulder. "Matt's really easygoing and not territorial. Plus, if it's a possible replant, he'll probably want ortho or plastics to take it."

"Who's covering trauma?"

"That would be Sheila McConnell. She's not gonna want to keep it. The evaluation will just tie up the trauma unit, and they won't want that if something big comes in."

"I better check."

"You know where they are," Emery said. "I'll clear things with Matt."

The trauma unit adjoined the regular emergency room but, unlike the ER, had a full operating room as well as a separate entrance, a turnaround for the emergency vehicles outside, and the closest access to the elevators to the rooftop helipad. Grady went through the connecting doors and walked over to a slim guy with close-cropped gray hair, in scrubs and a blue cover gown, sitting at a countertop computer adjacent to trauma bay one.

"Hey," Grady said when he looked up questioningly, "I'm Grady McClure, one of the surgical attendings. The ER just got a call there's a hand amputation coming in. Are you guys gonna want to see it?"

The guy held out a hand. "Jerry Kwan. I'm a PA on the trauma team. Nice to meet you. I'll give the trauma fellow a page—she might want to stick her head in for a look, but doesn't sound like it's going to be anything for us."

"Sounds good to me. I'll make sure somebody gives you a shout when he arrives."

"Will do, and welcome aboard. I'm sure I'll be seeing you down here."

"Roger that." Grady hustled back to the ER and pulled a green cover gown on over her street clothes.

Emery passed her on the way to check another new patient. "Matt said he's got a septic patient in the SICU, so you'll be doing him a favor if you triage this guy. He's sending his resident down."

"Great," Grady said.

Ten minutes later, Brody and another member of the flight crew brought in a heavyset guy with thinning brown hair, dressed in khaki shirt and pants and work boots, off the elevator. Grady went to help steer the gurney to a treatment room.

"Hi, Brody," she said as she grabbed a corner of the stretcher.

"Hey, Grady. This is Fred Murtaugh, fifty-four, a mechanics foreman at a boxing plant in Whitehall. Crush injury to the right dominant hand, partial amputation of the third, fourth, and fifth digits." Brody gestured to a plastic bag filled with ice at the foot of the bed. Inside was another bag with several portions of digits.

From what Grady could see at a quick glance, the amputated portions were fairly mangled. She turned to the patient as Emery met them to transfer the patient to a treatment table.

"I'm Dr. McClure," Grady said. "As soon as we get you settled, I'll need to get a look at that hand."

"Sooner the better. It's a mess." He glanced down at his bandaged hand where a white gauze wrap completely obscured the injury. All except the bright red blood soaking through the bandage.

"Has he had anything for pain?" Grady asked Brody, who was busy handing lines off to Emery and another ER staff member.

"Two mg. of morphine, IV, thirty minutes ago," Brody said.

"Let's give him another four," Grady said to Emery.

"On it," he said and disappeared into the hall.

A young blonde with striking deep brown eyes appeared behind Brody's shoulder. "I'm the surgery resident on call. How about I check the digits while we wait?"

Grady recognized the resident who'd been in the OR last night. Courtney something.

"Sure," Grady said. "Then unwrap this wound."

Her eyes glinted. "Absolutely."

"Do you have any medical problems?" Grady asked Mr. Murtaugh while Emery pushed the morphine. The flight medics would've already gotten all that information, but besides wanting to hear for herself, the more she talked to him, the faster she could establish a relationship with him.

"Healthy as they come. Don't smoke, don't drink."

"No vices, huh?"

He grinned a little weakly and patted his middle. "Just food."

Courtney returned and adroitly stepped around Grady into the patient's field of vision. "Hi. I'm Dr. Courtney Valentine. You ought to be feeling a little more comfortable now, so I'm going to unwrap your hand."

"Sure thing."

Grady smiled to herself. She was pretty sure Valentine was a first year, but she had the moves down already. She'd be all elbows in the OR, pushing her way to the best position to see and assist. The mark of a good resident—only time would tell if she'd be a good surgeon.

Grady leaned over Courtney's shoulder to watch while Courtney donned gloves, carefully cut the bandage, and eased the dressing off Mr. Murtaugh's right hand.

He was right—it was a mess.

Neither she nor Courtney made any comments. Grady waited a beat, and sure enough, Courtney spoke.

"So how did this happen?" she asked as she began to irrigate the wound with sterile saline to wash away clots and fragments of what looked like metal.

"I was fixing one of the box presses. Power was off, I'm sure of that. But the gears must've been caught halfway through a revolution and the damn things jumped forward while my hand was inside. Rolled right over it."

"Are these little bits of metal?" Courtney asked neutrally.

"Yeah, that's pretty common inside the presses, just from wear and tear." He craned his head and looked down. "Those don't look too good."

Courtney didn't say anything this time. Someone had trained her well.

"The problem," Grady said calmly, "is that the parts of your fingers that were lost are crushed. That makes it really hard to reattach them. It doesn't help that all those little bits of metal are contaminating the wound, either. They're kind of an invitation for infection."

"So if you reattached my fingers, they're not gonna do very well, right?"

"There's a good chance that they won't survive if we do. The surgery itself could take as much as twenty-four hours. That's not great for the blood supply to the rest of your hand either."

"What about going back to work?" he asked. "I'm mostly a supervisor—I was just on the floor today because one of my guys was out sick."

"If we attempt to replant and it goes perfectly, you're looking at six months of rehab minimum. If things don't work and you need a revision, longer."

He swallowed. "And if you don't do anything?"

"The good news," Grady said, "is that your thumb is fine, and that's ninety percent of your hand function. With your index finger and your thumb, you can do pretty much anything you need with that hand except carry much of anything."

Murtagh's face visibly relaxed. "So then what are we looking at in terms of recovery?"

"We'll clean things up and close all the wounds. Six weeks, maybe. Light duty only when you go back, for three months after that."

"Well, that's easy," he said. "Just get me back to work. I can tell just from looking at those things they're not gonna work right, so what's the point."

"We can get one of the hand specialists in here if you want another opinion."

"They're not going to tell me anything different, are they."

"I don't believe so."

"Then let's just do it."

Grady said, "You want to talk to anybody before you decide?"

He hesitated. "Well, I got a guy."

"I think you better call him first, then."

He grinned a little sheepishly. "Yeah, I guess I better."

Grady glanced at Courtney. "You interested in scrubbing?"

Courtney tilted her head and gave her a long half disdainful, half teasing look. "Is that a trick question?"

Grady laughed.

CHAPTER TEN

W hy don't you go ahead and get him prepped and draped while I scrub," Grady said after they got Mr. Murtaugh situated in the operating room.

"Will do." Courtney kneed the plate on the stainless OR sink to turn off the water, let the water drip from her elbows, and shouldered open the door to the operating room.

Grady watched her through the windows over the scrub sinks as Courtney worked with the OR nurses, techs, and anesthesia to get Mr. Murtaugh ready to go. You could tell a lot about a young resident by the way they interacted with the other staff. The ones who were the least confident internally often projected just the opposite, their self-assurance frequently tinged with an air of superiority or arrogance. Just from watching her, Grady could tell Courtney was at ease with her role on the team and knew what she was doing. Grady didn't know anything about her personally, but if she had to put money on it, she'd bet Courtney was a local. Everyone in the OR knew her, and the easy banter flowing between team members was clear, even through the glass. That kind of interaction usually took a lot longer to develop, especially where junior residents were concerned. Hell, *she'd* probably have to work pretty hard at it herself to achieve that level of camaraderie, although she'd always had a natural ability to get along with people. On the surface, at any rate. That was enough for her, those surface connections. Usually. And just like that, she thought of Blaise.

Easy banter, true. Effortless conversation, true. Simple pleasant time spent together. All true. But this time, with this woman, she wanted more than surface familiarity. She couldn't remember the last time she'd wanted to know a woman the way she wanted to know

Blaise. Inside, where it mattered. Maybe the urge was so strong simply because Blaise so obviously *didn't* want Grady to know her. Or maybe Blaise didn't want *anyone* close. And that appealed to Grady on some deeply primal level—one she could scarcely verbalize. But the feeling was clear. She wanted a woman who was hers.

The thought was like an ice-water shower. Where the hell did that thought even come from? That was not her—no way. Sure, she liked women. Loved women. Enjoyed them as people, and especially enjoyed them in bed, and why not. But for hers and all that meant? The very thought made her chest tighten.

Grady let out a breath of relief. Thank God for surgery. When she was in the operating room, there was nothing else in her mind but the case. The OR was an oasis of peace, despite the ever-present tension of making sure everything went right for someone who'd entrusted themselves to her.

And right now, she had a case to supervise and a reprieve from thoughts she couldn't begin to untangle. She finished her scrub and backed into the OR, hands out in front of her. A scrub tech draped a sterile towel over her hands, and she dried them off. By the time she was done, the tech had her gown open and was holding it up for her to slide into. As she went through the automatic motions of being gowned and gloved, she glanced over at the table where Courtney waited, and took in the patient's draped form. Courtney had positioned him with his arm extended on an arm board with a stool on either side. The tubes from a compression cuff snaked out from under the sterile sheets and towels. Good. Courtney'd remembered they'd need a tourniquet in order to see what they were doing once they started to clean up the mangled mess of his hand.

"Everybody set?" Grady asked, walking over to join Courtney.

The anesthetist, a young guy with a thin face whose almond-shaped brown eyes were the only things visible above his mask, nodded. "He's steady as a rock. Let me know when you want the tourniquet up."

"Right." Grady sat down across from Courtney. "Go ahead, Dr. Valentine, let's get started."

Courtney cut the sterile sleeve over Mr. Murtaugh's hand, and one of the circulating techs focused the overhead light down into the field.

"Tourniquet up," Courtney said with a glance at the clock. "5:05 p.m. Give us a heads-up in an hour, David."

"You got it, Court."

Forty-five minutes later, Courtney said, "I think that about does it except for his middle digit. What are we going to do about that exposed bone?"

Grady laughed. "Shouldn't that be my question?"

"It was kind of rhetorical. I *do* have a plan."

Grady held back another chuckle. Courtney was too damn confident for words, but she'd done a really good job. Still, not wise to encourage her hotdogging too much. Training programs were years long for good reason. Even the most natural surgeons like Courtney Valentine needed to see lots of cases with lots of potential complications before they would have enough experience to handle emergencies or the routine cases that suddenly went south.

"Well, rhetorically speaking," Grady said, "what are the options?"

Courtney was silent for a moment, thinking things over, and that was a good sign. The young ones—and some of the not-so-young ones, unfortunately—who tended to shoot from the hip often picked the flashy course of action because it was fun or challenging to do. That didn't always mean it was the best thing for the patient.

"Ordinarily," Courtney said after a minute, "you'd want to maintain length in order to leave him as much function as possible. Considering the loss of the fourth and fifth, and the injury to this one, his index finger is going to be his only working finger besides his thumb. Rather than swing a flap and immobilize his remaining good digit, I would just go ahead and shorten this back to the first available joint."

"Agreed. Why don't you draw out the incisions," Grady said.

Courtney used a sterile surgical marker to draw some lines on the tip of Mr. Murtaugh's partially amputated digit.

Grady pointed out a slight correction that would allow her a little bit more skin coverage and said, "Go for it."

Before the hour of tourniquet time was up, his hand was rewrapped, and he was on his way to the recovery room. Once Courtney got him settled, Grady said, "Nice job, Dr. Valentine."

"Thanks, that was great."

"Weren't you on call last night?" Grady said as they walked toward the surgeons' lounge.

"Uh, yes," Courtney said as she busied herself opening her locker.

"I thought you were supposed to be off call after a night on call."

"Well, yeah, but you know, if you're not here, you can't get the good cases, right?"

Grady paused in front of her locker. "Flann Rivers know you're working extra hours?"

"Maybe." Courtney hesitated. "Probably not. Are you going to tell her?"

"Well, I'm not the residency program director or the chief of surgery." Grady opened her locker and pulled off her scrub shirt. "I get where you're coming from. But," she said as she shrugged into her polo shirt, "if I thought it was affecting your work, I certainly would. You're right, if you not here, you can't get the good cases, but if you're too tired, you won't learn from them, and you might make mistakes."

"I'm off until Monday," Courtney said, facing Grady with her back to her open locker, "so I figured hanging around the ER for a couple hours wouldn't be a big deal, and it paid off. But I'm done for the weekend."

"Good."

"So, how are you liking life in town?" Courtney stripped off her scrub top and dropped it on the long, low bench between them.

Grady had a second's worth of seeing the lacy black bra that covered Courtney's full breasts before she turned her back. She'd been changing her clothes in locker rooms with other women for a decade, and some of them were women she'd been intimate with. Sex never came into the equation in these circumstances, regardless of how the other women identified sexually. But she didn't know Courtney, and while Courtney might not know she was a lesbian now, she surely would soon, since Grady didn't keep it a secret. The last thing she wanted was to give any hint of impropriety. As she shucked her scrub pants and pulled on her jeans, her back still turned, she said, "Living here is definitely different. Nothing like the city. But so far, I like it. What about you—you from around here?"

"Mmm. Close by. I grew up in Saratoga, but I went to high school here. I was a volunteer at the Rivers when I was young, so I'm pretty much part of the place, yeah."

"And you came back," Grady said, turning around as she closed her locker.

"Never considered anything else. Who wouldn't want to work here?"

"Beats me," Grady said.

Courtney had donned a short-sleeve white top that scooped low, but not so low Grady wanted to avert her gaze, and tight black jeans. She'd unclasped the gold barrette that had pinned her tawny curls up while she was operating and let her shoulder-length waves flow free. Grady guessed she was twenty-six or twenty-seven, not really all that much younger than her in age, but years younger in terms of experience. Courtney might not be interested in women, and even if she was, she was a resident. Not that Grady wasn't used to seeing residents and attendings getting involved, especially considering they were all adults, but if she *had* been interested, which she wasn't, she was new here, and the last thing she wanted to do was start in on a new reputation.

New place, new chance, new life.

"Well, I hope you enjoy the rest of your weekend," Grady said.

"Hey," Courtney said before Grady reached the door, "you know about the big game tonight, right?"

Grady turned back. "You mean the football game to be followed by the party of the century?"

Courtney grinned. She really was very pretty. "Every party is the party of the century around here, but it should be fun. You should go to the game."

Grady frowned. "Correct me if I'm wrong, but isn't this a high school football game?"

Laughing, Courtney followed Grady into the hall. "You've got a little bit to learn about living around here. Yes, it's a high school football game, but half the people in town are related to someone on the team or coaching the team or involved with the team in some other way. And more than half went to high school here and still consider Hudson Falls an archrival. That's who we're playing tonight. So it's not about high school—it's about us."

Us. As in the community. A concept Grady was completely unfamiliar with. She was used to the small tight elite social circles she'd grown up with, and she'd been intensely bonded to her fellow residents, who had functioned almost like a military squad. She'd depended on her peers for sanity and survival. But a whole community? Strange. Strangely enough, she was curious. And she had nothing else to do.

"So where is this game?" Grady asked.

"Just west on Union. That's the big street that divides the village." Courtney glanced at her watch. "And kickoff is in a little over half an hour. I'm headed over there after I grab a piece of pizza. Want to come?"

"Uh, well...I'll think about it."

"Okay." Courtney's tone was casual, but her gaze had that searching quality that so often accompanied the first overtures to making more meaningful contact. A bit of a question—*are you, do you want to, are you interested.* "On the off chance you might be wondering, there are fifteen surgery residents in the program. Defying statistics, three of us are queer. And I was only offering to show you around."

Feeling like an ass for being so transparent and so wrong, Grady felt herself blush. And wasn't that embarrassing. But she could at least be as up-front as Courtney. "Fair enough, and for the record, I don't date residents. But yeah, thanks, I'll take a ride. That would be great. I'll pass on the pizza, though. I had that for lunch."

Courtney raised an eyebrow. "And where is the problem?"

"No problem," Grady said, even though she could easily see Courtney Valentine being a very pleasant problem. Once upon a time. "No problem at all."

❖

Blaise woke a little after six with the unsettling sensation of grogginess and agitation. Maybe two blackberry cream filled doughnuts and then a second cup of coffee after a full night in the ER wasn't so conducive to a refreshing sleep.

Oh, who was she fooling?

She couldn't blame the doughnuts or her busy night for the restless agitation. The cause rested squarely with Grady McClure. A totally unexpected happening in her life. She could count on the fingers of one hand and not even use her thumb the number of times she'd met anyone, male or female, who'd instantly captured her attention the way Grady had. And the one time she had, she'd spent years regretting.

She hadn't even seen it coming until she'd been caught in Grady's thrall. Even if her first impressions *had* been mostly negative, and she hadn't really been wrong. Grady was confident, charming and aware of it, and maybe a little too sexually arrogant. But then there'd been all those moments when something else had surfaced to balance those things out, and maybe even suggested those suspicious traits were just surface trimming, covering up something that even Grady didn't know was there. She'd revealed intuitiveness, compassion, and an absolutely genuine kind of charm that fed a need Blaise had long ignored.

And the instant tingling in her middle as she recalled Grady's unabashed flirtation reminded her how susceptible she could be to some of those needs when she wasn't on guard. Blaise propelled herself from the bed and jumped into the shower while the water was still a little too cold. Just what she needed. Her brain woke up, along with her body.

Grady very likely projected that effortless charm to everyone, and the very last person Blaise was interested in was a practiced charmer.

What was it she'd told Abby she was looking for? Steady and unassuming and humble. Something like that. It didn't sound boring at all to her. She wanted someone she could count on. Someone who would be there no matter what. She hadn't had time when Taylor was a baby to even think about something like that. Who had time for romance with an infant to care for and then a toddler to raise, and a job to earn money for a roof over their head, and a crash course in motherhood that she hadn't anticipated at the ripe old age of nineteen? Her mother had swiftly departed the picture with a figurative brushing of her hands and a dismissive *obviously the acorn doesn't fall far from the tree.* As if Blaise was as fickle and unfaithful as her absent father had been. But she was determined to be exactly the opposite. She'd done her best to be there for Taylor every step of the way, even when that meant ignoring her own needs and wants.

She stepped out of the shower, reached for a towel hanging on the back of her bathroom door, and caught her reflection in the mirror over the vanity. She didn't make a habit of assessing herself, even when applying the light makeup she generally wore, the action so habitual she barely saw her face. Thirty-five, practically thirty-six. Not so bad, really. Her breasts were not as pert as they used to be, but a reasonable B cup size, and she'd managed to recover most of her skin tone following her pregnancy, although hey, not twenty anymore. She briskly wrapped the towel around herself and turned her back on the mirror. What was she doing? Her body served her well. Running kept her strong, a reasonable diet kept her healthy, and beyond that, what did it matter?

So what if Grady was likely a few years younger. So what if she looked more like a decade younger, her face unlined, her tight body toned, her every movement filled with confidence and power.

Okay, enough. Not going there anymore. Resolutely, Blaise pulled on black workout tights and a red workout top that fit her pretty damn well, damn it, and padded barefoot down to the kitchen. A note was propped up against the coffeemaker that was busily brewing coffee.

"Thank you, Taylor, someone raised you well," she murmured as she unfolded the piece of paper.

Morning mom. Don't forget the game. Dave picking us all up. See you there :)

As if she could forget the game. No one would let her. Besides, she wanted to go. She enjoyed the festive atmosphere, and the local sports event was one of the big social outings of the week for most of the community. An excuse to stand around in groups, drink coffee or hot chocolate, and gossip a little while watching the game. Business deals got done, relationships got started, and gossip flowed freely. The life of a small town.

After a quick cup of coffee, she slipped into running shoes and drove over to the field. The lot behind the school was already full, and band music drifted from the direction of the athletic field. Her spirits lifted as she trod along the well-worn path from the parking lot. The sun was setting earlier every night in mid-September, but they'd still have light until at least eight before the field halogens kicked on. The fall always made her feel a little wistful that another year was passing, but she loved the crisp air and the beauty of the fall foliage. Nothing ever came all of a piece—and that was fine, that was life. How could joy be fully appreciated without the occasional sadness, or victory without loss?

"Hey," Abby's familiar voice called. "Wondered when you'd show up."

Smiling, Blaise joined Abby, who stood with her sister-in-law Carson Harrington along the fifty yard line. Abby looked casually attractive in a red football jersey and jeans, and Carson, as usual, looked perfect with every curl in place and a black top edged in a little bit of lace tucked into black stretch jeans.

"Hi," Blaise said. "Have I missed anything important yet?"

Both teams were on the field, the blue and gold home team at one end and the green and white visiting Tigers at the other. Assistant coaches ambled up and down the sidelines, clipboards in hand, shouting instructions. She noticed the Tigers had one female coach. Good for them. Maybe attitudes really were changing. She knew Taylor and her friends saw things very differently than even her generation.

"Nothing too critical happening yet," Abby said.

"It must be great to have Bill back," Blaise said to Carson.

"It is, and I hope this time it's for longer than six months. The baby is old enough now to miss him when he's gone." Carson gave a wistful shrug. "Me too."

Abby slid an arm around Carson's shoulders and gave her a hug. "Well, he's home now, and that's what counts."

Carson nodded briskly. "You're absolutely right."

"I'm going to grab something to eat," Blaise said. "You two want anything?"

"I'm good for now," Abby said, and Carson echoed it.

Blaise gave a little wave and headed toward the trio of food carts parked at the end of the field that sold hot dogs, fish fries, coffee, hot chocolate, and the like. She paused to consider what evil she wanted to try when Grady McClure and Courtney Valentine walked into view.

She shouldn't have felt anything at all, and certainly not the instant wash of disappointment. Hadn't she just been telling herself that effortless charmers never lacked for company?

CHAPTER ELEVEN

"Wow," Grady said as she followed Courtney onto the sprawling high school athletic field. "You weren't kidding that the entire town was going to be here."

People of all ages, including many carrying toddlers and wearing slings with infants, packed the tiers of aluminum bleachers that flanked both sides of the field and congregated on the sidelines in milling clumps. The colors of the day appeared to be green and white or blue and gold. At a guess, she would've put the crowd size near five hundred.

"I had no idea this many people could possibly be interested in a high school football game." But then, the whole week had been full of surprises. When she'd arrived in town, she never would have imagined being captivated by a woman who clearly wasn't taken with her, or *not* being ready to pursue a very attractive one who had at least hinted at availability, or ending up in the midst of a cultural phenomenon so far beyond her experience she felt decidedly out of place.

"Oh yeah," Courtney said offhandedly. "Two towns, really. And you figure with all the kids, their parents, the previous players who are still hanging on to their glory days..." Courtney chuckled. "Plenty *of them* in both towns...plus the townspeople who just get into the spirit of the thing."

"I guess I'm going to have to work on my spirit," Grady muttered.

"Oh, don't worry. It sneaks up on you." Courtney grabbed Grady's arm. "Hey. Let's go this way. The apple cider doughnut cart is here, and I want to get a couple."

Grady groaned. "You're kidding, right? Not more doughnuts."

"Oh, I see you've been introduced to our local vice."

"Yeah, at the bakery this morning. Honestly, I don't think I can have another doughnut for at least a month."

"Well, I missed doughnut call," Courtney said, tugging the hem of Grady's shirt as she maneuvered like a heat-seeking missile through the crowd toward the white food truck with a big blue doughnut logo on the side and a line of fifty people waiting to order. "And I guarantee you'll take back those words before long."

"Good thing we got here early," Grady said, taking in the line.

"All part of the experience."

Courtney dodged into a breach in the crowd and dragged Grady along in her undertow. Trying mostly unsuccessfully to avoid knocking people about, Grady shot another look toward the field, hoping to find a little space, and almost stumbled to a halt.

Blaise stood twenty feet away, staring at them. At least, Grady thought she'd been staring, but she quickly averted her gaze and then her body, turning at a right angle and abruptly disappearing into the mass of people. The whole thing happened so fast if the woman had been anyone but Blaise, Grady might've thought she'd imagined it. But there was no way she could ever mistake anyone else for Blaise. She couldn't mistake the expression on her face, either, half angry, half disdainful. *Great. Something else to add to her super first impression list.*

Mercifully, Courtney slowed down, released her shirt, and queued up at the end of a line so long Grady couldn't even count how many people were ahead of them.

"Sure you don't want anything?" Courtney asked.

Oh yeah, she wanted something all right, but so far she wasn't making very good progress. In fact, she was kind of screwing up all over the place without quite knowing where she was going wrong. But then, what the hell, she wasn't doing anything wrong right at the moment. Blaise had already told her she wasn't interested in seeing her tonight. Or ever, maybe. And she wasn't with Courtney that way, anyhow. Besides being interesting and attractive, Courtney was one of those effortlessly friendly types, and there was nothing wrong with being friendly. Whatever Blaise surmised was not her problem.

"Thanks," Grady said, "but I think I'd better have something where the protein to carb ratio is just a little bit higher, like maybe four or five to one for a change."

"The fish cart is pretty good. If you're into that," Courtney said.

"I think I'll actually try to find a burger. That place at the far end, they've got that, right?"

"Until they sell out, which will be pretty quick. You better hustle."

"Okay." Grady hesitated. "Listen, if you've got plans or something, I don't want to get in your way."

Courtney cocked a hip and narrowed one eye, the other brow rising. "Believe it or not, the football game is not the best place to pick up a date for the night."

"Uh, I just thought—"

"You need to relax more," Courtney said with a shake of her head. "I don't have any plans. It will be fun to watch the game with you. Unless *you've* got other plans."

"Nope, no plans." Grady couldn't think of any reason she should avoid Courtney's company. And why should she? "Where will you be?"

"Top of the bleachers on the blue and gold side."

Grady squinted in that direction. "That's packed over there."

Courtney grinned. "Trust me, there's always room at the top."

Grady couldn't help but laugh. Courtney's self-confidence was infectious. "All right then. I'll meet you there."

"Don't take too long. Kickoff in six minutes," Courtney said.

"I'll make it. And hey, get me a doughnut," Grady called and plunged into the crowd.

❖

Well, that didn't take her very long.

Blaise put one shoulder forward and edged her way through the mass of people milling about in front of the food trucks. Why should she be surprised? Grady was new in town, young and attractive, and anyone with a heartbeat would take notice. And of course it would be Courtney.

Blaise sighed. If she was a betting person, and she wasn't—who could afford to throw good money after bad? *Thanks, Mother, for that handy life lesson*—she'd lay odds that Courtney was just exactly Grady's type. Young, smart, confident, sexy. Huh. All the things she was not.

She'd also never been the competing type even when that might have been a possibility in her life plans, and she definitely wasn't entertaining competing with Courtney Valentine. She was closer in age to Courtney's cousin Sydney, but she'd known Court since Court was twelve years old and starting middle school, and she'd been earning extra money assistant coaching girls' soccer—in between finishing her degree and raising a baby. By the time Court hit high school, she was every boy's heartthrob and every girl's secret envy. Thinking back, Courtney'd probably been the heartthrob of a few girls too, but Blaise had been willfully blind to that at the time. But Court? She'd always known who she was and enjoyed letting it show—vivacious, smart, and funny with a lighthearted sexuality that was just playful enough not to be offensive. The Valentines were both seductively beautiful, but where Val had all the heat, Courtney had the devil-may-care attitude. She managed to be a heartbreaker without really hurting anyone and ended up with more friends because of it. Val hadn't been so lucky and gained a reputation for burning hot and fast and leaving a trail of ashes in her wake. Blaise had never been convinced Val deserved the criticism, but high school was like that. Once you had a name, you never lived it down. Not for a decade or so, anyhow.

Now that Courtney was a resident, Blaise had to adjust her memories of the adolescent to the reality of the adult. Court hadn't changed all that much—still confident and naturally seductive—but she was also reliable and serious about her work. That was enough for Blaise.

But Grady and Court weren't in the hospital tonight. Blaise would bet a hundred dollars she could not afford to lose that Courtney had taken one look at Grady and lasered in on her faster than a New York minute.

And, as if she needed reminding, why shouldn't Grady return the interest? *She'd* certainly been clear enough that she wasn't interested. And she wasn't. So uninterested, to be precise, that when she saw Grady headed her way, she immediately faced the back of the person in front of her in line, completely determined not to care the slightest what Grady was up to.

Blaise couldn't see her, but she knew the instant Grady stepped up beside her. She didn't know how, but her skin actually tingled the way it did in an electric storm right before all hell broke loose. And wasn't that just the truth?

"Hey," Grady said, "how's it going."

Blaise's heart gave a little jump, damn it, but at least she managed not to squeak.

"Fine. Enjoying the local color?" There, she could be friendly.

"It's quite a shindig," Grady said. "I think if I stayed home, I'd be the only person in town who wasn't here."

Blaise couldn't help it—she felt her shoulders relaxing. Grady didn't deserve the back end of her discontent. She should make an effort to be friends. They were going to be working together, after all. "Well, you're right about that. I hope you have fun. It might take a little getting used to. I can't imagine it's anything like what you usually do on a Saturday night."

"Believe me," Grady said, "my Saturday nights are often not this exciting."

Blaise faced her and narrowed her eyes. "Somehow I cannot believe that."

Grady gave her that innocent look that was all charm with a side of sexy. "If I'm not working or catching up on sleep, I'm usually trying to scare up a game on the internet."

"What kind of game?" Blaise asked, a sudden flush of jealousy making her tone sharp. She had visions of those really voluptuous women who popped up in ads when she was trying to buy housewares online, offering to do…whatever. Grady couldn't possibly mean…

"You don't think…" Grady laughed loud enough that several people craned their necks to see what the joke was. In a choked voice, she said, "Do I look like the type to frequent online massage parlors?"

"I'm sure I wouldn't know what type that might be," Blaise said, barely suppressing her own laughter. Grady grinned and she couldn't hold back a smile. Damn it all, she was easy to play with. Blaise caught her breath. Was that what she was doing? Playing with fire, more like it. But oh, the flames were pretty.

"Whatever type that is, I'm not it," Grady said. "I mean *game* games, you know—digital board games."

Blaise's eyes widened. "You've got to be kidding me. You are a gamer?"

"Well, mostly online because I really don't have time, but yeah, I like it." Grady's eyes flashed. "You?"

"By default initially—Taylor wanted someone to play with when she couldn't get enough of her friends at the same time. Now I'm hooked." Blaise shook her head. "It's hard to believe, but my daughter and her friends have actually given up video games and are into board games instead. Like, what I was playing in college. It's so weird."

"Yeah, there's something about the give-and-take, the…I don't know, togetherness of it. It's cool."

"I don't have much time to play," Blaise said, "especially working nights. Once in a while…"

"What?" Grady asked.

Blaise just *knew* she was blushing, damn it. "There's a twenty-four-hour game room in Troy. Sometimes when I get off work and I'm still wound up from a busy night, I stop in there for an hour or two."

"Wow, you are serious." Grady shoved her hands in her pockets and rocked on her heels. "So, maybe one morning…"

"You don't miss a step, do you?" Blaise said with a wry smile.

Grady shrugged. "When I have a goal in mind, I'm pretty persistent."

"A goal, huh? I'm not sure that's a flattering description."

Grady leaned closer. "You want flattering? How about when I want to get to know a beautiful, sexy, intriguing woman better, I'm relentless."

"Relentless I believe." Blaise moved up to the front of the line as the man ahead of her ordered and stepped away. "But in my case, flattery is appreciated, but not likely to work."

She wanted to mention that Grady had a beautiful, sexy young woman waiting for her somewhere on the field, but that really, truly was not her business. Besides, she didn't want Grady to think she cared. If Grady knew just how much she enjoyed the way Grady looked at her, she would just be encouraged to be even more relentless, and Blaise was not available for pursuit. She had two years before Taylor left for college, and nowhere in her blueprint for the future was there room for a flirtation that had all the earmarks of being trouble.

"Well…" Grady raised her voice as Blaise stepped up to the counter. "I'm also inventive and flexible."

The broad-faced, balding food vendor raised a brow and nodded with an appreciative grunt. "That sounds pretty good to me."

"Charlie," Blaise said with a laugh, "she would run you ragged. And besides—Mildred would murder you."

He chuckled. "True enough. You having fries with the double cheese?"

"Of course."

"Make that two," Grady called, "and I'm buying."

"Sure," Charlie said.

"You don't have to do that, Grady," Blaise said.

"I know," Grady said, sliding her hands into her pockets. "But I'd appreciate it if you'd let me."

"All right, but next time it's on me."

"Next time," Grady said with a little rumble of satisfaction. "Deal."

Blaise sighed. She'd been outmaneuvered, and she didn't really mind. Grady was easy to talk to. Easy to look at. Easy to give in to. Too damn easy in too many ways.

Chapter Twelve

Grady carried her cardboard tray of burger and fries along with a bottle of water through the crowd, which had changed direction and begun surging toward the field like a pack of lemmings heading for the cliff edge. Rather than try to set a course, she just let herself be carried along with the flow and finally reached the bleachers Courtney had pointed out earlier. She scanned the ten levels of aluminum benches, despairing of ever finding Courtney, but there she was, half standing and waving her arm. Grady nodded to let her know she'd seen her and plotted out a course of how to get there. Two rows from the top.

An insurmountable challenge at first glance, considering people were packed shoulder to shoulder wherever she looked, but she'd never been one to give up easily. Only hoping she could make it before halftime, she took a breath and plunged in. She needn't have worried. As she began to climb, muttering *excuse me, sorry* as she tried not to tread on sitting people, a path appeared as those already settled in simply shifted an inch or two one way or the other before resuming their positions. Holding her own food aloft, she stepped gingerly over seats or on seats while tiptoeing through the obstacle course of strategically positioned food and drink containers. When she reached the row below Courtney's with nary a crushed French fry or spilled soda in her wake, she exhaled for the first time, only to discover a pair of lace-up, calf-high black boots topped by skinny blue jean–clad legs occupying the ten inches of bench next to Courtney.

"Hey!" Courtney said brightly. "You made it."

"I did, and I'm still not sure how." Hesitating, Grady smiled at the blonde from the pizza parlor who belonged to the feet on the bench.

Taylor Richelieu tilted her head, for an instant looking very much like her mother with her open, appraising gaze, and shifted her feet off the seat. "How you doing."

"Great, thanks. I'm Grady."

"Taylor."

Courtney scooted over a couple of inches, and a space appeared beside her.

Grady dropped down with a whoosh of relief. "Did I miss anything?"

Courtney laughed. "You made it just in time for kickoff."

Now that she was sitting, she realized she was starving. Pizza felt like a long time ago. Trying the burger—not at all bad for truck food— Grady checked the field. Three refs stood in a semicircle in the middle of the field at the fifty yard line with the two teams lined up on their own sidelines. Two or three players from each team jogged out for the traditional coin toss. She finished off the burger as the players went through the motion of choosing who'd kick off first.

"Excellent burger," Grady said as she wiped her hands on the paper napkins she'd shoved in her pocket.

"Here." Courtney handed her a brown paper bag. "Have a doughnut."

"Maybe a little later. Thanks."

Courtney shifted the bag a bit higher and shook it under her nose. "They're much better when they're hot."

Maybe it was the inviting tone in her voice, but Grady chalked it up to the irresistible odor of apples, brown sugar, spices, and warm dough. Really, who could resist. She stuck her hand in the bag, extracted a plain-looking doughnut dusted with sugar that smelled like heaven, and took a bite. Better than heaven. "You're right. Much better this way."

"Trust me, I know these things." Courtney handed her the bag. "Pass these to the hungry crew behind you. Payment for saving seats."

Grady twisted as much as she was able without elbowing the guy beside her and held up the bag. "You guys want doughnuts?"

Three voices simultaneously chorused *totally, yes*. Taylor, seated in the middle of the trio, snaked out a hand and the bag promptly disappeared.

"So, ah, when did you arrange to have them save seats?" Grady asked Courtney. "'Cause I've been with you since we left the hospital, and I don't recall you making any plans."

Laughing, Courtney said, "I just commandeered the space when I saw these guys hogging the bench. The one who looks a lot like Flann, only cuter, is Margie Rivers, the beanpole on the end is Tim Brunel, and the one with the kick-ass boots is Taylor Richelieu."

The teens made sounds resembling greetings as the doughnut bag deflated.

"Appreciate you saving some space," Grady said over her shoulder.

"No problem." Taylor crumpled up the empty bag and stuffed it into one of the ubiquitous cardboard food carriers on the floor between her kick-ass boots. "We were mostly holding them until someone we knew came along."

Tim snorted, and Taylor elbowed him.

"What?" he asked, affronted.

"It's all cool," Taylor muttered.

Courtney glanced back. "Something up?"

Margie shrugged. "Nothing new. We just didn't want to have to put up with some of Taylor's fans for the whole game."

"Please," Taylor said with a dramatic snort. "Billy Riley is a jerk."

"That too," Margie said.

"It's not a big deal, Court," Taylor said. "Plus, you had doughnuts."

Taylor's grin reminded her of Blaise's rare smile, and heat stirred in her center. She turned to watch the kickoff before she went any further with her mental musings and totally lost her focus.

Courtney leaned forward, her shoulder brushing Grady's.

Grady had no room to move away. Courtney's bare arm rested against hers, warm and firm. She hadn't been this close to a woman in months. Courtney smelled good too. Oranges or something citrusy like that, fresh and sparkling. All of it—the touch, the scent, the casual togetherness—was nice. And that was all. Nice.

She wasn't getting any of the usual internal vibes from being around a sexy, possibly available woman in a situation where something more might develop. She felt like pinching herself. As if she didn't know exactly why she wasn't acting like herself. She plucked up a fry and watched the players run up and down the field, trying really hard not to think about Blaise.

❖

Blaise forced herself to focus on the game and not on Courtney and Grady sitting a few rows behind her in the adjacent section. If she turned her head just a little, she could see Court and Grady perfectly, looking like an attractive couple enjoying a date. She was not in the habit of self-torture, and this was crazy-making. Not looking was the logical option.

Besides, she'd already seen them together when they'd arrived. She knew they were watching the game together. There was nothing to be gained by noticing them, *together*, again. And she definitely didn't need Taylor catching her watching and assuming she was keeping an eye on her and her friends. A cardinal sin in public situations, and one she tried hard not to commit, even though she couldn't shake all the worry, ever since Billy Riley had taken to pursuing her. The anxiety had gotten worse after Margie and Blake had been hassled a couple of times by some of Billy's crowd. Taylor was careful and rarely went anywhere without some of her friends along, but physical confrontations weren't the only dangers any longer. Bullying came in many forms, some of them deadly. Taylor swore nothing out of hand had been happening, and that Billy was just a nuisance and, to quote her, a dipwad. Still, Billy Riley showed all the signs of harboring an angry, aggressive streak when denied the attention he wanted.

"What's the matter?" Abby said quietly.

Blaise jumped. "What? Nothing."

"You sure? Because I've seen you hip-deep in emergencies and not look so tense."

Blaise let out a breath. On her other side, Carson was so engrossed in watching the game and her newly returned Army husband that Blaise doubted she was listening. "Billy Riley has been hassling Taylor a little bit. He's interested in her, and she's not interested in return. His way of getting her attention is to make remarks about her friends—or me. He accused her of being a dyke, like her mother, a few days ago. I don't think Taylor wanted to tell me that, but she was angry enough it came out."

"He's friends with a couple of the senior boys who were giving Blake a problem, isn't he."

"Yes." Blaise grimaced. "He's been in trouble since he was ten or twelve. Shoplifting, minor vandalism. The kinds of things an unsupervised, unhappy kid gets into. But now he's almost a young man, and nothing excuses his behavior."

Abby squeezed Blaise's knee. "Taylor will tell you if anything else happens, won't she?"

"Yes. I'm sure of it. I just worry."

Abby huffed. "Believe me, I do know about that."

•

"Of course you do. God, it's hard." She shook her head. "And I think they handle it better than we do most of the time."

"I know—it's kind of amazing. They have each other, and they're not only smart, but they know they can come to us."

"You're right. And I need to remember that."

After a moment, Abby said nonchalantly, "I don't suppose part of what has you so wound up has anything to do with Grady being here."

"It most certainly doesn't," Blaise said a little too quickly.

"Okay. Just wondering."

"You can stop wondering. We had a friendly conversation over doughnuts, for heaven's sakes. Hardly anything romantic."

"Oh, I dunno, I had doughnuts this morning, and it was very romantic."

Laughing, Blaise shoved against Abby's shoulder. "Don't gloat."

Carson leaned around Blaise and pointed a finger at Abby. "I heard that. And you're talking about my sister. Ew."

Abby grinned. "Oh, I'm so sorry, because I'm sure up until this very moment you didn't think Flann had ever had sex."

Someone a row in front of them laughed out loud.

Carson rolled her eyes. "All the same, I don't have to have the picture in my mind. Where *is* my sister anyhow?"

Looking self-satisfied, Abby said, "She waited at the hospital while Blake finished up helping with a patient he was following to give him a ride. They're probably down there on the sidelines somewhere."

The action on the field picked up and everyone went back to watching the game until a few minutes later Abby pulled her phone from her pocket and checked a text.

"Damn it," she said after a second. "The ER."

"You're not on call, are you?" Blaise said.

"No, but Marcus Winston's mother fell, and they're bringing her in for evaluation. He asked me personally if I would see her."

"Gladys is living in the senior residence facility out on 372 now, isn't she?" Blaise said.

"Yes," Carson said. "After Archie died, she really couldn't keep up the house on her own."

"Well," Abby said, "I can hardly tell a staff member I can't be bothered to come and see his mother. Hopefully, I'll just need to poke my head in. Glenn is there and can handle anything."

"Sorry you have to leave, but that's what happens when you get to be the doctors' doctor," Blaise said.

"Probably has more to do with me being the chief. Either way, I have to go. Can you take the kids to the Rivers place when the game is done?" Abby said.

"Sure," Blaise said, even though she hadn't been planning to show up until it was time to take them all home at the end of the night. She could always make two trips.

Carson said, "I'll take them, but they'll have to wait until Bill is done and gets the equipment squared away."

"No," Blaise said, "that's silly. I'm here. I've got room for them."

"All right," Abby said. "I'll meet you all later if I can."

"Call me," Blaise said, "but I'll handle the transport tonight."

"Thanks." Abby threaded her way down the bleachers and disappeared.

"Abby is quickly becoming a major force at the hospital," Carson said.

"She's great, and everybody knows it."

"We are lucky to have her," Carson said. "And of course, my sister is doubly lucky."

"It seems that's mutual where those two are concerned," Blaise said. The pang of longing that rose up out of nowhere was not unfamiliar, but usually she could ignore it. She loved that her friends were happy, and every time someone she knew celebrated a new relationship, she hoped for their happiness. Sure, every now and then she wished she had someone waiting at home to hear about her day, or help her think through a problem, or make her feel wanted. Or hell, sexy even.

She just hadn't felt so many of those things all at once in such a short period of time. And she knew exactly who to blame. Funny, the last thing she felt when she thought of Grady was anger. If only she could figure out exactly what she *did* feel.

Chapter Thirteen

Grady jumped to her feet along with everyone else in the bleachers and cheered as the home team quarterback threw a Hail Mary pass with twenty seconds left on the clock, and somehow, the wide receiver, a middling-sized guy even in all his football pads who ran like a deer, managed to catch it, threaded his way through half a dozen defenders, and crossed into the end zone with ten seconds on the clock. Courtney threw her arms around Grady and hugged her as she simultaneously jumped up and down. Laughing, Grady hugged her back.

"Up by two," Courtney shouted. "Up by two."

"With the extra point, even if the other team somehow manages to get into field goal range, it will only send the game into overtime," Grady shouted back, as jubilant as if she'd had money riding on the outcome. A few hours ago she'd never laid eyes on any of these kids, and now they had somehow become *her* team.

"No way we'll end in a tie," Taylor yelled from behind them. She braced her hand on Grady's shoulder and leaned forward to see around the big guy to Grady's right. "Dave's got a shotgun arm. I bet they fake the kick, and Dave passes it for two," Taylor said.

"I wouldn't take that bet," Courtney said.

Grady stayed on her feet, the excitement of the crowd contagious. She hadn't seen a live football game since she'd watched the Redskins play at FedExField five years ago on one of her rare Sundays off. Professional football had nothing on this. *This* was a whole town turned out to cheer for a bunch of kids.

The quarterback, Dave, faked the toss to the kicker, ran to his right, and floated a sweet pass into the end zone. The buzzer sounded and the home team won. The eruption from the home side was deafening. For a good five minutes, Grady couldn't hear anything except shouting and foot stomping and the roar of victory. Finally everyone quieted, and she dropped down next to Courtney, breathless and weirdly exuberant.

"That was great," Grady said.

Courtney shifted to face her, her thigh pressing against Grady's. Her face was flushed, her eyes bright, her grin incandescent. "Totally. I'm really glad you got to see it. This was a big one."

"Me too," Grady said, surprised to realize she meant it. She'd had a good time when she'd thought she was only going to be killing time.

Taylor leaned forward between them, a hand on each of their shoulders. "Court, are you going to the Homestead after this?"

"After this?" Courtney laughed. "You kidding? Wouldn't miss it. I'd give you guys a ride, but no way will you fit in the Miata."

"No problem. We'll find a ride."

Margie crowded in beside Taylor. "It looks like a ride's on the way."

She pointed, and Grady automatically followed the direction she indicated. The bleacher crowd had slowly begun to dissipate, and Blaise climbed toward them, stepping from one empty seat to the next. Grady hadn't expected to see her, even though she'd known exactly where she was sitting during the whole game. Whenever she'd sensed a break in the action, she'd snuck a peek in Blaise's direction, trying to figure out who the woman sitting on Blaise's right side was. The three of them—Blaise, Abby, and the mystery woman—were obviously together. But just friends? Had to be. Blaise had said no girlfriend. That didn't mean no dating, though, did it? That scenario had niggled away uncomfortably at her mind as she watched the game.

Blaise was alone now, and as Grady absorbed the impact of her suddenly being right there in front of her just a few feet away, the world went silent. The lingering sounds of celebration, car horns honking as vehicles jostled to get out of the parking lot, and the occasional shout from the football field all faded away. Nothing registered but the thundering of her heart and the roaring in her ears. A totally new, somewhat mystifying, and downright fascinating development.

"Hey, Blaise," Courtney said as Blaise stopped a row below them, her head just at Grady's level.

They *should* have been looking into each other's eyes, but Blaise focused past Grady to the teenagers behind her. "You three want a ride to the party?"

They looked at one another, and Margie spoke up. "We could wait for Dave, but you know he'll be an hour while they review the game. So yeah, that would be cool."

"Great. I'm in the lot, the closest corner to the field. You know the car. I'll wait for you there."

For a second, Grady thought Blaise was going to turn around and walk away without even acknowledging her. Invisibility was a rare sensation for her. She didn't like it. "Hi, Blaise. Great game, huh?" She flinched inwardly. Not the greatest line of all time, but if it got Blaise to give her a look, she'd take it. Somehow, that connection felt important.

Blaise's expression didn't change for a second, as if she was considering whether to stop or keep going, and then she smiled. Her smile changed everything and made every lame line in the world worth trying, just for a glimpse of that light in her eyes.

Grady held her breath, as if the next words were the most important ones she would ever hear.

"It was. Terrific." For a few seconds that stretched to eternity, Blaise held Grady's gaze. Her eyes were *not* blue. They were what blue should be but rarely was—vibrant and warm and crystalline bright.

When Blaise glanced at Courtney, Grady felt the link between them snap with the sharp pang of a broken bone.

Blaise's smile shadowed as she said to Courtney, "Good way to introduce her to all the excitement around here."

Courtney laughed. "It's a start. Next up is the after-game party. That ought to really cement the town's reputation as a jumping place."

"No doubt," Blaise said with a hint of coolness returning to her tone.

Grady winced inwardly. No way was Blaise not going to think she and Courtney were together in some way. Blaise had to know that Courtney was into women, and she definitely knew Grady was. Anyone would get four out of two and two under those circumstances. She could hardly blurt out, *It's not a date, we've just met.* That wouldn't work, considering she hadn't known Blaise all that much longer, even though every cell of her being lit up at the mere thought of her. Actually being near her was excruciating in a very good way.

"Court's been kind enough to introduce me to the local entertainment." Grady instantly wanted to close her eyes and rewind the whole conversation, because *that* didn't come out all wrong at all.

"Well, I'm sure you'll have a great time. I've never been to anything out at the Homestead that wasn't fabulous." Blaise motioned to the kids. "Meet me at the car. We've got room for a few more if you find anyone else along the way who needs a lift."

With that she turned, walked down the nearly empty bleachers, and disappeared.

"Sorry I didn't actually check with you about the party," Court said. "I just assumed you'd want to go. Really, though, you should. It'll be fun, and I guarantee great food."

"Is food the primary source of bribe around here?" Grady asked, still off-balance from the less than stellar exchange with Blaise. When had she gotten so lame around women?

"Usually works, and it's an innocent vice."

Grady grinned. Time to get back on her game—at least acting like it. "I'm not so sure. I've only been here a few days and I'm going to have to start running a whole lot more than I have been."

Courtney gave her a slow once-over. "I dunno. You look pretty… fit to me."

One of the kids behind them gave a little snort.

Courtney laughed again, totally confident and amused. She held out her hand to Grady. "Come on. Let's go before we end up behind twenty cars and can't find anyplace to park when we get there except in the middle of the cornfield."

Grady took her hand because it would've been churlish not to, and Courtney pulled her to her feet, gave her hand a little squeeze, and let go. The teens trooped down behind them.

Halfway to the lot, a dark-haired boy in pale blue shorts, a red T-shirt, and sockless running shoes called out, "Hey, Margie," and jogged over to join the others.

"Hi, Court," he said and nodded to Grady. "Hi. I'm Blake."

"Grady McClure."

Blake broke into a blazing smile and stuck out his hand. "You're one of the new staff. I'm an extern in the ER. My mom's—"

"The boss." Grady shook his hand. "I see the resemblance now."

Blake's smile was shy and maybe a bit pleased. "Well, I hope I get to work with you."

"Suck-up," Margie muttered just loud enough to be heard, and Blake laughed.

"Margie's an extern too. We usually share shifts."

Grady grinned. "I'm sure we'll spend plenty of time together."

Blake tossed an arm around Tim's shoulders and looped the other around Taylor. Margie walked backward as the four drifted over to where Blaise leaned against her Suburban, watching them with an amused smile as they all drew near.

Courtney's small yellow sports car was parked not far away, and as the kids piled into the Suburban, Grady felt Blaise's eyes on her back as she and Courtney waved and kept going, together, to Courtney's car. When she looked back, though, Blaise had gotten into the Suburban and closed the door.

Dismissed.

"Did you forget something?" Court asked, and Grady realized she'd stopped walking.

Yes. I forgot to say any of the things that mattered. Like, I can't stop thinking about you, and I really, really want to see you...alone... again, and would you mind very much if I kissed you?

"Nope," Grady said, picking up her pace and climbing into the passenger seat of the sports coupe. "All good."

Courtney pulled out before Blaise and a line of slower moving vehicles, and once they'd cleared the congestion right around the high school and reached the two-lane leaving town, she let the little car loose. Grady powered her windows down, Courtney did the same, and they zoomed through the night. Cool air tinged with the scent of hay and corn and cows whipped through the small interior. A few miles from town, the inky sky blanketed them in black velvet and wisps of moonlight. They were alone, not just in the close interior of the car, but alone in the whole universe, it seemed. Grady couldn't help notice the sense of intimacy and anticipation that wrapped them in the night.

"So," Courtney said as she passed a slow-moving vehicle without reducing her speed and pulled back onto her side of the highway in a smooth, unhurried move, "what I was saying earlier, about wanting your company?"

Grady pressed both hands flat on her thighs. She never liked having these conversations about expectations, although she always did. Usually she started them. "Yeah?"

"I meant that."

"Okay." Grady waited, noting the past tense.

"But now I'm thinking," Courtney said, turning her head to glance in Grady's direction. She only lingered for a second or two before looking back at the road, but in the reflected light off the dash, her expression was clear. She'd gone from open and friendly and casual to intense and seductive. "I think I might like something a little more personal."

"Courtney…"

"Not tonight. I'm not asking for a hookup." Court laughed. "I'm way past that, believe me. And I'm not getting those vibes from you, anyhow. But I'd like to see you again, not just as friends."

Grady let out a breath. "Can we slow things down just a bit? There's the little matter of you being a resident and me being staff."

"Oh, come on. I'm twenty-seven. You're what, thirty-one?"

"Almost thirty-two."

"That makes us grown-ups. You're not my supervisor or the program director. I suppose you could get me in some kind of trouble if you really tried, but"—she lifted a shoulder—"I'm kind of, you know, the hometown girl, and it gives me an edge."

Grady laughed. "What you are is very sure of yourself."

"Okay, that too." Courtney's smile was visible even though she still watched the road as they shot down the highway. "So let's just be adult. Do I hear a maybe?"

"For tonight, let's keep it the way we started."

"All right. For tonight."

Court turned left onto a dirt road that, Grady realized after a few seconds when they rounded a bend, was actually an approach road to a rambling four-story farmhouse with dozens of glowing windows nestled in a semicircle of huge trees. Cars parked two deep beside a big barn silhouetted in moonlight a bit past the house, and lined either side of the road, which she guessed was a driveway, although she'd never seen anything so long considered a driveway.

For tonight, Court had said. That was about as far ahead as she could plan. In fact, her life seemed to change hour by hour, and wasn't that totally strange. A month ago, even, she wouldn't have hesitated to say yes to Court's offer.

She had no real reason to hesitate now, and she'd always followed her instincts where women were concerned. Courtney was exactly the kind of woman she usually pursued. And she liked her. And it'd been a long time. All perfectly good reasons. She should have said yes. Weirdly, she wasn't sorry. And she had plenty of time to change her mind.

Chapter Fourteen

B laise pulled out of the parking lot three cars behind Courtney's very recognizable yellow Miata. From the vantage point of her high-riding SUV, she couldn't actually see Grady and Courtney, but she could imagine them, inches apart, enjoying the first stages of getting to know one another. It might've been a long time since she'd actually experienced that herself, but she certainly remembered the exhilaration and excitement that the promise of someone new brought with them. Never mind that was exactly how she'd felt after a silly cup of coffee and a doughnut with Grady earlier that morning. She'd felt that same rush then and spent the hours after pretending that she hadn't. But that was on her. Maybe she couldn't always control what she felt, but she certainly could control what she did about it—which did *not* include chasing after the source of the excitement without considering the consequences. That was a lesson learned long ago.

Once on the two lane, she fell well behind the Miata and soon lost sight of it as Courtney sped away. No surprise there. If she had a car like that, she'd be driving with the wind as well. All the same, she wasn't that far behind when she pulled down the long drive to the Homestead. Courtney and Grady were just getting out of the Miata, which Courtney had adroitly wedged between a couple of larger trucks pulled off on the side of the drive. They were walking close together, but at least they weren't holding hands.

Blaise mentally slapped herself in the forehead. She really had to stop regressing to the stage where hormones dictated her actions. Hadn't she put that well behind her after Taylor came along?

She pulled over adjacent to the curving stone walk that wended through the sloping lawn encircling the house. A dozen people exited cars and headed for the back porch, the unofficial main door.

Turning on the seat, she said, "All right, you know the drill. If you plan on going elsewhere later, you'll need to check in with all parents. I'll come back and pick you up if you're calling it a night, or I can drop you off at your next destination. But if it's a house party somewhere else—no deal. It needs to be at one of your places."

"Mom," Taylor said with exaggerated exasperation, "we've heard this before. We all know."

She couldn't see Taylor's face very well in the shadowy back seat, but she could feel the eye roll.

"Besides," Margie said, reaching over the seat to pluck at Blaise's sleeve, "you're coming in now, right? You have to get something to eat at least."

"Well," Blaise said hesitantly, wondering just exactly how much she didn't want to see any more of Courtney and Blaise together. As soon as she thought it, she knew that was ridiculous. Absolutely irrational knee-jerk reaction to a situation that not only had nothing to do with her, but might not even be what she thought.

Ha. As if it was going to be something else. Really.

"Well," she said again, still weighing practicality versus potential discomfort. She *was* pretty hungry, and was she really willing to put herself out just so she could avoid what she couldn't change anyhow? She'd come a lot further than that, hadn't she? She jumped at a rap on her half-open side window and twisted around.

Flann peered in. "Y'all coming in, or what?"

Blaise decided she was far outnumbered and couldn't even come up with a good reason to herself, let alone her friends, as to why she wouldn't go in. She didn't have to stay. She wouldn't stay. With any luck, Ida had made cornbread, and one slice of that and maybe, with even more luck, some chili or mac and cheese, and she could sneak away. Have a cold beer. Deal.

She cracked her door, Flann stepped back, and she jumped out as the teens piled out behind her. The kids took off as she fell in beside Flann.

"How you doing, Flann," she said.

"Great. Where's Abby? I thought she was with you."

"She was supposed to text you," Blaise said as they walked around to the back porch. No one ever used front doors, all of which opened into formal living areas that also didn't get all that much use, except sometimes on holidays or when distant family or casual acquaintances came to visit. But for everyday use, for family and friends, the kitchen—

inevitably accessed by the back door—was the heart of the house. The Riverses' back porch was as long and wide as some front porches, without the formality of colonnades and elaborate woodworking. Plain wide plank floor, unadorned posts, and a sturdy railing just made for behinds to rest upon—and showing the decades of wear to prove it. A number of rockers, other comfortable chairs, and side tables were scattered about, many of them already filled with folks.

"I didn't get anything from her," Flann said, after pulling her phone from her back pocket and checking the screen.

"I'm not surprised," Blaise said. "You know how bad the cell reception is in that part of town. Anyway, Marcus Winston's mother fell, and he contacted Abby to come in and see her."

"Smart guy, although with the crew that she's got down there, anybody could handle it."

"Marcus probably knows that too," Blaise said, "but you know as well as I do what he needs is hand-holding. Treating the anxiety matters sometimes too."

Flann grabbed the screen door and held it open for Blaise. "Yeah, I get it. I've even held a few hands myself. This ought to go on awhile, so hopefully she'll make it."

Blaise blinked as she stepped from the shadows of the porch into the brightly lit kitchen, already jammed with people milling about, collecting drinks and food. The yellow plaster walls vibrated with the rise and fall of excited voices. The sounds, the throngs of bodies pressing closer, the sudden claustrophobia had her taking a step back. If she hadn't sensed others just behind her, inexorably moving inside, she might have backed all the way out the door and disappeared into the anonymous comfort of the warm, dark night. Easier to retreat than steel herself for the inevitable discomfort, and she'd retreated a lot over the years, but she'd usually had better excuses than she had tonight. After all, hard to argue with a baby at home, or a sick kid, or an extra shift at the hospital. All legitimate reasons she avoided parties, even innocent ones like this one. As if there was really any other kind around here.

But she'd never quite managed to shake the anxiety that surfaced with the onslaught of too many too loud voices and the fraying of boundaries that went along with the lowering of inhibitions or plain old carelessness. She took a breath. That wasn't the here and the now. This was the Homestead, and these were not strangers. These were friends she could trust, and she was careful. Always. With another, easier breath, she plunged into the chaos.

❖

Grady filled a paper plate with way too much food—wings, a wicked looking mac and cheese with what looked like buffalo chicken bits scattered through it, a nod to well-rounded nutrition with some leafy green salad, and a brownie square that she definitely didn't need after a day replete with many doughnuts. Somehow, the hours in the crisp air, the lingering excitement from the game, and the general exuberant atmosphere of everyone around her kicked her appetite into overdrive. She grabbed a paper cup from a big stack on a long oak sideboard and filled it with beer from a keg just inside the back door. When she finally turned around, she'd lost sight of Courtney and craned her neck to find her. Her gaze fell instead on Blaise standing just inside the back door, a look on her face that meant she was assessing and considering. Grady was getting to know her looks—not a big surprise seeing how she spent a lot of time surreptitiously watching her. When Blaise appeared to be on the verge of leaving, Grady took a couple steps in her direction. She couldn't move far or fast considering the crowd around the keg.

"Get everything you needed?" Courtney asked brightly, slipping in beside her. She too carried a cup of beer and a laden plate. "We're probably still early enough to find a place inside to sit and eat, unless you want to try for the back porch."

"I'm good either way," Grady said, throwing one more quick look in Blaise's direction. Blaise had somehow managed to make it to the long oak table in the center of the kitchen filled with platters and casserole dishes. She *wasn't* leaving. Grady relaxed on a surge of relief and focused on Courtney. "Your call."

"Let's eat inside," Court said. "That will give me a chance to introduce you to some people, if you want. Or," she said with that sly smile, "I can keep you all to myself. However you choose."

Grady laughed. "Let's just go eat."

Courtney's smile widened. "Follow me, then."

Grady kept close behind her as the house continued to fill with people, more people than she expected. Teenagers, young kids, and adults of all ages swarmed in the back door, around the food and drink tables, and throughout the downstairs, which was fortunately expansive. The door from the kitchen led to a wide hall that ran all the way through the house to the front door. She could see archways on either side that she assumed went to the main living areas. Courtney adroitly wended her way through the throng, nodding and returning greetings, until they reached the far end of the hall, where she ducked through a set of open, ten-foot-high walnut doors into the library. Dark wood floor-to-ceiling bookshelves flanked a central fireplace with a wide stone mantel. A landscape oil painting depicting a winding river flowing beneath a red covered bridge against a soaring mountain vista dominated the space above. A high-backed floral-patterned sofa stood beneath a trio of front windows, matching armchairs faced the huge hearth set with logs for when the nights chilled enough for a fire, and an oversized desk took up the far end. Taylor, Margie, Blake, and Tim occupied the sofa, legs and arms tossed willy-nilly as they talked and ate. Margie waved a fork in their direction.

"We saved you some floor."

The teens shifted their feet, and Court and Grady settled down on the floor with their backs against the arms of the sofa.

Grady balanced her food on her lap and looked over her shoulder. "Just waiting for us, right?"

"Right." Margie grinned, looking a lot like an amused Flann.

"Where's Dave?" Court asked.

Blake answered, "He just texted me. They're still with the coaches, reviewing the game." He shrugged. "He'll show up sooner or later."

A pair of steel-toed shitkickers topped by faded blue jeans stopped an inch from Grady's outstretched legs. A young guy in a Budweiser T-shirt, a bit of scruff along his jaw, a buzz cut, and a burly build stared down at her before fixing on someone behind her. She pulled her feet back a little.

"Hey, Taylor," he said in a gravelly baritone.

Grady put him anywhere between sixteen and nineteen. Possibly older, but there was still a little softness around his face that suggested the bones hadn't quite matured yet.

"Hi, Billy," Taylor said flatly.

Grady didn't need much in the way of deductive powers to figure out this was Billy Riley, the guy who'd been hitting on Taylor.

Billy said, "Some of us are going to go to a real party in a couple minutes. Why don't you come."

Grady didn't have to see his face to hear the sneer.

"No thanks," Taylor said, again without inflection.

Tim's knee where it rested against the back of Grady's shoulder jostled up and down, but he kept quiet. Letting Taylor handle the guy.

"Come on," Billy pressed. "There's nothing going on here, unless you *like* hanging around with a bunch of old fu...farts." He snorted. "And queers. But we already know about that, don't we?"

Grady cleared her throat and set her plate aside. He was big and looming over her, not the best vantage point, and she slowly eased up until she could plant her butt on the arm of the sofa. Not a particularly aggressive movement, but it gave her room to maneuver if she had to.

"Excuse me," she said. "We haven't met. I'm Grady." She held out her hand.

He looked at her, puzzled, as if he couldn't quite decipher what she was about. He shoved his hands in his back pockets. "So?"

"Well, I thought you should at least know my name. And, by the way, I'm queer."

He stared at her. "What?"

"Well, since that seems to be important to you for some reason, I thought I'd let you know. Is there anything you'd like to share?"

"What?" His voice rose along with his brows.

"You know, something personal about yourself, since you seem to think that matters somehow."

He looked at Taylor. "What the fuck?"

"Billy, I don't want to go to the party with you," Taylor said. "Or anywhere else. So could you please just stop asking me."

He shifted his gaze back to Grady. "You're crazy."

"It was nice meeting you too."

"You know, Taylor, you're gonna find out sooner or later it's not a smart thing to hang around with...freaks." He spun on his heel and stalked away.

For second, there was silence, then Grady said, "Well, he was charming."

"That was...awesome," Taylor said softly.

"Yeah," Margie echoed.

"I couldn't let him toss around slurs," Grady said, reaching for her plate. Court got to it first and handed it over to her, letting her fingers brush over Grady's thigh as they exchanged a hold on it. "But I really haven't any interest in escalating anything physical. He is pretty big."

"Tell me about it," Taylor muttered.

Grady studied her. "What has he done?"

Margie, Tim, and Blake shot up straight.

"Taylor?" Blake said urgently. "What's happened?"

"Nothing," Taylor said quickly. She blushed. "Really, nothing. Just this one time at school…"

Court rose, sat on the other end of the sofa, and rested her hand on the back of Taylor's neck. "You want to go someplace and talk?"

"No, it's okay." Taylor shook her head, her blond hair swirling around her shoulders. "A couple of weeks ago after field hockey practice, I was coming out of the locker room and it was late—five, maybe? It was pretty deserted and Billy…Billy was waiting. He wanted me to go for a ride with him. Get some pizza or something."

She fell silent, and Blake took her hand. "I'm sorry. He's hassling you because of me."

"No," Taylor said adamantly. "He's hassling me because he's a jerk and I said no."

"Go ahead," Court said. "What else did he do?"

"Nothing, except…something about him was scary, and I backed up and realized I was right against the lockers, not a great position, but it was too late and he put his arms on either side of me. I was kind of trapped."

"Did he touch you?" Margie asked. "If he did…"

Taylor took a deep breath. "No. He just…scared me."

Anger, *rage*, boiled in Grady's stomach. She wanted to say something, but she didn't know Taylor and Taylor didn't know her.

"Did you tell your mom?" Courtney asked.

"No," Taylor said in a small voice. "Nothing really happened. I promised her I would tell her if anything happened, but that wasn't something."

Margie blurted, "Yes, it was. It was intimidating and scary, and someone needs to kick his ass."

Taylor smiled. "Uh-huh. Well, it won't be you, shrimpboat."

"Excuse me, but I'm an inch taller than you are."

"Maybe nobody should try ass kicking," Grady suggested. "How about reporting him to someone?"

Taylor shrugged. "And say what? That he asked me to go have pizza with him and I said no? He didn't do anything. It was just the way he sounded, and those few seconds. Then he backed away, and I left."

"It's not safe to be alone with him," Court said.

"I *know*," Taylor said, emphasizing the word. "And I'm careful."

"It's true," Tim piped up. "We've got kind of a buddy system going. We all know where everyone else is, and we meet up coming and going to school and stuff."

Blake said quietly, "But it's not fair that we have to."

"You're right," Grady said. "It's not. But sometimes it's not about being fair. It's about being safe. And that's about being smart."

"Yeah," Blake said. "Tell me about it."

"So we're all agreed that you guys have this under control, right?" Court asked.

"We've got it," Taylor said.

"Okay then, I'm going to get some seltzer." She glanced at Grady. "I can drive you home if you want another beer."

"I'll go with you." As they worked their way back toward the kitchen, Grady said, "You think we should say something to someone?"

"Blake's parents already know he's been hassled, and they've talked with him."

"I sort of got that he's been targeted. Why is that?" Grady asked.

"He's trans."

"Ah. And he's one of the cool kids too."

"Yeah," Court said. "Double whammy. I'm not sure anything we say would make any difference right now, and I'd hate to undermine the kids' trust in us. They're doing all the right things. If Blaise knew about the school thing, she couldn't do anything differently except worry more."

"Yeah, I suppose you're right. What about the school board or someone?"

"Carson Harrington—Flann's middle sister? She's on the board, and she's aware of Blake's situation. She's a good friend of Blaise's too, so I'm sure she already knows."

"Good to know."

"Hey, Court." A woman in blue jeans, a short-sleeved blue-and-white checked shirt, and work boots angled her way over to them.

Courtney stopped, smiling, "Hey, Mel. How you doing?"

"Great. Busy. The usual." She glanced at Grady and back to Court. Curious, and questioning.

"Oh, hey," Courtney said, "Mel, this is Grady McClure. She's a new surgeon at the hospital. This is Melanie Cochran—she's got the farm next to the Rivers place."

Grady held out her hand. "Great to meet you."

"You too." Mel turned back to Courtney. "Listen, when you get a chance, I wanted to let you know about that litter of pups you were asking about."

"Oh, hey, did they whelp?"

Mel grinned. "Any day now."

"You'll call me right away?"

"Sure." Mel hesitated. "It might be the middle of the night, though."

"Not a problem...let me make sure you have my cell number."

"I'll catch you later, Court," Grady said, easing away. Court and Melanie might just be friends, but something in the way Melanie focused on Courtney said maybe she was thinking differently. Putting a little distance between her and Courtney might be a good idea before half the town decided they were dating.

"Sure," Court called as Grady faded back. "I'll be around if you need that ride."

Grady made it to the kitchen, grabbed a beer, and drifted out onto the back porch. By some miracle, a rocker half hidden in shadows at the far end of the porch was unoccupied, and she sank into it. The night was too dark for her to see very far down the sloped lawn, but the slap of the river against the shore and the slivers of moonlight reflecting off the water lulled her into a pleasant haze. The lights and noise from the gathering inside faded, and she slowly relaxed, sipping her beer and rocking a little. She hadn't seen Blaise on the way out. She wondered if she'd left. She wondered if she'd left alone. She wondered when she would see her again. As questions drifted through her mind, she closed her eyes for just a second.

Chapter Fifteen

Courtney stuck her head around the corner into the library. Tim and Taylor had disappeared, but Blake and Margie were in the same place, side by side on the sofa, heads bent over Margie's phone. Probably texting someone else in their crew. "Hey, have you seen Grady?"

"No, not since she left with you," Margie said.

"Okay. If you see her, will you tell her I'm looking for her. Mel just got a call from the farm. Sadie is about to deliver."

Blake shot up as if he'd been ejected from a rocket launcher. "Really? Can I come?"

"I'll have to check with Mel. You know sometimes the bitches get really touchy when they're whelping." The eager look on his face was so compelling, she wanted to say yes right there. But she really did need to check with Mel.

"I know. I can stay way out of the way."

"Really, Blake." Margie nudged his arm with hers. "You're going to ditch a party for puppies?"

Blake grinned, tossed his arm around her shoulders, and gave her a jubilant kiss. "Come on. It's puppies."

Margie's stunned expression almost made Courtney laugh. Wasn't expecting that, was she?

The wide-eyed look on Blake's face said he wasn't either. He vaulted off the sofa and immediately shoved his hands in his pockets. "Um."

"Yeah." Half laughing and half perplexed, Margie frowned up at him. "Like, what *was* that?"

"I dunno…exactly. Happy?" Blake actually shuffled his feet. "It just sort of…popped out."

"Popped." Margie rolled her eyes. "Go watch the puppies arrive. Nerd."

Court said, "Uh, I'll just go look for Mel. Come find me in a minute, Blake."

She backed out of the room, smiling to herself. She'd been a teenager once, and maybe as awkward as them, but she didn't like to think so. She preferred to see herself in her memory as cool and sophisticated and above being flummoxed by her first kiss. Her first kiss. Archie Camillo. Not a great kisser. Still, she remembered it. Fortunately, she'd soon discovered she much preferred kissing girls, and she was positive she'd been a world-class snogger from the start.

Mel waited out of the way against the staircase leading up to the second floor.

"All set?" Mel asked.

"Just about. Listen, Blake Remy asked if he could tag along. He's a really good kid, and you know he volunteers a lot at Val's clinic, so he knows how to be around animals."

"Sure. We need to go, though, if we don't want to miss it all."

"Okay, I can't find Grady, and I don't want to leave her without a ride. Let me text her and—Wait a second. Hey, Blaise!" She waved to Blaise. "Talk to you a minute?"

"Sure." Blaise, holding her cup of wine in the air to keep it from sloshing on her shirt when someone inevitably bumped into her, headed for Courtney. Expecting to see Grady close by, the undeniable relief when she didn't caught her by surprise. A pleasant surprise for a change. "What do you need?"

"Mel's retriever is about to have puppies, and I want to be there. I gave Grady a ride over, but I can't find her. If you see her, can you have her text me, and we'll figure something out. We need to go right now."

"No problem. I'm sure she won't have any trouble getting a ride home, though, but I'll see if I can find her."

"Great. You have my number, right?"

Blaise laughed. "Of course. Along with just about every other staff person I might have to tag for the ER."

Courtney waved at Blake to join them and, with her other hand on Mel's wrist, took off toward the front door. Blaise turned the other way and worked her way back toward the kitchen, checking the rooms on either side of the hall as she passed. No sign of Grady. She bumped into Abby just as she made it into the kitchen.

"Hi," Blaise said. "Everything turn out okay?"

Abby nodded. "Gladys was stable, and crotchety." She grinned. "She couldn't understand what all the fuss was about just because she had a little bruise on her...bum, I believe the term was."

Blaise laughed. "Nothing broken?"

"No. I think the folks at the residence were reacting out of an abundance of caution. She really did have a pretty nice bruise on her hip, but fortunately, she's got good bones and nothing's broken. We're not even going to keep her for observation."

"Oh, that's great news."

"And now," Abby said, grabbing a disposable cup and a jug of red wine, "I'm going to have a drink."

"I'd join you," Blaise said, tossing her mostly empty cup into the big recycling barrel, "but I've already had my one."

"Are you headed out?" Abby asked. "I wasn't sure you'd be here when I got back."

"I'm not sure what's happening with the kids just yet. I haven't seen Taylor or Tim for a while. Blake just went off with Mel Cochran and Courtney to watch some puppies being born."

"I just saw Dave and some of the team pull up. It will be a while before they sort out their next stop." Abby sipped her wine and made an appreciative noise. "I can handle transporting them if Dave isn't driving."

"I'll find you in a while, and we can coordinate. Flann is looking for you too." For some reason, Blaise didn't want to mention that she was actually searching for Grady. She *did* have to deliver a message, after all. It wasn't as if it was her idea to look for her. Just doing Courtney a favor. Never mind knowing Grady and Court had parted ways. That was just a little bit of added happy.

She poured herself some seltzer, passed on the brownies after some serious deliberation—the memory of doughnuts still fresh enough to sway her to exercise restraint—and continued on her circuit through the first floor. Someone had propped the kitchen door open with an old cast iron shoe scraper, with just the screen to keep out the moths who insisted on trying to get inside to the light. Unlike them, Blaise was drawn to the dark and the promise of quiet outside and let herself out onto the porch. The crowd had already started to thin. Farmers' hours meant an early start in the morning, even though the next day was Sunday. Plenty of people would be in the fields or the barns at first light to put in a few hours' work before church or family midday dinner or however else they celebrated the day of rest. Mostly, rest came after a good deal of work.

Blaise walked toward the far end of the porch, where she'd be unlikely to run into anyone who wanted to chat. She didn't mind friendly talk with neighbors, but her mind had been buzzing all day with too many thoughts and too many feelings, and right now she'd just like to empty her head. That was a wish she wasn't going to get fulfilled.

Grady slouched in a rocker at the far end of the porch, and as soon as Blaise saw her, all the noise and chaos and crazy lightning sparks flared bright and hot in her entire body. Quiet was the last thing she felt when looking at Grady. Asleep—at least that's how she seemed as Blaise drew near and got a closer look—she was even more distracting. Grady was definitely fast asleep—fast asleep with a half-full cup of beer in her hand, balanced on her thigh. How had she managed not to spill that?

Blaise eased against the railing across from Grady and tried to decide if she should wake her or not. She looked peaceful. And frighteningly, quite a bit younger in her unguarded moments. She really oughtn't watch her this way, unawares. She'd just sneak away again. In just a second. Just one more brief glance, to satisfy the strange sense of longing mixed with wonder.

Moonlight struck Grady's face at an angle, leaving one side in shadow and the other bathed in soft, silver light. Smooth skin, strong bones, delicate angles and—Blaise leaned forward, just to get a better look—incredibly long, dark eyelashes.

Those lashes fluttered, and Grady's eyes opened.

"Hi," Grady said, her voice a little husky from sleep.

Husky and very sexy.

Blaise straightened abruptly. "Um, you were asleep."

Grady grinned and moved her cup of beer to a little table beside her rocker. "I guess I was. How long have you been there?"

"A millisecond. Hardly any time at all. And I was not staring."

"Really? Because it looked like you were."

Blaise tried not to grind her teeth. "I was just trying to see if you were really asleep."

"You mean as opposed to faking being asleep when there was nobody else around?"

"All right, if you must know," Blaise said, flustered—which was completely unlike her—and annoyed, and tired of being *both* on top of it all, "I was looking at your eyelashes."

Frowning, Grady rubbed her eyes with one hand. "What's wrong with them?"

"Nothing. They're gorgeous."

Grady's grin widened, and the moonlight danced in her eyes as she sat forward a little. "Is that what you think?"

"About your *eyelashes*," Blaise said slowly and distinctly. "And can we just forget about that right now."

"Oh, I don't think so."

Damn it, she should have left when she'd had the chance. At least she could take care of Court's request. "I have a message for you from your girlfriend."

The playfulness left Grady's face. "I don't have a girlfriend. I told you that."

"If you say so."

Grady stood so quickly and stepped so close, Blaise leaned back, but with her butt against the railing, she had nowhere to go. Grady was very, very close. Way too close.

"Do you think I would lie to you about something like that?" Grady's voice was pitched low. Her face, no longer young or vulnerable, all sharp angles, her eyes dark and serious. "About anything at all?"

"No," Blaise said softly. "I don't. So I apologize. I'm not…quite myself. Long day, I guess."

"You don't need to apologize." Grady stroked a finger along the edge of Blaise's jaw and rested her fingertips lightly on her throat. "And while we're on the subject, you don't just have gorgeous eyelashes, you're gorgeous everywhere."

Blaise's breath came fast and shallow. The beat of her heart was a flutter of wings in her chest, a trapped bird struggling to escape a predator, or taking flight toward freedom. She wasn't sure which. She couldn't back up anymore, and she didn't want to. The heat of Grady's gaze drifting languidly, arrogantly, over her face, stoked a heat inside her she'd never felt. Had never even known she wanted to feel. Other things she wanted, she shied away from thinking about, but she couldn't stop looking at Grady's mouth. Her lips were full and ever so slightly amused—as if she enjoyed Blaise's quandary. Go. Stay. Yield. Take. Risk. Flee.

"Grady," Blaise said quietly.

"Yes, Blaise?"

Had she moved even closer? Blaise's body hummed with anticipation. No uncertainty there.

Blaise took a breath. Steadied herself. "I don't kiss women I just met."

The corner of Grady's mouth turned up fully. Not just amused. Inviting. "Are you going to kiss me?"

"No."

"Did you think I was going to kiss you?"

"The thought crossed my mind."

"When I kiss you, you won't have time to wonder."

"What makes you think I'll want you to?"

"Don't you?"

Yes. No. How could I?

Grady leaned a little closer. She couldn't stop herself. Indecision warred in Blaise's eyes. A pulse beat in Blaise's throat, a ripple like the river far below them, flowing sultry and slow in the pale moonlight. Haunting, seductive, beautiful. Her fingertips barely touched Blaise's throat over that pounding pulse, but the force of it shot through her, making her thighs tremble and something deep inside her clench until she ached. Oh, she wanted to kiss her all right. She wanted to kiss her and not stop.

"Are you sure you don't want me to kiss you?" Grady murmured.

"Do you think I would lie to you about something like that?" Blaise whispered.

"No. Not to me."

Blaze pressed her hand to the center of Grady's chest. Grady's heart pounded beneath her palm as wildly as her own. She had thought she might push her away, but she didn't. Couldn't. The way her muscles tightened, the way her breath caught, when she'd touched her just then. Oh, she liked knowing she could unsettle Grady. She wasn't alone in the wild wanting. And she wanted...more. Her fingertips drifted a little higher, found the delicate arch of collarbone, skimmed over the vulnerable hollow at the base of her throat.

"Blaise," Grady groaned. "Kiss me, then."

"I can't do this like this." Blaise dropped her hand.

"All right," Grady said, blinking hard to clear her head and tamp down the fire. She eased back, letting her fingers trail down Blaise's throat until the contact broke. Something wild and primitive raged inside her, howling in frustration. "I will kiss you," Grady said. "But I'll wait until you ask, if that's what you want."

Blaise shivered. What did she want? Not this whirlwind of conflicting sensations—desire, hunger—spinning out of control. Grasping for solid ground, she cleared her throat, swallowing back the desire that threatened to choke her. "Courtney...Courtney left with Mel. Something about puppies."

"That's a lot more novel than etchings," Grady muttered.

Blaze laughed and, suddenly, being with Grady was easy again. Grady laughed too, and the stark lines in her face eased. "Really, around here that wouldn't even be a line."

"I heard Mel talking about it earlier. Thanks for letting me know."

"She wanted to make sure you had a ride home. I can text her if you want to meet her or..."

Grady shook her head. "No, I don't. I'm sure she's busy."

Grady didn't seem the least bit upset that Court had disappeared with another woman. Not a date, then.

"I have to check with Abby and the kids," Blaise said, "but I can drop you off in town if you need a ride later. I'm not sure when I'll be leaving, though."

"Doesn't matter. I don't have any plans," Grady said in a rush before Blaise could change her mind.

"Well, if you're sure, I'll text Court and let her know."

"I'm sure." Grady followed Blaise as she turned to go back inside. She was sure, all right, even if waiting wasn't her game. But then, where Blaise was concerned, all the rules had changed.

CHAPTER SIXTEEN

Flann dropped a kiss on her mother's cheek. "Have you seen my wife?"

Ida Rivers slid a tray of warm apple pies onto the stone trivets at one end of the table. In seconds, the stack of plates she'd put out was gone and the pies were rapidly following. "She was headed into the hall about ten minutes ago."

"You need help down here?"

Ida pushed a lock of midnight hair threaded with silver behind her ear and surveyed the remaining food. "I think we might have filled everyone up—for the moment."

"Yell if you need a hand. Dad here?"

"Hiding in his study, I think." Ida smiled. "There may be poker."

"Oh yeah?" Flann considered. Maybe she could fit in a hand or two. Better clear it with Abby first. "I'll catch him later, then."

"Mm-hmm." Ida patted Flann's cheek. "You were up most of the night, I hear. Get some rest."

Flann didn't even ask how her mother knew she'd had a case the night before. Her mother always knew. The Rivers was in her blood, just like all the rest of them. "I'm good, but I might grab Abby and take off a little early. Haven't seen her much the last few days."

"All the more reason to skip the poker—go."

Grinning, Flann circuited through the downstairs, ending up in the library. Margie was curled in the corner of the sofa, and Flann dropped down beside her. "Hey. Have you seen Abby?"

"No," Margie said in kind of a weird flat tone, "not since the game."

"Oh, well, she's probably hiding somewhere so she doesn't have to talk shop with half the people here."

"Uh-huh."

Flann angled her back to the arm of the sofa and stretched one leg out on the seat, her bent knee just nudging Margie's. "Where's Blake and the rest of your crew?"

"Um, Taylor and Tim went to find Dave. Blake is delivering puppies."

"Come again?" Flann sipped her beer. Something was off with her sister. Margie's usual exuberance had disappeared, like the bubbles in champagne gone flat when set aside for other pleasures. She immediately substituted an image of seltzer left out on the counter, feeling somehow guilty thinking about champagne and sex and her sister in the same mental breath, but all the same—something was not right here. "I didn't think you guys were on call for Val. Some kind of emergency?"

"Not Val, Courtney."

"Okay, now I'm really not following. What's going on with Blake and puppies?"

Margie heaved a sigh. "Mel Cochran's bitch, Sadie, is having pups. Right now. Blake ran off to observe."

"Well, of course he did." Flann grinned. "Are you upset puppies won out over your company?"

She'd meant it as just some good-natured poking, but Margie's expression took another odd turn, as if she wasn't quite sure whether she was upset, angry, or confused. Totally not her sister.

"Nope."

Margie—reduced to sentences of one word? Flann straightened, giving Margie a little space between them, but in a position where she could watch her face. Margie, like all her sisters, was pretty easy to read when you'd grown up with them. "So what's the problem?"

"No problem," Margie said, her forced enthusiasm obvious.

"Uh-huh. Are you two fighting or something?"

Margie shook her head.

"I can keep on guessing all night." Flann took another sip of her beer, anxiety starting to roil in her innards. "Has there been another altercation? Somebody giving you or Blake trouble?"

"No," Margie said. "Not really."

"Define *not really*," Flann said through clenched teeth.

Margie heaved a sigh and dropped her head onto the back of the sofa, staring at the ceiling in a posture Flann was coming to recognize as the universal teenage sign for *my parents are bothering me and I'm so bored with it all.* She wasn't Margie's parent, but she was her big sister, and as far as she was concerned, that gave her a legitimate reason to poke and prod until she got answers.

"Spill it, Rivers."

"Billy Riley. He's such an ass."

"Agreed. What else?"

"He keeps bugging Taylor to go out with him, and she said no a million times."

"Okay," Flann said slowly. "Some guys—some women too—don't take no for an answer right away. It's annoying. But is something happening that's a lot more than annoying?"

"Not really." Margie sighed and rolled her head to the side to meet Flann's gaze. "But he feels wrong. Like, something more could happen."

"I think I know what you mean," Flann said quietly. "Like he could do more than just be a jerk verbally. Like that?"

"Maybe," Margie said softly. "I don't really know for sure. He's just…a creep."

"I get that. Is there anything else? Something I should know, or Abby or Blaise?"

"No, you guys already know. It's nothing new."

"Was Blake on Billy's a-hole radar tonight?"

"No more than usual. Just the usual *oh hey, you all like queers* kind of thing."

Flann sighed. "You're right, he's an ass."

"You know, lots of us, like, I don't know, half, somewhere like that, don't even think in terms of straight or gay. It's kind of, just, you know, flexible."

"Hmm," Flann said, starting to tread out onto the thin ice again. Why did she always end up here when she started talking to a teenager? Of course, if she remembered right, being a teenager was a whole lot about sex. Other things mattered, sure, but sex? Pretty much up at the top of the list. "So how about you?"

Margie grinned. "You don't really want to know that, do you?"

Oh boy. Flann's stomach produced a lot more acid, if that was even possible. "Yeah, I do. Just because it's you. You're my sister, and I love you and I want to know you."

"That's corny."

Flann sighed. "Okay, yeah. Maybe. But it's still true."

Margie's expression softened, and for an instant she looked like the much younger kid Flann remembered. Always bold and brave and filled with enthusiasm, but still learning about the world.

"Come on, Margie. It's me, remember?"

"I'm mostly coming down on the liking guys side of things."

Flann pressed a hand to her heart and stared. "Oh my God. No."

Margie's grin widened. "I know, weird, huh? Of course, that makes it fifty-fifty for the four of us. So maybe not."

"It's not weird, babe." Flann leaned over and touched the tip of her index finger to Margie's nose, the way she used to do when Margie was much younger, just to get a giggle out of her. "It's you. That's all that matters."

"Blake kissed me."

Flann froze, as immobile as if she had suddenly turned into an ice statue. She shook her head, certain she'd misheard. "Come again?"

"Blake. Your kid, you know the one? Dark hair, awesome blue eyes, really nice to everyone? He kissed me."

Flann carefully leaned back, drained the rest of her beer, and set the cup on the floor. She needed a lot more than that ten seconds to gather her thoughts, which had scattered to the wind like chaff in a summer gale. She took a deep breath. This she could not fuck up. "Okay. How do you feel about it?"

"That's my question," Margie said with a spark of her usual attitude.

"No fair," Flann said, "I asked you first."

"I don't know," Margie said after a long minute. "Mostly good. I mean, it's Blake. And it was really quick. I'm not sure it actually counts as a kiss."

"Well, were there lips involved?"

Margie rolled her eyes. "Well, duh, yes."

Flann couldn't bring herself to ask any more.

Margie laughed. "But that was all, and Courtney was standing right there. It's not like it was, you know, going anywhere."

Flann wanted to clap her hands over her ears. Oh, fuck. Did she really want to hear this? She couldn't not, now that they were here finally, thin ice be damned. "Okay, about the going somewhere. Is that in the cards, do you think?"

There, she just put it out there. Time to stop pussyfooting around the subject.

"I don't know that either," Margie said. "But I didn't want there to be any big secret about anything, just in case. Because, you know, it's complicated. You and Abby and Blake and me."

"You know what," Flann said, the storm finally settling, the air growing still, and her thoughts clearing. "It's not really complicated. Abby and I care about both of you, a lot. We love you. And you're both terrific. And if there's more, and it's what you both want, that'll be just fine."

Margie studied her with that way-too-old expression she sometimes got in her eyes, even back when she'd been a kid. So smart, always so scary smart. "You're not the same as you used to be, you know."

"Oh. Am I about to be insulted?"

"Well, you're still, you know, a little bit of a know-it-all, so you're still you, the one who is always certain, always ready to jump into any situation and fix it, but you're…I dunno, you see more now."

"I see more now," Flann said quietly. "I think that's because of Abby. I think that's what happens when you fall in love, and you learn a lot more about yourself when you do."

"Well, I'm not there yet," Margie said. "But I'm good."

Flann shoved over, flung an arm around Margie's shoulders, and dragged her close. She kissed the top of her head. "Kiddo, you're a lot more than good. You're a Rivers."

Margie threaded her arm around Flann's waist and rested her head on her shoulder. "Yeah. I am."

❖

Blaise finally tracked down Abby sharing a beer with Carson and a couple of other hospital staff in the upstairs sitting room.

Abby noticed her at the edge of the crowd and joined her. "Hi! Did you track down our errant offspring?"

Blaise shook her head. "We've still got three unaccounted for… Dave, Tim, and Taylor."

"If you're ready to go home," Abby said, "why don't you just go. I'll be here for a while unwinding anyhow. I'll catch up with Flann, and we'll make sure the kids all get sorted out. I'll have Taylor text you with her plans."

"Are you sure?" Blaise waffled, and she didn't like that. She hadn't even intended to stay when she'd arrived, and here she was, an hour or more later. Now she was more than ready to leave, and she hesitated. All because of the little matter of Grady McClure. She'd offered Grady a ride and now what? Leave with her, alone? The memory of a mesmerizing face in the moonlight, warm fingers, and her still thundering heart decided her. "Maybe I'll just stay and wait for the kids."

Abby tilted her head. "Okay, so what now?"

Blaise knew she was blushing, damn it. "Nothing, really. I told Grady I'd give her a ride home because Courtney's off with Mel having puppies. But I'm sure she can get a ride with someone else."

"Oh, okay." Abby gave her a look. "So you want to hang around here, waiting to possibly give the kids a ride somewhere, even though you've had your fill of the party, and I can do it just as easily, all so you don't have to give Grady a ride home?"

"It's not like that."

"Um. How is it, then?"

"Damn it." Blaise glanced around, happy that no one was close enough to overhear the conversation. The sitting room was as large as the formal living room downstairs, with big bay windows opposite the entrance, another huge fireplace, and a scattering of sofas and overstuffed chairs. Even though the party seemed to be slowing down, at least half a dozen people were sprinkled around the room. None close, though.

"It's the weirdest thing," Blaise said. "I can't quite figure out whether I like her or not."

"Has she done something that you don't care for?"

"She's an outrageous flirt. And she seemed so sure of herself—and of me, as if I'm just going to give in at any second and let her kiss me."

"Oh." Abby nodded approvingly. "Well, that's progress, then."

Blaise laughed. Dramatic much? "I hate you."

Abby grinned. "That's allowed. I am your best friend, right?"

"I just don't know how to feel around her."

"Well, maybe you should stop thinking about it and just go with whatever it is you're feeling when you're with her."

An icy tentacle wrapped itself around Blaise's spine. "I can't do that."

Abby studied her. "Why not?"

"Because I can't."

Abby gently grasped her wrist. Her fingers were warm, the touch comforting in its gentleness. "All right. Then go slow and be careful, but try to trust your feelings and not think everything to death."

Blaise sighed. "I'm not sure I know how."

"Well, I think you do," Abby said, lightness in her voice, "so you can just trust me."

Blaise took a deep breath. If only it was that easy. "Make sure Taylor texts me, okay? And I can come back if I need to."

Abby squeezed her wrist ever so slightly and let go. "I will. Now, go do something for yourself."

As Blaise made her way back downstairs, pausing only slightly when someone called her name, to smile and return the greeting, she thought about what Abby had said. Something for herself. What would that look like?

She *had* done something for herself all of her adult life, hadn't she? She'd had her child because she wanted her, and she'd raised an amazing daughter. She had a job she loved that let her give something to her friends and her community by doing it. She had a home—an entire community that she cared about. Weren't all those things for herself? And yet—there were those moments that snuck up on her in the quiet hours when the world slowed down enough for her to feel the absence of...something.

She walked into the kitchen, and Grady pushed away from the wall by the door where she'd been leaning back out of the crowd. Half a dozen people filled the space between them, but Grady's gaze caught hers instantly and held it. As if she'd been waiting. Not just for a few minutes, but for far longer.

Chapter Seventeen

Grady had been passing the time waiting for Blaise by people watching. She wasn't a big partygoer in general—mostly because she didn't have a lot of time, and she'd never had many intimates, just colleagues, not like best friends or people she'd hang out with after work. For years, her whole life, all her personal interactions, had been with people at the hospital, and most of those had been her fellow residents. *Fellow* being the accurate description. There were some women, of course, and a lot more than there used to be, but in surgery, still, lots of men. And the further along in her training she went, the more that seemed to be the case. The subgroup of surgery residents formed a small community within the larger hospital circle, and the dozen or so in her year were the individuals she ate with, worked with, and slept with. She got along with them fine and never felt the need to hide who she was or much of anything about her private life except the details of what and with whom. But the hours she kept, the odd competitive camaraderie she shared with her peers, and the transitory nature of most of her sexual interactions didn't make for much in the way of long-term friendships. So parties always struck her as being a gathering of strangers all hoping to connect.

The people at the Homestead celebration seemed different—not as disposed to congregate in separate little islands ignoring everyone else. Of course that might be because most of them had grown up together or had lived there for a long time. Maybe that wasn't true, either, but she didn't think there was anything particularly magical about the place. Maybe a shared history was enough to overcome other differences, at least when face-to-face. She wondered how long *she'd* be considered the outsider—not exactly an unusual situation for her, but one she unexpectedly wanted to change.

She'd figured out right away who the matriarch of the Rivers family was. Ida Rivers was a handsome woman, midnight hair faintly silvered, a mostly unlined face, strong graceful body, and a gently commanding air that said she was in charge without needing to demonstrate her authority. People, old and young, congregated around her. Grady recognized Harper and her wife Presley Worth when they stopped to chat with Ida before grabbing food and drinks and disappearing. She'd met Presley briefly the day she'd started on staff. Harper was an easy call, since she looked a lot like Flann with contrasting coloring.

Although a stranger and essentially alone in the crowd, Grady felt comfortable hanging back, unnoticed.

Everything changed the instant Blaise appeared in the doorway. The air sharpened, the soft orange glow from the open hearth at one end of the room blazed brighter, and her skin tingled as each tiny hair vibrated with an electric charge. Blaise was beautiful. Grady wondered if she even knew that and decided she probably didn't. Everything she'd learned about Blaise said she rarely thought about herself. As if everything that mattered were the things outside her, like her daughter or the hospital or even her friendships with the people around her. Whatever seethed inside her, whatever wants she had—and she must have them, there were too many sparks of passion glimmering beneath her surface for that not to be the case—she kept hidden. From everyone.

And that was a challenge. What did Blaise want—for herself, from a woman? Intriguing, fascinating, exciting. Blaise caught her watching and stared back, bold and intense. She didn't look away, the way she might have just a day before. Was she searching for Grady's secrets, the same way Grady searched? And if she was, what did she see? Grady knew what Blaise *thought* she saw. A woman who was into casual relationships; confident—maybe, no, *definitely* more than was warranted; sexy, she hoped, but not the kind to commit. Grady knew she projected that. Mostly it was true, and partly it was just easier.

And for the first time, that wasn't what she wanted another woman to see. She wasn't sure exactly what she *did* want Blaise to see, except she was serious. Serious about getting to know her. And damn serious about kissing her. If Blaise wanted the first before the second, she'd be as patient as she could. Maybe.

She kept her gaze on Blaise as Blaise threaded her way across the room to her.

"Sorry that took me a little while," Blaise said.

"No problem," Grady said. "I was having a good time just watching the natives."

Blaise chuckled. "I can't imagine that occupied your interest for more than thirty seconds."

"Not true," Grady said. "I like sorting out the power structure. It tells you a lot about the people."

"Oh?" Blaise raised an eyebrow. "And what did you discern?"

"Well, as near as I could tell, Ida Rivers is probably the mayor, and if she isn't, she is unofficially. Flann and Harper—in fact, all her kids—are her honor guard. Harper's in line for the throne, Flann, she's the first sword. Carson, the advisor, and young Margie…" Grady laughed. "She will be the strategist."

"Let me guess, you've been reading epic fantasy in your off hours."

"I don't have much time to read," Grady said, "but I confess that I do have a liking for the politics and intrigue of those kind of big-canvas stories."

"Well, I can't say that you're wrong in your assessment. Very good indeed."

"You want to know what I think about you?" Grady said.

Blaise shook her head. "Absolutely not."

"Why not? I know you're not a coward."

"Well, thank you very much," Blaise said tartly. "First, if you got it wrong, I'd be insulted. And if you got it right, I'd be even more insulted that I was so easy to read. So it's a no-win scenario. Are you still looking for a ride home?"

Grady laughed. "Nice deflection. You're really good at that, and since I've already said it, that's not news."

"And you are really good at not answering questions."

"You're right," Grady said. "That maybe sums us both up, don't you think?"

Blaise regarded her with her eyes slightly narrowed, assessing. "Yes. Definitely not compatible."

"Oh no," Grady said, "I wouldn't necessarily draw that conclusion. Complementary might be a better word."

"A ride home?" Blaise repeated, determined not to get into another personal conversation that she never wanted to have and couldn't seem to avoid where Grady was concerned.

"Persistent, I'll add that too," Grady said. "But we share that one. Only I want to see more of you, and you want…less?"

The question in her eyes and the shadow of uncertainty in her tone demanded truth. Blaise sighed. "I never said that. Can we—for the moment—stick with the present question? As in a ride home. Are you ready?"

"Sure, if you are."

When Grady didn't push the issue of anything more personal, Blaise snuffed out a spark of disappointment. Really, could she not stay with a single decision when Grady was around? Casual, friendly, nothing more. "I've been ready since I got here. I have no idea how I ended up staying, when all I was going to do was drop the kids off."

"I think it was preordained," Grady said as she held the door open for Blaise. They walked out side by side and down the steps into the refreshingly cool darkness. "So you could give me a ride home."

"Of course, that must be it."

Grady laughed.

The knots in Blaise's neck loosened the moment they left the lights and noise behind, and she took a deep breath, letting the scent of pine and wood smoke soothe her. "God, it's a beautiful night."

"It is," Grady said softly.

Blaise glanced her way. Grady was watching her. Impulsively, she asked, "What do you think of it?"

"The night, the party, the town…you?" Grady asked.

"All except the last," Blaise said as she remoted her door locks.

"One of these times you're going to let me tell you what I think of when I see you."

"Tonight is not that night." Blaise climbed into the SUV as Grady, shaking her head, swung around the front to get in the opposite side.

As Grady buckled in, she said, "It's a gorgeous night. I love the fall. I'm not really super keen on the dead of winter, but I love the briskness of nights like this."

"Mm, me too. Perfect for a hayride."

"Um," Grady said skeptically, "I'm not sure how I feel about hay in my…you know…anywhere."

Blaise snorted. "I was talking about riding in a big hay wagon with neighbors, decorated with a few pumpkins, that kind of thing. Not sex."

"Oh. Okay. Really?"

"You'll see in October." Smiling at the image of Grady in a hay wagon, Blaise pulled out and headed toward the two lane back to town.

"The town," Grady said, "I like it. At least what I've seen so far.

And the hospital is totally awesome. Amazing opportunities. Great staff, excellent referral sources, plenty of challenges, especially with the medeva—"

Blaise reached across the center console and squeezed Grady's forearm. "No shop talk, Doctor. You're off call for the moment."

"Roger that." Grady stiffened at the touch on her arm, hoping Blaise wouldn't move her hand. Of course, she did after just a few seconds. Grady figured she had maybe ten minutes more of Blaise's company. She wanted to make the most of them, and she wanted Blaise to know they meant something to her.

"Did you ever find Taylor?" Grady asked.

"No. Taylor, Tim, and Dave were somewhere else in the house. Abby is on kid search. She'll have Taylor text me."

Grady hesitated. "Listen, I don't think it's a major issue, but that kid, Billy Riley—"

Blaise snapped her attention from the road to Grady. "You know Billy?"

"Met him tonight."

"What happened?"

"Actually, nothing. I happened to be in the library with Courtney, eating. Taylor was there with her friends, and Riley came in. He wanted Taylor to go with him to another party. She said no."

Blaise muttered an oath under her breath. "He is so persistent. That worries me."

"I get that," Grady said. "Some people just don't know when to quit."

Blaise raised a brow. "Oh, really?"

"That's not me, Blaise."

"I know that." Blaise sighed. "I'm sorry. You didn't deserve that. I'm just angry at Billy."

"No apology needed. Taylor said she'd already told you he was pestering her, but just so you know. She said she was handling it, and she was."

"It's funny, that your children want to protect you." Blaise shook her head. "I'm sure there are dozens of things she doesn't tell me. Some of them she probably should, but I guarantee she tells me a whole lot more than I ever told my mother."

"Well, if she tells you anything, it's more than I ever told mine," Grady said.

"Not close?"

"Not the heart-to-heart-talk kind of close, no." Grady smiled wryly. "More like you're the symbol of my success, so don't screw up kind of thing."

"Ouch," Blaise said. "I'm sorry."

"Thanks, but growing a thick skin has its advantages." Grady saw the red light marking the center of town. A few more blocks and they'd be at her place. "Is there anything open around here?"

"Now? Well, there's a bar that serves burgers and such. Are you hungry?"

"No," Grady said, her voice laced with frustration. "I'm just not ready for the night to be over yet."

"Oh," Blaise said. Funny, neither was she. "All right then, how about a nightcap?"

"I've had my quota of beer for the night, and I can't imagine the bar is going to have anything else I would want to drink."

"That's a bet I wouldn't take, but how do you feel about port?"

Grady sat up straight and the seat belt snapped across her chest. "Port? Oh, I feel really good about that."

Blaise put on her blinker, turned onto Union Street, drove down three houses, and pulled into a narrow drive between a two-story yellow house and a similarly styled white clapboard one on the opposite side. "All right then. I'll meet you on the porch in just a couple of minutes."

"This is your house?" Grady said as she got out and followed Blaise to the front porch.

Blaise smiled at her. "Uh-huh."

"Okay, dumb question. Sorry, being around you tends to reduce me to a bumbling idiot at times."

"I've never noticed that. Go, get comfortable on the porch, and I'll get the drinks." Blaise hurried through the house to the kitchen. She could've invited her in, but if she did, the intimacy would be far too frightening. And there was the little matter that she didn't trust herself inside, in the middle of the night, alone with Grady.

Grady stirred her up too much.

Blaise carried the port back outside and handed Grady the small glass. Grady took a sip and sighed. "Okay, that's perfect."

Grady had chosen the porch swing to sit on. Blaise could play it safe and take the rocker next to it, or she could sit beside her. That would still leave at least a foot of space between them. And the glider was fun. She sat down, put a foot on the floor, and gently pushed the rocker into motion. "Thanks for telling me about Taylor's encounter with Billy. That was thoughtful of you."

"I don't think it was anything dangerous," Grady repeated. "Courtney was there, and she explained you already knew he was a bit of a problem. She also said Taylor was the kind of kid who'd tell you about anything more serious."

"I would've understood if you hadn't said anything. And Courtney's not wrong. Courtney is—well, Courtney is a lot of things. I'm sure you noticed."

"I like Courtney," Grady said, sipping her port. "But she's not you."

Blaise huffed. "She most certainly isn't."

"No, she's not anything like you." Grady tilted her head back, half closed her eyes. No lights shone from the neighboring houses, the trees on either side of Blaise's house blocked the porch from casual view, and the bit of sky visible over the silhouettes of rooftops and chimneys glittered with a swath of sparkling stars like diamonds on black velvet. The gentle sway of the rocker, the port warming her despite the faint chill, and Blaise's citrusy scent cocooned her in lush sensation. Pleasantly overloaded, she spoke without thinking. "Courtney's fun. She's bright and energetic and—"

"Sexy," Blaise said. "You can say it."

Grady laughed and turned her head toward Blaise. "Sexy. Yes, in a general sort of way. But I'm not interested in general—I'm much more interested in specifics. As in, specifically you. Like I said, Courtney would be fun, but you, you would be—*are*—unforgettable. First, but not last, you're sensual and sexy down to your bones. Everything about you fires me up—your certainty, your determination, even your damn blueprint for the future, and I know you have one. Your smile, the look in your eyes when you're weighing the consequences of your next move, the fact that you do—I want to know why. I want to know what you dream that no one else knows. I want to know all of it."

"No, you don't," Blaise said quietly.

"I do," Grady said, "whenever, whatever you want to tell me."

"And if I repeat I don't plan on sharing any of that?" Blaise wanted to hear just one answer, the sane smart answer, and dreaded it at the same time.

"I'll wait."

Not what she wanted to hear, despite the rush of relief. "Why? Why bother?"

Grady smiled. "Because you're determined and certain, and I *know* when you feel that way about a woman, it will be everything."

Blaise's chest tightened. Everything. She could barely remember when she'd believed passion, love, would be everything she wanted. Grady had no idea what she was asking of her.

CHAPTER EIGHTEEN

Blaise's phone vibrated, and she slid it from her pocket. The sinking in her stomach could have been disappointment, or relief. She cleared her throat, searched for steady ground when the world seemed to have tilted. "That's Taylor. Dave is dropping her off at home. She'll be here in a few minutes."

"Why do I get the feeling you're happy about that?" Grady's tone was teasing, but Blaise couldn't find the words to tease back. She wanted—needed—Grady to know what Grady'd just said had touched her. What she wouldn't say was how much her being touched frightened her. Feeding a need only made the hunger greater.

"Maybe because I don't know what to say," Blaise said. "You can't know these things you believe about me, and yet…somehow you know more than you should."

"More than you want me to?" Grady asked softly.

"I don't know that either." Blaise smiled wryly. "Hence my cowardly retreat into silence."

Grady chuckled. "Cowardly you are not. Cautious, maybe?"

"Mm. That sounds better."

"Tell you what. Don't say anything." Grady set her port glass on the railing as she rose. "I had a great day today. Actually, just about every minute since I met you has been amazing. That would be"— she checked the sports watch she wore—"one thousand, six hundred and eighty minutes. And I've thought of you for at least half of them. That might be more time than I've ever spent thinking of anyone that intensely. In fact, I know it is."

"You see why I don't know what to say?" Blaise laughed in desperation. "No one says those things. I can't…you confound me."

"I'm going to take that as another compliment."

Blaise snorted, but she couldn't help smiling. "Of course you are."

"And since your daughter is on her way, I'm going to go home now." Grady stepped in front of Blaise and leaned over with one hand on the arm of the glider. Her body blocked out the stars. "And before I go, I'd really, really like to kiss you good night. If you don't mind."

Blaise stopped the motion of the glider with her foot flat on the porch floor. Her knees were just between Grady's spread legs. If she reached out a few inches, she could grip her hip. She didn't move, not one muscle. "I ought to mind. But," she said before Grady could straighten and move away, "I think I'll mind a lot more if you don't."

"Good," Grady murmured and leaned closer, inch by slow, powerful inch. "Because if I don't kiss you, I'll never sleep again. I'll just lie awake hungry."

Blaise imagined those endless minutes ticking by, waiting for sleep, waiting for the promise of a kiss, for the taste and texture of it. Grady was barely moving now—close, so very close. Waiting. Blaise could still say no. If she didn't stop Grady now, she could never pretend she didn't want this. Not now, and not later when *she* waited for sleep, remembering the husky timbre of Grady's voice and the dark glimmer in her gaze. She could never pretend Grady hadn't awakened something in her she'd kept locked away behind bitter walls of disappointment and anger. Grady gave her the choice, and the answer must be truth, for she would not live a lie.

"What do you say, Blaise?" Grady murmured. "Will you rescue me from my sleepless night?"

"I don't think you need rescuing," Blaise said.

"You'd be surprised."

Blaise couldn't look away from the stark planes of Grady's face, sharp and taut with hunger. For her. She gasped.

Grady's mouth curved in that half-amused, half-satisfied smile, and Blaise had the insane urge to nip at that full, sensuous lower lip. Instead, she brushed her thumb over it, and Grady groaned.

"Don't tease, not now," Grady said. "Take it—or tell me to go. I can't hold back much longer."

Blaise's heart leapt into her throat. Grady's desire burned through her, birthing a bright raw power she adored.

"You'll survive. Patience." Blaise slipped the tip of her thumb along the inner surface of Grady's lip, felt the flick of tongue against her skin. Grady's eyes fluttered closed, her breath quickened, harsh and shallow. The sight of her need stoked Blaise's arousal, thick and languorous, pulsing between her thighs. Oh yes, she liked the power Grady unleashed in her.

She brushed the line of Grady's jaw, felt her muscles quiver and jump, and nearly laughed. So gorgeous. Want crashed through her, shaking her control. She hungered now, deep and aching. She thirsted. So long denied.

"I want you to kiss me," Blaise whispered.

"Show me," Grady said.

With her fingers wrapped around Grady's nape, Blaise pulled her down the last few inches. Grady braced her other arm on the back of the glider, framing Blaise in her embrace.

Blaise breathed out at the last second, drawing in Grady's scent as their lips touched. Dark and rich—bergamot and amber—potent and intoxicating. Every part of her exploded into awareness at once, drowning her in sensation. First her lips shimmered with the featherlight glide of Grady's mouth over hers, then the pressure of Grady's kiss demanding more, shifting to claim her completely. The thread of desire twisting through her thickened, tugging her deeper and deeper into the heat of Grady's mouth, the silken sweep of Grady's lips plundering hers with delicate fury.

Grady kissed with her eyes open, and the beauty nearly undid her. Blaise stroked her face, and the tremor beneath her fingers turned her liquid inside. This was not desire. This was something far more crucial—terrifying and irresistible. Too much.

Blaise gasped and murmured, "I think—"

"Don't," Grady whispered, keeping a white-knuckled grip on the glider with both hands. If she touched Blaise anywhere else, she'd never be able to stop. The sweet, tart taste of Blaise's kisses sank claws of need into her belly. She wanted to touch her, taste her, everywhere. She wanted to lose herself in the wild wonder of her. The enormity of her wanting turned her body to stone. She would kiss her and nothing more. Not yet. "Don't think."

Grady's mouth took hers again, firm and demanding but oh, so careful. Blaise surrendered to impulse and nipped at her lip. Grady jerked as if shocked, and Blaise exulted. She sucked Grady's lower lip and nibbled at it again, teasing Grady until Grady's tongue swept into her mouth and drove all thought of teasing from her mind. Grady's power stormed her control, and she drew her in. Opened for her. Welcomed her.

Headlights slashed through the dark, shattering the shadows that secluded them in the night. Blair murmured and pressed a hand against Grady's chest. "Taylor."

"Fuck." Grady straightened, breathing like she'd just finished a marathon.

The instant their lips parted, the cool night air brushed across Blaise's mouth like an icy hand on a fevered brow. How was it she'd never noticed that kisses could be so warm? How was it she'd never before ignited from the simple brush of lips over lips? The silky glide, the teasing touches, the exquisite, taunting torment of a tongue playing against her own. How could she not have known?

"I need a minute," Blaise said, half laughing. "I don't want to face my daughter looking guilty or...worse."

"I might need more than that," Grady muttered, backing up until she hit the railing behind her. "You are...fuck, I can't find the right word. Exceptional."

Blaise laughed again, the lingering thrill of desire and the heady power of arousing Grady making her shudder. "I have to say I've never experienced a good-night kiss quite like that before."

"Good." Grady's tone held a hint of satisfaction and unexpected possessiveness that Blaise found surprisingly exciting.

The headlights grew brighter, more focused, as the pickup truck pulled over to the curb in front of the house.

"I should go," Grady said quietly, and when she moved, Blaise didn't call her back.

For the moment, she wanted only the lingering memory of Grady in the moonlight, before reality intruded.

"Good night," Blaise said softly.

Blaise watched Grady turn and walk down the porch steps as Taylor came up the sidewalk. They passed, exchanged quiet greetings, and then Taylor dropped onto the swing beside her.

"I didn't know you knew Grady," Taylor said.

"Oh," Blaise said, doing her best to shift into parent-gear now that her heart wasn't pounding its way out of her chest. Ignoring the other parts of her anatomy that hadn't yet calmed down would have been a lot harder if she hadn't had to converse with her teenager. "She's a doctor at the hospital. One of the new surgeons."

"Yeah, I knew that. Courtney mentioned it. She was with Courtney, right, at the game?"

"Mm-hmm."

"Yeah." Taylor pointed a foot at the port glass on the railing and looked down at Blaise's wineglass on the floor. "I guess you two got home a while ago, huh?"

Blaise smothered her smile. This was new. This not-so-subtle third degree. "I gave her a ride home. Court had to leave."

"Oh, I know. Blake took off too. Just thought, you know, you should know. About Court."

"Well, thank you," Blaise said, "and I will duly note it."

"Okay. Good."

"Honey," Blaise said, "there's nothing serious going on between Grady and me."

"Geez, Mom." Taylor heaved a sigh. "It's not like I don't think you might, you know, want a date or something. Which would be great, since you never do. But if she's going out with Court too…just saying."

"You've never shown any interest in my personal life before. Why now?"

"Maybe because you didn't have one?"

Blaise nodded. "Fair point. Grady and I are not dating. And neither are Grady and Court."

"Good. I'm going to bed." Taylor grabbed Grady's port glass and headed for the house. "She's cool, by the way. In case you wondered. Night."

"Night, honey."

The night closed in and silence reigned. Blaise swung the glider, thinking about one thousand, six hundred and eighty minutes. She'd probably spent as many of them as Grady had, maybe more, thinking about the long night in the hospital handling a surgical crisis with Grady, and the moments in the waiting room with Wilbur Hopkins, and the magical moments in the café sharing doughnuts, and tonight… finding Grady asleep, the car ride, the quiet conversation, the kiss that never should have been and was more than she could have dreamed.

She pushed the glider steadily, back and forth, back and forth, far from ready to sleep. How many more minutes would she spend reliving the softness of Grady's mouth, the tremor of Grady's muscles beneath her palm, the soft murmur of pleasure that escaped Grady's throat as she'd touched her? More than the minutes in a day. Countless.

❖

After midnight, the village was nearly deserted. Even the pharmacy on the corner of the main crossroads was closed. The bar

Blaise had mentioned—Bottoms Up—was still open, but only two pickups remained in the parking lot, probably belonging to the staff. Grady's apartment was two blocks away from Blaise's home, a quick five-minute walk in the opposite direction from which she'd come. Not nearly a long enough walk to dispel her simmering agitation. She hadn't worn a jacket, and the air held enough chill to dry the sweat on the back of her neck, but it did little to dissipate the heat that streamed beneath her skin. She'd kissed plenty of women before, and always found it enjoyable. How could she not? A woman's lips were warm, delicious, as enticing as an age-old mystery, and just as impossible to solve.

But this was a kiss beyond her experience.

This kiss caught her by surprise, nearly knocked her off her feet. A kiss that fired every nerve and left her light-headed, a little disoriented, and a whole hell of a lot turned on. If a simple kiss left her reeling, she had a hard time imagining what would happen when she finally put her hands on Blaise. Hell, when Blaise put her hands on *her*. She was likely to end up a cinder.

Arousal like that almost never happened to her. Of course she got turned on when women touched her, and she enjoyed orgasms as much as anyone, but she rarely—all right, almost never—lost the thread of her control. She always sensed, deep inside, that she was leading the dance. From the moment she'd met Blaise, she'd been following. And the funny thing was, she didn't mind. Every second was too damn interesting. Fascinating.

And now, exciting in a way she hadn't been excited in her life. Physically, absolutely, but more than that. Her thoughts were all of Blaise—what was she doing right now, what was she thinking, feeling, hoping. Was she thinking about the kiss? Did she want another?

"I'm screwed," Grady muttered and loved the insane euphoria that bubbled inside her.

She'd reached the end of the main thoroughfare with nowhere else to go and turned around to walk back. In twenty minutes, she could be at the hospital, and there was always something going on there. Another day, another night, another time, she would've done that. But this night she had nothing she wanted to escape, or forget, or prove.

What she wanted was to go home, stretch out, and imagine the next kiss. Because there'd be one, there'd *have* to be, now that she knew what it was to kiss the woman she wanted. Not for an hour, or a few days, or a week. When she thought of Blaise, she didn't think of time, or limits. Only possibility.

CHAPTER NINETEEN

The screen door closed with a bang as Taylor came out carrying a muffin and her usual morning hot chocolate.

"Hi," Blaise said, sipping her second cup of coffee of the day.

Taylor sat beside her on the swing. "Isn't this where I left you last night?"

"Mm-hmm." She'd finally gone to bed when her body had overruled her mind, and the buzz—the tornado, actually—of Grady's good-night kiss had finally waned. Even then, she'd lain awake, not reliving the kiss as she'd imagined she might, but wondering what she wanted next. Oh, she knew what she *wanted*—she just didn't know if she should. She wasn't against spending time with an attractive, funny, interesting, great-kissing woman. She just…didn't all that often. Grady, though, Grady was more than that. Grady instigated. That's what it was—she started things she had no business starting. Like the warmth in the pit of Blaise's stomach at the merest reminder of Grady's teasing voice, or appraising glance, or…God…her mouth.

"Mom?"

"Hmm? Sorry?"

"You're not working today, right?"

"No," Blaise said, almost glad she wasn't, and that was definitely new. She liked her job. Loved it. She'd spent years studying part-time while raising Taylor when other twenty-year-olds were still cloistered in the protected world of college. Today, though, she was happy not to have a shift. Grady was a lot like her—work was part of who she was, and she'd likely take any excuse to show up at the hospital. So if she went to work, she might see Grady.

Blaise mentally rolled her eyes. Kidding herself much? She'd been sitting there thinking about her for the last hour. No use denying that she *wanted* to see Grady. Curiosity, that's what it was. What a strange feeling to have about a woman. Curiosity. Wondering what Grady'd do next, say next, make her feel next. That was the hook, of course. Grady made her feel things. Things she hadn't expected to feel, ever, or had forgotten that she wanted to. And then of course there was the kiss. If Taylor hadn't come home when she did, the kiss might have become more. Thank goodness they'd been sitting on the front porch. And how smart had she been not to invite Grady inside for that nightcap? She'd known herself better than she'd let herself acknowledge.

How long had she been pretending to herself about what she didn't want? That was not a thought that made her very happy.

"So, I'm meeting up with everybody at Blake's to study this afternoon," Taylor said.

"Is that what you call it now," Blaise teased. "No marathon Risk game on the schedule?"

"No really, we're serious." Taylor drew her feet up to the glider and wrapped her arms around her bent knees. Somehow her mug remained balanced on the broad wooden arm.

Blaise instantly pictured Grady's hand on the arm of the glider last night, the other braced on the back. Caging her in. She could have escaped, like a bird through an open window, any time she'd wanted. But she hadn't.

"Besides, Dave needs help with math," Taylor said. "He has to raise his SATs if he's going to get into Duke."

College. Like an unexpected rush of cold water in the midst of a hot shower, reality snapped into sharp focus. There it was, the next big step in their lives. She was close to having what she needed for Taylor to go pretty much anywhere she wanted, at least to start, though she secretly prayed for scholarships. She didn't tell her that. She'd vowed when Taylor was born that her daughter would have the opportunities she'd never had. And there was no price tag attached. Her love was free.

You've made your bed, now you can go lie in it. You'll get no help from me.

Blaise shrugged off the memory. "I didn't know he wanted to go there."

"Well, everybody thinks it's because of the football."

Blaise turned to Taylor. She knew that tone—something on her mind. "Isn't it?"

"This is kind of, you know, personal. Private," Taylor said.

"Before you tell me, if it's something that is likely to put any of you in danger, I can't swear to silence."

"*Mom.*" Eye roll.

"I know, I know, but it's best that we're clear with each other."

"It's nothing bad. Dave wants to be a minister."

"Ah. Wow. That's great. Is it a secret?"

"Well, sort of. Everybody just sees him as the quarterback, you know?"

"I do," Blaise said steadily. "But it's not exactly something to be ashamed of."

"Totally. But it's just hard, when you're different in any way at all."

"Sometimes it is. As long as the rest of you give him plenty of support, he'll be fine."

"We're totally cool with it."

"Good." Blaise swallowed the rest of her cooling coffee. "So, Mom time now. Any more problems with Billy last night? After he asked you to go to another party, and you said no?"

Taylor glanced at her sideways through a fall of blond hair. "Okay, who told you about Billy jerk-face Riley?"

"Grady, and she made it clear you'd already handled things, so don't be angry with her. I just wanted to make sure there wasn't something else later."

"No, there wasn't. He was just doing his usual thing, pretending there was nobody else around when he talked to me and insulting everyone. Then refusing to hear the word *no*. What is *with* that?"

"Billy's behavior is not typical. Sure, some people are going to ask more than once even if you say no. Maybe not right away, but a few days later…a week…they'll ask again, just hoping you might have changed your mind. But most people will quit after the second time. This is a little extreme. But I know you know it, and as annoying as it is, I think it's something you'll just have to wait out."

"I know. It's a pain."

Blaise reached over and gave her hand a squeeze. "Believe me, I know."

"So, can I ask you a question?"

"Of course."

"When you were in high school, did you know you liked girls?"

Blaise took a breath. Well, that was a new question. They'd talked about sex, of course, and sexual identity, but they'd never actually talked about her life. "I did, but I pretended to myself that I didn't."

"How come?" Taylor asked quietly.

"You never got to meet your grandmother, and I'm sorry that you didn't experience having a grandmother, but my mother was very rigid in her opinions about what was right and appropriate. That's how she raised me to think, even though a lot of what she said never felt right to me. It took me quite a long time to realize that what she thought was good and bad wasn't necessarily true at all. After you were born, she didn't want anything to do with me, or you. And I'm sorry about that."

"Wasn't your fault, Mom," Taylor said with a practical note.

Blaise laughed softly. "No, I suppose you're absolutely right. But when I was your age, I guess I wasn't—well, no, I don't just guess, I know—I wasn't as brave as any of you kids are today. So I just ignored the feelings I was told I shouldn't have and tried to have the feelings that I thought I should have."

"Well, first of all, that's bullshit about not being brave. Because here you are, and look at us. And if that's not gutsy, I don't know what is."

Grateful for the excuse of the slanting sunlight, Blaise shaded her eyes and swiped at a few tears. If there was one person in the world whose respect and love she wanted, it was Taylor. Just to know that she hadn't let her down. "Well, I realized a little later than most that I was a lesbian. And that answered a lot of questions for me, about things that had never felt quite right that suddenly did. Are you questioning?"

"Me?" Taylor shook her head. "No. I'm not all that interested in anybody right now, I mean, not for the sex part. I'm really happy with my friends. I think a couple of them are pretty hot, but I'm not interested in, you know, getting with anybody right away."

"Okay. Could I ask who you think is pretty hot?"

Taylor laughed. "That's really subtle, Mom. I think Margie is really hot, for a smartass, but I don't get any of those *feelings*, you know, for her. Dave, he's really hot. I could see that."

"Okay," Blaise said. "I think I got it. As long as you're comfortable with whatever you feel, I'm good with that."

"So, same here."

"Sorry?"

"You know, if you want to date someone."

"Ah. Well. I will definitely keep that in mind." Blaise hesitated.

The day seemed a day for heart-to-hearts. "You haven't asked me anything about your biological father since you were nine."

Taylor frowned. "Uh-huh. You said he was a guy you sort of dated for just a little while and that getting married was never an option. What more is there to say?"

"Some people want to know more about birth parents. If you do, there's not much I can tell you because I really don't know all that much, but you should know you can ask."

"I don't really care," Taylor said. "He's not part of our lives. He's just the past, right?"

"Right," Blaise said, "he's very much part of the past."

"I'm good with that," Taylor said as she grabbed her mug and jumped up. "No worries."

"Text me if your plans change," Blaise called after her as Taylor disappeared through the door. The faint response, only slightly world-weary, left her smiling. She'd made some doozy mistakes growing up, but ensuring that her past never shadowed Taylor's world wasn't one of them, and she planned to keep it that way.

❖

Flann found Abby on the back deck, coffee in hand, wrapped in the handcrafted multicolor patchwork quilt she'd purchased for Abby at the fair that summer. She leaned down to kiss her, grabbed the coffee cup, and took a sip. Still warm, still dark and rich. "Mm, thanks."

Abby laughed and held out her hand. "Give it back."

Grinning, Flann returned the cup and pulled over another chair close to Abby's. She reached for her hand and interlocked their fingers. "Hi."

"Hi. Everything good at the hospital?" Abby asked.

"Yeah. Quiet for now."

"Did you happen to stop by the ER?"

"'Course." Flann raised Abby's hand and kissed her fingers, relaxing at the prospect of a day at home.

"Of course you did. Always looking for business."

"Just trying to avoid that second trip back."

"I think we're giving you plenty of advance notice when something's brewing," Abby said. "No complaining, Rivers."

"About half the rooms were occupied when I passed through,"

Flann said, "but I didn't see anything that looked worthy of the chief just yet."

"Good. I could use a lazy morning. Especially if you don't have any plans."

Flann waggled a brow. "I could have."

"Blake is still asleep. I don't think he got in until almost five. Which means we have a window of a few hours all to ourselves."

"Finish your coffee," Flann said, "and we'll take advantage of it."

"Oh, I do love the sound of that." Abby drained her cup. "And that's that."

Flann searched around for a good opening and couldn't find one. "So…Blake and Margie."

"Hmm?" Abby said absently.

"They've progressed to the kissing stage."

"And you know this how?" Abby asked casually.

"Margie."

"Really?" Abby released Flann's hand, set her coffee cup aside, and faced in Flann's direction. "Was she upset by it?"

"No. I think surprised would probably be the better word. She told me and didn't seem particularly concerned, but it was enough of an event that she mentioned it."

"And how do you feel about it?"

Flann shrugged. "Well, it's really not about me, is it."

Abby smiled gently. "Isn't it?"

"Oh, come on. I know that teenagers have sex. Even though it makes me want to put my fingers in my ears when they talk about it."

"But…Margie, sister, Blake, kid. All loaded issues there." Abby paused. "Are you thinking about saying something to Blake?"

"Well, Margie didn't say it was a private conversation, but it sorta was."

"Okay, let's just take this to one ultimate conclusion, even though it might not necessarily be where it's going. Are you opposed if they have a sexual relationship?"

Flann winced.

"And you can't put your fingers in your ears on this one."

"No," Flann said after a few seconds. That was enough time for her to see the picture and then unsee it. "They're both terrific, smart kids. And I know they care about each other." She studied Abby. "What about you?"

"They talk to us when they need to. As near as I can tell they're honest with themselves, which is, really, amazing. Better than I did for a long time."

"So you're okay with it."

"Do you trust Margie? Do you trust Blake?"

"Yes," Flann said instantly.

"So do I. So yeah, I'm okay with it."

"So we don't say anything to him unless he says something to us."

"I think that's a good place to start."

"Okay then," Flann said getting to her feet. She held out her hand. "Let's go have wild, crazy sex."

Laughing, Abby got to her feet and took Flann's hand. "Let's."

Grady spent the day mostly killing time. When she'd finally fallen asleep, she'd slept soundly and, amazingly, hadn't dreamed. She almost wished she had. She wouldn't have minded having a nice sexy dream about Blaise, although she didn't really need to be asleep to have sexy dreams about Blaise. Every other minute she seemed to be having some fantasy that featured Blaise. Kisses with the addition of the small sounds she made that she probably wasn't even aware of and flashes of the way she smelled and tasted.

Needing to get out and move around, she ate breakfast at the diner and went for a five-mile run that turned into ten miles when she couldn't burn the agitation out of her system. She recognized the feeling. Horny. *Wonderful.* Not something that usually disturbed her equilibrium, but nothing was business as usual any longer.

All of that took up the morning, so she spent the afternoon catching up on journal reading. By the time dinnertime rolled around, she was ready to lose her mind. She'd reached for her phone fifty times to call Blaise, and then thought better of it. Blaise was a jumble of conflicting messages. She said she wasn't interested in anything intimate, or wasn't *ready* to be interested, and Grady had to believe that Blaise believed that. But that's not what Blaise's body said. When they'd kissed, Blaise had been right there, one hundred percent present, so fucking hot and sexy and...tempting. Teasing. Hungry. Blaise had wanted her, and Grady had felt it.

If she knew anything about Blaise, and she'd learned more about Blaise in the time they'd spent together than she'd ever cared to learn about anyone else, she knew Blaise would want to process. If she pushed now, Blaise would back away. A defensive reflex. Why, Grady didn't know, but she wanted to. She wanted to know what Blaise feared might happen if they kissed again, if they did more than that. Was it just Grady radiating not serious, commitment-phobic? Something in the way she handled herself, or was it something else? If Blaise was vulnerable in some way, she needed to go easy, she needed to be patient.

When a ding signaled a text at seven, she dove for her phone. A spear of disappointment hit when she saw it wasn't Blaise. She knew it wouldn't be, but she'd been hoping in the back of her mind all day that it might be. It was a reprieve, though. The ER.

She called immediately.

"McClure," she said. "Someone page me?"

"Hi, Dr. McClure, it's Mari Mateo, one of the PAs in the ER. We've got a probable appendicitis here, and Dr. O'Malley just took an open tib fracture to the OR for a debridement. I thought I'd call before it got too late, in case something else comes in. The surgery resident is on the way down, and since you're backup—"

"Yep, no problem," Grady said. "I'll be right over."

She quickly changed into jeans, a fresh shirt, and running shoes, and made it to the hospital, walking fast, in fifteen minutes. The ER, as always, was brightly lit and looked the same at any time of day. Closed curtains on half a dozen cubicles indicated patients being worked up. Courtney, in scrubs, her hair caught back in a ponytail, sat at the nurses' station, tapping on the computer.

"Hi, Court," Grady said.

"Hey." She looked up with a smile. "Are you here to see the appy?"

"Yeah. Did you do the workup?"

"Fifteen-year-old boy, belly pain for three days, vomiting for the last few hours."

"Three-day history, huh. Kind of long for appendicitis."

"Kids around here are tough, and they grow up working through minor injuries and illnesses. But he lost his appetite tonight, and that's what got them in here."

"Definitely a serious symptom," Grady said with a wry smile. "White count?"

"22,000 with a shift. Temp's a hundred point five, and he's got localized tenderness. I don't think there's any question what's going on."

"All right, let's take a look at him." As Court led the way, she asked, "Did you see his plain films?"

"Yeah. A few distended loops of bowel, but no free air. If he's perfed, it's not free."

"That's a point in our favor."

Court pulled a curtain aside and introduced her to Clete Orono.

"Hi, Clete," Grady said, holding out her hand. "I'm Dr. Grady McClure. You mind if I take a look at your belly?"

"No," Clete said.

Even lying down, he was big, probably six feet, two hundred pounds, dark hair, dark eyes, and an inquisitive, trusting expression. He was tough too. When Grady felt his belly, the muscles were rigid, but he showed no sign of discomfort even when she pressed a little in the area of his appendix. When she released her fingers, though, he winced.

"Rebound," she murmured. She didn't need much more evidence of what was going on. "So, Clete, you've got appendicitis. It could be a couple of other things, but the chances are really high that's what it is."

"Okay," he said. "So, can I go home tomorrow?"

"Well"—Grady glanced at Court, who smothered a grin—"there *is* the little matter of the OR first."

"Yeah, my sister had the same thing a couple years ago. Three days before the fair and she was showing her sheep. She made them let her go home the next day, so she could make the show. Took two blue ribbons that year too."

His voice brimmed with pride.

"Right, okay then," Grady said. Sheep. Really? "We'll get you out of here soon as we can."

Back at the nurses' station, Grady leaned against the counter while Court called the OR.

When Court finished, she looked up at Grady. "Sorry I abandoned you last night. I've been on a waiting list for one of Mel's puppies forever, and I wanted to be there when they were born."

"No problem. Blaise gave me a ride home."

"Oh, excellent." Court looked around. Murmured voices came from down the hall, but no one was in sight. "So we never did finish the conversation about next time. I was thinking, there's a concert in Albany next weekend. How do you feel about pop?"

"Thanks, but no."

Courtney said, "Not into music?"

"That sounds like a date," Grady said, "and I'm not dating right now."

"Really. Okay." Court stood with a smile. For a second she looked like she was going to say more, and then gave a good-natured shrug. "Worth a try. I'll go talk to the nurses about Clete."

"Great," Grady said, "I'll see you in the OR."

Court disappeared down the hall, and Grady leaned over the counter to check the call sheet laid out on the worktop. Some things never changed, including the handwritten calendars every unit used to pencil in staff on call.

Grady sighed. Blaise's name wasn't there for the eleven to seven shift.

Chapter Twenty

Hey," Abby said from the doorway of the break room just as Blaise slid a fresh coffee filter into the brewer, "about ready to take your dinner break?"

"Hi," Blaise said, turning around. "Yes. Just making my last caffeinated cup for the night. You have time for one?"

"Unless something major comes in, I might even have an hour to catch up on paperwork. One of the best things about these night shifts is it's either quiet or chaos." Abby, in scrubs and her trademark bright yellow rubber Crocs, leaned against the doorjamb, eyeing her with a quizzical expression. "So, how's Grady?"

"Um…" Blaise slid her phone from her rear pocket as it buzzed, signaling a text. "Grady?"

"You know the one," Abby said casually, her gaze sharpening, "five seven, five eight, brunette, amazingly dark blue eyes, a bit of a roguish grin. Overall pretty hot?"

"Abby"—Blaise palmed her phone and tried sneaking a look at the screen—"haven't we had this conversation before about you being married and no longer drooling over hot women?"

Abby raised both hands, her brows arched in an appearance of total innocence. "Me? Drooling? Oh no, just making an aesthetic observation. But you *do* know the one I'm talking about, right?"

Blaise blew out a breath. "Yes, I know the one."

"So?" Abby said, drawing out the word.

"She's fine. I haven't seen her since the night of the football game. You know I've been working my four on, and since I'm here nights and she's a surgeon working days, we don't exactly bump into each other very often."

"So you haven't heard from her, then."

Blaze squeezed her phone. "Not exactly."

"Okay. What does that mean—exactly?" Abby made a come-on gesture with her hand. Her smile began to resemble that of a cat with a canary. Or rather, what used to be a canary and now was lunch.

"We've been sort of talking, I guess you'd say." Blaise resisted the urge to shuffle her feet. Good Lord, what was she—fifteen again? Although sometimes, she almost felt that way. Ridiculously giddy when a smiley face emoji could make her heart race. Sometimes she didn't even ask herself why she felt what she felt, or if she should, or shouldn't. She couldn't remember a time when she had the freedom to just *be*.

"There's some question about that? Talking seems fairly identifiable."

Blaise gritted her teeth. "Well, if texting is talking, then yes, we have been talking."

Abby burst out laughing. "You know what the kids call talking when they text, right?"

Of course she knew. She had a teenager, didn't she? One who was constantly on her phone, texting her friends from the second she arrived home, even though she'd just seen them five minutes before. The internet provided a wealth of information for parents who wanted some glimmer of understanding about the world their teens inhabited, and a brief search explained that when teens were interested in a one-on-one relationship, they didn't necessarily date—they *talked*, via text.

"It's not the same thing," Blaise said defensively.

"You mean you're not exactly dating, just sort of pairing off, I believe it means."

"She's just been chatting, you know, when she's between cases or if I'm awake or sometimes in the evening when I'm at work, she'll just say, *How are things in the ER?* Being friendly." She was talking too fast, as if trying to explain away what didn't need to be explained. They were just texting, for heaven's sake. Silly, harmless texting.

"Aha. So you *are* talking."

"You know you're annoying, right?" Blaise surreptitiously glanced at her phone.

How's the night going?

Blaise smiled and, guiltily for absolutely no reason, slid her phone into her back pocket.

"Well," Abby said, "we're *all* going to be talking soon, because she's out in the lobby, and she has food. It looks like a lot of food, and you know, a lot of hungry people around here and all. Can't keep that a secret."

Blaise stared. "She's out in the lobby? It's three o'clock in the morning!"

"Well, there are a lot of all-night takeout places too, and whatever she has, it smells really good, and I want some. So do Brody and Glenn and a few other people who caught a whiff."

"Why didn't you bring her back? What if she leaves?" Blaise hurried for the door. Grady was here. Why didn't she say she was coming? Why not text her? For almost a week, she'd been getting texts. Casual chatty texts, which struck her as odd at first, because most of her friends never texted her unless they were asking what time she was going to pick up the kids or had she heard from the kids or something about the kids. But they didn't *talk* to each other that way. Surprised the first few times, she'd replied perfunctorily.

Busy here. The usual

Just got home

Going for a run before work

But then, then she'd begun looking for the texts, and sharing more. When she'd said she was reading a book, Grady had asked what it was about, and they'd ended up discussing fiction. Then other things—snippets of articles they'd read or bits about interesting cases. What had started out as weird had become nice, in a very strange way.

Abby grinned and moved out of her path. "I told her I'd send you out, but believe me, that woman is not going anywhere until she sees you. She'll just sit out there making us all drool." She called down the hall after her, "Over the *food*. So don't you dare send her away. Remember, hungry people are cranky people."

"I'm not going to send her away," Blaise said. "You don't mind if she comes back here, do you?"

"Why would I mind? She works here. And she was smart enough to know if she was bringing food, she needed to bring a lot. I'm half in love with her."

Laughing, Blaise hurried down the hall, hit the button for the auto doors, and searched the lobby. Grady, in dark jeans, running shoes, and a navy V-neck sweater with the sleeves pushed up to midforearm, leaned on the counter by the reception desk, chatting to the clerk. Two huge bags with the logo of a Thai takeout place sat on the floor by her feet. When she saw Blaise, her smile widened. "Hi. Did I catch you at break time?"

"You did. And I packed a salad and yogurt."

"That sounds good."

Blaise pointed at the takeout bags. "That smells better."

Grady bent to pick them up, and Blaise grabbed one. Grady held out the other. "You want to take them back?"

She could, and everyone would be happy. Except her. She didn't give a damn what was in the bags. "No, you bring them back. Come on."

"Hold up a sec." Grady fished around in a bag, took out a small cardboard container and a pair of chopsticks, and passed them through the window. "Pineapple fried rice. That's what you wanted, right?"

Warren nodded vigorously. "Hey, thanks, Dr. McClure."

Grady waved and followed Blaise.

"Did you actually take orders?" Blaise asked as they walked down the hall.

"Just for him. I figured the rest of you could just fight it out."

"That was really nice of you." Blaise slowed. The break room was guaranteed to be busy, and she just wanted a minute alone with her. It had only been a few days, but somehow that seemed far longer. "It's the middle of the night, though. What are you doing here?"

"I wanted to see you." Grady shrugged. "And it's really hard, you know, with you working nights and me mostly here days except when I'm in the OR with an emergency. I know you have to sleep, but you have to eat too."

"You need to sleep too," Blaise pointed out.

"I do, but I'm one of those diphasic people. I sleep in shifts usually. I think it's just habit after years of being on call and getting habituated to being up half the night. Now I just sleep that way. Don't worry."

"I'm glad you're here," Blaise said hurriedly as they walked into the break room.

Sure enough, Brody, Glenn, and two of the other night nurses sat around a table with expectant expressions. Abby leaned against the counter drinking coffee.

"Thai? Oh yeah." Brody rose to take one of the bags from Grady, carried it over to the table, and pulled the containers out. "Excellent choice."

Abby dragged a chair out at another table, and Blaise and Grady joined her with the second bag.

"This will be all over the hospital tomorrow," Abby said, digging into a carton of curry chicken. "You'll be knighted or vilified."

"How so?" Grady said.

"Some people are going to be very annoyed, considering they'll feel duty bound to outdo you in some way."

Grady laughed. "Well, in this particular instance, everybody wins."

Laughing, Abby said, "Very true. You're definitely due a knight-hood in my book."

"I'm satisfied, then," Grady said.

Abby stood. "If you don't mind me being rude, I'm going to take this back to my office and finish it while I try to answer a few emails. 'Night, Grady."

"'Night."

"Abby is a fan," Blaise said.

"Good person to have on my side," Grady said, munching on a spring roll. "The ER chief, and your bestie."

"Ha." Blaise shook her head. "You don't need any help charming people."

"Really? What about you?"

"This was rather unexpected," Blaise said after a few seconds, "and very nice."

"I told you," Grady said in a low voice. "I wanted to see you."

"It's good to see you too." Blaise ducked her head. She wasn't actually blushing, was she?

"When's your next day off?" Grady asked.

"Tomorrow night," Blaise said.

"You have some time in the morning, then, right? Since you'll probably push your schedule forward a little?"

Blaise tilted her head. "How did you know that?"

"Oh, I've been researching the usual sleep schedules of people who routinely work night shifts. That's what it said you should do on your days off."

"That's very bizarre, you know that, right?"

"Well, when I don't know something, I try to figure it out." Grady skimmed her fingers over the top of Blaise's hand. "And when I want to know someone better, I pay attention."

"I mentioned I loved Thai, didn't I," Blaise murmured. And why did something so offhand, so casual, suddenly feel so special? "Why didn't you ever consider just asking me about my schedule?"

Grady leaned on her palm, her expression pensive as she studied Blaise. "Would you have told me?"

"Yes, why wouldn't I?"

"Because you don't like to talk about personal things."

Blaise tensed. "My sleep schedule is hardly personal."

"I didn't want to take any chances."

"Chances how?"

"That you might stop talking to me."

"Grady," Blaise said quietly, "I like talking to you. I just…I'm not used to it."

"Used to what, Blaise?" Grady murmured.

"Talking about personal things."

"I bet you do with Abby."

"Abby is my best friend," Blaise said.

"And?"

"You don't feel like that."

Grady's eyes glinted. "Not like a friend, you mean."

"You know what I mean," Blaise said. "I don't kiss my friends."

"I'm really glad to hear that. I mean, it's totally your business and everything, but I prefer to have a lock on the kissing thing."

Blaise laughed. Grady was so outrageous and so sure of herself, and Blaise liked it. She liked the way Grady presumed, all the while knowing if she pushed back, Grady would ease off. That's what all the texting had been about. Remote enough for her to feel safe, but intimate too. "At the moment, you happen to be the only one I'm kissing. Or have kissed, past tense."

"I'd like very much to make that present tense," Grady said. "And the sooner the better."

Blaise put her food aside and leaned forward until she was certain no one could overhear. Grady was so unlike her. If she asked anything, she knew Grady would answer. Grady gave her the power to explore—herself, Grady, the two of them. "Why?"

"Because I can't stop thinking about you. I can't stop thinking about kissing you. I can't stop thinking about touching you. And it's making me crazy."

"So you resorted to seduction by Thai?"

"Is it working?"

Why pretend otherwise, when she didn't want to. "I really love Thai."

"And kissing, how do you feel about that?"

Blaise might have hesitated, not all that long ago. But there'd been a kiss, and conversations, and texts, and Grady so certain. "I think I feel inclined to try another kiss."

"When?"

Up to her still. When had anything been completely up to her? More power, sweet and seductive. Blaise leaned back, and Grady's gaze fixed on her face. "Do you have a case in the morning?"

"Nothing on the schedule until I have to staff the residents' clinic at two," Grady said. "Once I'm done with rounds at seven, unless there's an emergency, I'm free."

"I'm off at seven."

"I know."

"I have to see Taylor before she leaves for school at seven thirty."

"Come to my apartment after that," Grady said instantly. "I'll make you breakfast. And we'll see."

We'll see.

Blaise nodded. She wanted to see. "How can I say no to a woman who offers to feed me?"

Grady smiled. "I have no idea."

CHAPTER TWENTY-ONE

Want to come over for coffee and gossip?" Abby said as she grabbed her backpack and joined Blaise on the way out of the conference room while the day shift headed off to their various duties.

"Oh," Blaise said, "um, thanks. I can't this morning."

"Okay." When they reached the door, Abby held it open. "Got a date?"

Blaise jumped and made a show of sliding her sunglasses on while she hid her surprise. Not all for show, either—too much bright morning sun pretty much guaranteed her biorhythms would revert to a normal day-night cycle, and she'd never get to sleep. Although the way her blood buzzed and her body tingled with anticipation, she doubted she'd sleep for a week. She cast a sidelong glance at Abby, who pulled her shades out as well. "Why do you say that?"

Abby smiled. "I can feel the vibrations from here. And, come on, Grady showed up at three o'clock in the morning with food. She didn't do it because she thought *we* were hungry. She's courting you."

"Courting?" Blaise laughed. "Somehow, I can't see that in relationship to Grady."

"Why not?" Abby slowed by a stone bench. "Sit for five minutes. She'll wait."

Blaise realized she wanted to talk. And as anxious as she was for whatever was about to happen to *happen*, she sat.

"You like her, don't you," Abby said quietly.

"I do," Blaise said just as quietly. "And I'm not sure that's a smart idea at all."

"And maybe you're letting your initial impressions cloud your vision."

"Ouch. That sounds…shallow." Blaise wished she could argue, but whenever she thought about Grady, the past fogged the present, fear obscured reality, and need overshadowed desire. Such a jumble of emotions she couldn't be sure *what* she felt.

Abby threw an arm around her shoulders. "I don't mean that in a bad way, and you know it. What I mean is, something about Grady put you off at first, but do you even know what that was? Or why you can't let it go?"

Blaise remembered the knee-jerk reaction, but that was over quickly, as soon as she saw Grady. Maybe, just maybe, some of what she'd tried to bury had resurfaced and colored her judgment. But she hadn't been completely irrational, either. Some of her reactions had been accurate. "I think I told you once before that overly confident, super-charming, sexually aggressive women are just not my type."

"Well, viewed that way, I can't argue. But you could also think of them as strong, attentive, and just plain old sexy," Abby said. "The opposite side of those first impressions."

"Are you trying to talk her up to me for some reason?" Blaise asked, deflecting as best she could since she had no argument there either. Grady was confident and capable, perceptive and sensitive, and damned attractive. And Blaise liked all of that very much.

"Maybe I'm just pointing out she's got some stellar qualities." Abby shrugged. "But mostly—and even though I haven't known you a long time, I like to think I know you pretty well—I've never seen you react this way to anyone. And maybe you don't notice, but there have been plenty of people who have been trying to get your attention."

Blaise felt the blush. "Who?"

"Rakelle in the OR, Taisha in the lab, and Juan from radiology."

"I think you're imagining things." Blaise would have noticed if someone was interested. Wouldn't she?

"I hear what you're thinking." Abby poked her arm. "I think you've conditioned yourself not to notice. But you noticed Grady, and you noticed her noticing you. That says to me there's a connection there that matters. Those don't come along very often, and when you click with someone, it's worth exploring."

"I hardly know the woman," Blaise protested, knowing it sounded thin even as she said it.

Abby rolled her eyes. "Oh, come on. That's another one of those excuses people make when they're afraid of what they feel. We can talk to someone for a year and never know anything about them, or spend a night with them, talking about things that really matter, and learn more. *Feel* more. Which is it?"

"You should've been a psychiatrist or something."

"God forbid," Abby said. "I'm far too meddling for that. I'd be trying to solve everyone's problems instead of letting them work to their own conclusions. Fortunately, you don't need a psychiatrist. You just need me."

"All right," Blaise said, "you're right, and I've known it almost from the start. We connected. More than that. Grady opened doors I've kept firmly closed for a long time, and that's what I'm not sure I want to face." She took a breath. "Being vulnerable is scary. And disruptive. I've worked very hard to have a safe, stable life."

"I think I understand that. Especially when you have a child. I spent a lot of years thinking only about Blake, avoiding complicating relationships, and I don't regret a second of it. I know you feel the same way about Taylor. But sometimes, we're better parents when we let other things into our life. If they're the right things. The right people."

"How do you know what's right?" Blaise stared down at her hands. "I'm a little bit afraid of how much I might feel. And maybe I'm wrong."

"All the more reason to find out. Because it might be wonderful."

"I'm not much of a risk taker anymore," Blaise said.

"And I don't blame you, but from where I'm sitting, Grady looks like a pretty good risk. I've seen the way she looks at you. She's seriously smitten."

"Smitten," Blaise said softly and shook her head. That pretty much described *her*. "I'm having breakfast with her this morning. I promise I'll try to be open to new experiences."

"Well, that's one way of putting it. Here's to new experiences." Abby stood and threaded her arm around Blaise's waist as they headed down toward the parking lot. "Trust yourself. You'll know what's right."

Trust herself. The words echoed in her head all the way home.

Could she? Wasn't it finally time?

When she walked in the house, the scent of coffee drew her to the kitchen. Taylor munched on toast as she packed her lunch.

"Hi," Taylor mumbled, waving a crust at the toast on the table. "Still warm."

"Thanks." Blaise kissed her on the cheek but passed on the toast. Too many butterflies to eat. "Everything okay?"

"Mom," Taylor said, stuffing a bag of chips into her backpack. "I texted you when I went to bed last night, and I've been up for exactly"—she looked at the wall clock—"eighteen minutes. There's nothing new."

"A lot can happen in eighteen minutes," Blaise said lightly.

"Well, nothing has this morning. I gotta go."

Taylor headed out the door, and Blaise called after her, "Have a good day. Let me know what you're doing after school."

"I know, I know," Taylor called back.

Smiling to herself, Blaise hurried upstairs and hopped into the shower. Ten minutes later, she stood in front of the bathroom vanity, trying to decide what to do with her face. She didn't want to look as if she was dressing for a date.

Except she was, wasn't she. This was a date. No, an assignation. Because Grady's implications had been clear.

Grady had mentioned kisses. And kisses very often led to something else, especially between two consenting adults who had been dancing around their attraction since the first minute they looked at each other.

She brushed on a lick of mascara, applied a touch of lipstick, and met her own gaze in the mirror.

"Own up to it, Richelieu. You want a new experience. And what could be so bad about that?"

Refusing to answer her own question, she made sure she wore the sexiest panties she owned, which weren't all that sexy but at least they were low-cut and had a little hint of lace to match her black bra, shimmied into tight black jeans, and finished with a deep green silk shirt. Could be construed as casual, but she was hoping for sexy. Maybe.

Black flats, and she was ready to go. As she walked out the door, she made herself a promise. For the next few hours she was going to turn off the censor in her head that constantly counseled caution. She hadn't done that in more than a decade.

❖

Grady watched the clock and paced. She checked her phone. No texts. That meant Blaise was still coming, didn't it? She ran through possible breakfast choices, considering her serviceable but somewhat limited repertoire of cooking skills, and finally decided she should just wait for Blaise to choose. She wasn't even hungry. Well, she was hungry, starving, really, but food was the last thing on her mind. A steady diet of fantasy and snippets of remembered kisses ambushing her out of the blue wasn't enough to quell the constant chorus of need that welled up every time she thought of Blaise.

She was pretty sure kisses would be on the menu today, though. She'd said that out loud, and Blaise hadn't said no. In fact, for a couple seconds there, it looked as if Blaise was going to say even more. The look in her eyes had signaled more.

Grady'd practiced about all the restraint she had at her command, and reserves were running low. The best solution she could figure was space if she wanted to respect Blaise's go-slow request. Like real physical distance. Her kitchen was about fifteen feet wide, one of those big ones that ran the back of the house. Not enough space—a football field wouldn't be big enough. Not the way she was feeling. A glimpse of Blaise left her good intentions in tatters. There was always the back porch, a semipublic spot. Her kitchen opened onto the porch with stairs that led down to a nice fenced-in yard. It was also completely empty— no table or chairs. No help.

But thinking about the porch took her mind off the bedroom, which just so happened to be between the front door and the kitchen, opening off the hall that ran from the front of the house to the back, shotgun style. No way to get to the kitchen without passing the bedroom.

The doorbell rang, and she jumped. Right…distance, space, patience. None of which she had in abundance. She hurried through to the front of her second-floor apartment, grateful that there were no neighbors above her and whoever lived below was gone for the day. Her front door opened off another porch, this one overlooking the street. Glancing out the front window, she caught sight of Blaise standing just outside her door, and Grady instantly forgot her mantra of self-control. The sun shone onto the porch from behind Blaise. Her hair was down, instead of the way she usually wore it pinned up at work, and shimmered with golden highlights as a light breeze lifted strands about her face. When she raised a hand to push aside the stray locks, the gesture was so quintessentially female, Grady's stomach tightened.

A tiny frown appeared between Blaise's brows, and the doorbell sounded again.

Grady yanked the door open. "Sorry. I was…admiring you."

Blaise tilted her head, gave her a quizzical look. "Do you realize you say the oddest things?"

"I wasn't aware of that until I met you." Grady extended her hand. "Come on in."

Blaise hesitated for the merest second, still absorbing the look in Grady's eyes. Part wonder, part dark swirling desire that matched the sensation pulsing in her depths. If she stepped over the threshold, there'd be no turning back. Not in this moment. Grady waited, hardly seeming to breathe. Blaise took her hand and followed her inside.

The large bright living room held minimal furniture, all of it quite functional but not exactly matched in any particular style, colorful rugs of different designs and textures scattered about, shades the only window treatments, walls bare.

"I haven't done a lot of decorating," Grady said a bit apologetically.

"It looks like you've got all the essentials," Blaise said.

"Um, the kitchen's back here. I thought I'd make whatever you wanted."

"Did you?" Blaise said softly as they walked down the hall.

Grady slowed, turning so she was facing Blaise, her back to the kitchen. She wasn't working any plan now, wasn't reining herself in, wasn't running from—or toward—anything. She was standing in the sunlight with a beautiful, amazing woman right now—in this moment. And she knew exactly what she wanted. "Anything. Whatever you want."

Blaise's lips parted ever so slightly, and she studied Grady's face in that way she had of reading beneath the surface, speaking volumes without words.

"How much time do we have?" Blaise asked.

Grady swallowed. "Today? Three or four hours. After that? As long as you want."

Blaise's smile was part wistful, part temptress. She pressed her hand to Grady's cheek, her fingers lightly brushing along her cheekbone, diving ever so lightly into the hair at her temple. "You know, if you let me make all the decisions, you might be at a disadvantage."

"I don't think so." Grady sucked in a breath. Her heart was hammering. She'd never felt so unsure of herself in her life, and so certain at the same time. Her only recourse was honesty. "I want you. You're all I can think about. I've lost count of the hours and minutes and seconds I've thought about you. If I have to wait to kiss you, to touch you, I will, but I can't promise I won't bother you every chance I get."

Blaise laughed and the hint of shadow in her eyes cleared like clouds disappearing in a summer breeze. "I've discovered I rather like it when you bother me. The last thing I feel is annoyed."

"What do you feel?" Grady asked.

"Desirable, desired. Wanted. And even better than all of that," Blaise mused, "appreciated. Seen."

"You're all those things, Blaise, for me."

"But right now, Grady," Blaise said softly, "what I really want?"

"Anything," Grady repeated urgently.

"I want to be touched." Blaise slipped her hand behind Grady's neck. "By you."

CHAPTER TWENTY-TWO

I want to be touched...by you.

Blaise's words severed the tethers of Grady's restraint with the swift, pure slash of a scalpel blade. Grady's heart pounded so fiercely she couldn't hear, could scarcely breathe. Reason fled, but every other sense was honed to a razor's edge. Blaise's eyes, a misty blue like the sky on a hot summer morning after the last wisps of clouds had blown away, held hers, languorous and beckoning. Blaise's lips, flushed a deep rose, parted slightly, and her breath whispered across Grady's cheek in featherlight invitation. With a soft groan of blessed surrender, Grady slipped her fingers into Blaise's hair and cradled her head, angling her face to hers as she lowered her mouth to kiss her.

At the barest touch of Grady's lips, Blaise surged into Grady's arms, lacing her fingers at the nape of Grady's neck, her embrace breathtakingly possessive. Grady gasped as Blaise's tongue swept between her lips, demanding entrance, claiming her with swift, urgent strokes.

Grady meant to go slow, one careful step at a time, pacing herself to match Blaise's tempo, following Blaise's lead, but Blaise's hands on her skin, Blaise's breasts pressed to hers, Blaise's kiss—urgent and hot—burned through her like a wildfire sweeping across a barren plain. Grady's thighs trembled, and she stumbled back a step until her shoulders hit the wall, grateful for the support when her bones turned to jelly. Blaise cleaved to her, hands sweeping over her shoulders, down her chest, relentless and electrifying.

"Blaise," Grady gasped, "what—"

"Bedroom," Blaise said, nibbling on Grady's mouth. Blaise reached between them, yanked Grady's shirt free of her waistband, and slipped her hand underneath, her fingers hot on Grady's skin.

Grady twitched, a white haze searing her awareness until only Blaise remained. Blindly, she flailed with one arm, found the partially open door to her bedroom just inches away, and shoved it wide. Blaise clutched her shoulders, her mouth still molded to Grady's, and dragged her over the threshold. Grady stumbled for a second, a drowning woman suddenly tossed onto a foreign shore, searching for steady ground. The open window beside her bed allowed the morning air, fresh and brisk, to carry in the scent of pine and roses, and Blaise came into stunning focus. Hazy eyes in an unforgettable face, her pupils wide and dark, her cheeks flushed. A pulse rippled in Blaise's throat, skittering beneath the creamy column.

"Blaise," Grady croaked, her throat tight with need. "Are you—"

"Yes, yes, God, yes." Blaise pushed Grady across the room, somehow managing to keep kissing her. "I'm sure. God. You're gorgeous."

Blaise pulled away when they reached the bed, the covers still turned down from that morning, and fumbled at the buttons on Grady's shirt. "Why couldn't you be wearing a T-shirt or something."

Laughing unsteadily, Grady left Blaise to work on her shirt while she unbuttoned Blaise's. She pushed the silk from her shoulders along with the straps of her bra, and in an instant, or what felt like a heartbeat, Blaise's breasts were bare. She was pretty sure her heart stopped for a few beats. Blaise's breasts glowed pink with arousal, her nipples a darker rose, taut and tight.

"Incredible," Grady murmured, spreading her hands on Blaise's back, stroking down the slope of soft skin and firm muscles to the dip at the base of her spine. Blaise threw her head back, lifting her breasts in silent offering. Vision clouding, Grady answered with her hands and her mouth. Holding Blaise tight to the curve of her body, she cupped Blaise's breast and took a nipple into her mouth, teasing lightly with her tongue, grazing with her teeth. Blaise gave a little incoherent cry and gripped her shoulders, digging into the muscles. Blaise's need arrowed deep into Grady's core.

"Yes," Blaise said again, pressing her breast more firmly into Grady's mouth, "just like that."

Grady slid her hand from Blaise's back and unbuttoned Blaise's pants. When she fumbled at the zipper and muttered a curse against Blaise's warm, pliant flesh, Blaise laughed and pushed her hand aside. In an instant, Blaise pushed her clothing down and kicked free as she cradled Grady's head in her palm, urging her to continue lavishing kisses on her breasts. Guided by the insistent pressure of Blaise's hand, Grady moved from one breast to the other, fondling and teasing. How many eons passed she had no idea and didn't care. She would have stayed there until nightfall, but Blaise finally pushed her backward again. When her legs hit the bed, she toppled onto her back and Blaise followed, straddling her hips, naked and glorious.

Grady'd lost her shirt somewhere in the last few steps to the bed, and when Blaise opened her pants, she hardly noticed. Blaise was naked. Naked and astride her and flushed with arousal. Grady struggled to breathe, trying to take in all of her magnificence at once, and failing. She reached for Blaise's breasts again, and Blaise grabbed her hands instead, intertwining their fingers. Blaise smiled down at her, her hair draping her face in a shimmering golden curtain.

"You can't keep doing that," Blaise said breathlessly. "It feels too good…and…" She leaned down, her hair brushing Grady's cheeks as she kissed her. A deep, slow, thorough kiss that left Grady reeling. If she'd been standing, she might've fallen. "It's been too long, and I don't want to come yet."

Grady groaned. "You're killing me."

Blaise's smile was triumphant. "Oh. Not yet, I'm not." She leaned back, brushing her sex over Grady's belly. "But maybe soon."

"Don't hurry," Grady muttered, clasping Blaise's hips. "I love looking at you."

"Mm. Me too." Blaise trailed her fingers along Grady's collarbones, down the center of her chest, and circled her breasts. Blaise had a fleeting, fragmented thought, that she'd never touched a woman, wanted a woman this way, but she couldn't focus enough to think beyond that. All she could see was Grady.

When she caressed Grady's breasts and stroked the smooth planes of her abdomen, Grady arched beneath her, pressing a thigh between hers. The soft fabric of Grady's pants brushed over her clitoris and triggered showers of pleasure. Gasping, Blaise cupped Grady's breasts and rubbed her thumbs over Grady's small tight nipples.

"Jesus." Grady bucked, the muscles in her stomach jumping, shoulders and chest straining. "That feels so damn good."

"I have to feel you." Blaise pushed back on her knees and grabbed the waistband of Grady's pants on either side of her hips. "Help me."

Grady half sat up, shoving her pants down, and Blaise finished pulling them off her legs.

"Yes," Blaise muttered again, sliding one thigh between Grady's and meeting her body-to-body. Grady's leg slipped between hers, sliding through her wetness, pressing just where she needed the pressure. The showers of pleasure became torrential, and she filled to bursting. Blaise gripped Grady's shoulders and canted her pelvis, increasing the friction.

When Grady gripped her hips and pulled her more tightly to her thigh, Blaise moaned. "You'll make me come."

"Don't hold back." Grady's eyes blazed, rocking into her, faster and harder. "You feel so good. Look so amazing. I want to feel you come. Please."

Blaise pushed upright and Grady grasped her hands, their fingers locking again. Blaise stared down, held Grady's gaze, rocking, thrusting, every muscle braced in anticipation. The storm coiled and snapped within her, and the power built. When the dam broke, she threw her head back, heard her own strangled cry, and arched as the orgasm tore through her. Before the last tremor shattered deep inside, she was falling and Grady was there, closing her in her arms, holding her tight to her chest.

"You're amazing," Grady murmured. "Incredible."

Blaise buried her face in the curve of Grady's shoulder, catching her breath. She grasped for words but none came.

"Blaise?" Grady said after a minute. "You okay?"

"Not sure. I think I've lost my mind."

Grady chuckled. "That had nothing to do with your mind."

Blaise laughed unsteadily, awareness slowly returning. She was wrapped around Grady, their legs entwined, Grady's arms around her, their breasts, their bellies, every possible place touching. Desire, never quite abated, stirred again.

"You do something to me," Blaise muttered.

"Something good?" Grady whispered against her ear.

"Something amazing, scary as hell."

"As long as it's good."

"Oh, very good." Blaise managed to push herself up on her elbow and kissed her. "I don't usually…I can't remember…I've never actually been so out of control before."

Grady grinned. "That's the nicest thing you could've said to me."

"Oh, really?" She leaned forward again and nipped at Grady's lip. "Easy to please, aren't you?"

"Oh, not at all." Grady rolled her over so deftly, Blaise hadn't realized she was moving until she was on her back and Grady rested on her elbows and knees above her, caging her in, dark eyes aflame again.

Grady brushed a hand down the center of Blaise's body and cupped between her thighs. Blaise caught her breath. She was swollen and wet and, oh my God, still ready.

"Grady, go slow." Blaise gasped. "You feel too good."

"How is that possible?" Grady kissed her and stroked through her wetness.

"You'll make me come," Blaise warned.

"I will." Grady slipped inside her, and Blaise lifted to take her deeper. "Right now."

Biting her lip, fighting the first tendrils of pleasure bursting free, Blaise slid her palm down Grady's flank, over her hip, and between her legs. She found her clitoris, full and firm and slick.

"Oh fuck." Grady's head snapped back, and she strained for control, fighting to hold on until Blaise came. Every time she stroked inside her, Blaise echoed her movements, sliding down to tease her with short shallow thrusts and returning to her clitoris. Grady gritted her teeth, but she was losing the battle. She was going to come all over, and there was no stopping it.

"Blaise," she gasped. "I'm close."

Blaise caught Grady's nipple in her mouth and sucked, fingers finding just the right spot on the shaft of Grady's clitoris. Grady came in hard, sharp thrusts, her orgasm streaming down her thighs and burning along her spine. Deep inside, Blaise closed around her, fluttering in swift, rapid contractions, joining her at the peak and beyond.

❖

Blaise drifted on a lazy current of contentment, a cool breeze blowing across her naked back and a riot of birdsong floating in through the open windows. Beneath the lingering pleasure, an overwhelming sense of peace slowly penetrated her decidedly stuporous brain. Minutes passed as strength slowly returned to her lifeless limbs along with the realization that she still sprawled bonelessly atop Grady. When she tried to shift her weight aside, Grady's arms tightened around her.

"You're good," Grady murmured, kissing the side of her neck.

"I'm heavy."

Grady laughed, and the sound reverberated into Blaise's chest along with a little thrill of excitement. The slow easy play of Grady's hands up and down her back soothed and aroused her at the same time.

Discovering she could actually move a little, Blaise managed to lift her head and kissed Grady, taking her time about it. "You make a really nice pillow."

Grady grinned, her usually sharp, always a little hungry, eyes looking hazy and decidedly self-satisfied.

"Proud of yourself, aren't you?" Blaise murmured, kissing the edge of her jaw.

Grady's grin widened. "Just a little. You?"

"Extremely." Blaise nipped at her lip. Catching a memory of herself astride Grady, riding her to the edge of orgasm, she felt her cheeks heat. "Although a little surprised. I don't think I've ever been quite so…"

"Wanton?" Grady stroked the curve of her breast and cupped her fullness. "Wild and abandoned?"

Blaise narrowed her eyes. "Don't get carried away."

"Too late," Grady murmured, kissing her with such unexpected tenderness Blaise trembled.

The passion she'd expected. Heat had simmered too close to the surface, too nearly out of control, every time Grady had looked at her from the moment they'd met. But the other side of her—the gentle regard—still made her ache. She stroked Grady's face. "You know, you're always surprising me."

"In a good way?"

"Mm. Very good."

"You didn't surprise me," Grady said. "I knew you were going to destroy me. And you did."

Blaise caught her breath. "I won't pretend I don't know what you mean. I didn't expect…" She dragged a hand through her hair, smiling wryly. "I had no idea what to expect. I didn't let myself really think about it too much, or I might not have come over here at all."

"I'm eternally grateful that you did," Grady said. "I don't know how much longer I could have waited without exploding."

"I've never actually believed in the concept of chemistry," Blaise said, "but I also never experienced anything—or anyone—like being with you this way. I don't usually lose my mind quite so thoroughly."

"I don't usually surrender every morsel of control, either. I think I should thank you for that," Grady said. "I feel…freaking amazing."

Blaise said, "I'm not sure I could have gone to the places I went if you hadn't made me feel so safe. As if everything I did was what you wanted."

"It was, and *you* are everything I want." Grady took a long breath and framed Blaise's face with both hands. "You couldn't have said anything more perfect to me. Trusting me, that's a gift. So thank you."

Blaise propped her chin in her hand, still stretched out on Grady and, since Grady didn't seem to mind, having no desire to move. Their legs entwined, their bodies touching almost everywhere, couldn't have felt more natural. That made no sense, but she couldn't argue with the rightness of it.

"I believed you wanted me, and that let me be…free. That was a gift too." Blaise shook her head. "I don't know how everything can feel so right."

"I know you enough to know what I feel whenever I think of you," Grady said. "Whenever I touch you. Blaise, I'm—"

"Grady," Blaise said, the tightness in her chest not denial, but the fear of wanting too much to hear what Grady was going to say. "Too soon."

"If you think so," Grady said, "but I don't."

Blaise sighed and settled back into her arms, resting her cheek on Grady's chest, listening to her heart beat. "How did you come to be so sure all the time?"

"I'm not, not really. It's just armor—I learned to seem sure even when I wasn't."

"How so?" Blaise went back to drawing aimless circles on Grady's chest as Grady stroked her hair lazily.

"My life has mostly been about getting to where I am now—goal-oriented, no matter what it cost."

"Why so driven, then?" Blaise asked, fascinated by the way Grady's stomach tightened when she moved her hand lower.

Grady covered Blaise's hand when she would've stroked lower. "If you want me to talk, you can't do that."

Blaise smiled to herself. She could wait a little while, but she planned to do that again soon.

"I grew up believing achievement was a symbol of worth—my worth, I guess—and that what I accomplished was what mattered most."

"Mattered to your family, you mean?"

"I think I mentioned before that we were a competitive lot. It's pretty much the family legacy, living up to the family name." Grady laughed, but there was no pleasure in it. "It's funny, when I met Flann, I thought we'd have a lot in common. I knew she came from a family of doctors, so I figured we'd be a lot alike. But we weren't."

Blaise stilled. "I didn't know that your family were doctors too."

"That's one of the nice things about being here," Grady said. "It's the first time I haven't actually been following in my father's and brother's footsteps. It's nice not to—"

Blaise sat up quickly, a cold chill making her tremble. She pulled the sheet up and covered herself. "What did you just say?"

"What?" Grady's brow furrowed.

"What did you just say, about your brother." Blaise gripped the thin cotton sheet so hard her fingers ached.

"Oh," Grady said, looking momentarily confused as Blaise edged over to the side of the bed, "he's quite a bit older than me, so growing up I hero-worshipped him at first, and then sibling rivalry kicked in. I went from wanting to be like him to wanting to beat him." She snorted. "Every McClure for generations probably went through the same thing. We all went to the same medical school and had residencies at the same hospitals, so every step of the way someone was comparing me to Gav."

"Gavin McClure." Blaise fought down a bubble of horror, praying this was a nightmare and she'd waken in a moment. But she wouldn't, would she. She slid from the bed and searched in the pile on the floor for her clothes.

Fool me once, shame on you. Fool me twice, shame on me. Fool. Fool.

"Blaise, what the hell are you doing?" Grady jumped out of bed, and Blaise flinched away, clutching her shirt to her chest.

Stunned by the wide-eyed shock on Blaise's face, Grady went statue still. She put her empty hands up, trying to look reassuring. "Talk to me, what's happening?"

"It doesn't matter. I have to go." Blaise pulled on her shirt and fumbled through the discarded clothes, found her pants and pulled them on, not even bothering with panties. "It doesn't matter."

"The hell it doesn't." Grady yanked on her own pants. "A minute ago we were just talking—now you look like you're ready to jump out the window."

"I have to go," Blaise repeated, grabbing her shoes.

"Wait, just wait. Tell me what the hell is going on."

"It doesn't matter—it was just a mistake."

"What mistake?" The roaring in Grady's head threatened to shatter her control, and she took a couple of deep breaths to steady her voice. "Us? Is that what has you in a panic?"

Blaise snapped, "There is no us. There never was, and there never will be."

"You know that's not true. You felt the connection, just like I did. I know you did. Jesus, Blaise—what's wrong?"

"This shouldn't have happened. I'm sorry."

Grady knew better than to touch her. She looked like she might come apart at any second, but she couldn't let her just walk out. She edged around Blaise until she was standing between Blaise and the bedroom door. "At least tell me why. What did I do?"

"You didn't do anything. I did." Blaise took a shuddering breath. How could she have been so blind? How could she have let herself be carried away by her need to be wanted again? God, she hadn't learned a thing. "Please move."

"Just tell me why," Grady said. "I deserve to hear what it is I've done. Give me a chance to make up for it."

"I can't."

"Why not?"

"You just have to believe me, that this can't happen again."

Grady raked a hand through her hair. "Why? Why, Blaise?"

If she hadn't just been in Grady's arms, if she hadn't just opened herself to her, held her and been held by her, she would have had the strength to keep silent, but the pain in Grady's eyes broke her. "Because your brother is Taylor's father."

Chapter Twenty-three

Grady braced her arm on the wall beside the door, the roaring in her head switching to silence so profound she was without thought. Blaise's words, though, echoed through her entire body as if she'd been hollowed out and left to wither on a desert floor.

"Gavin?" Grady said quietly. "Gavin is Taylor's father?"

"Aren't you going to ask me if I'm sure?" Blaise said bitterly, still standing barefoot with her shoes in one hand, the top button of her shirt undone, her hair in disarray from where Grady had run her hands through it. Her eyes were bruised, not angry, but tinged with a weary sadness the depths of which Grady had only guessed at before.

"Why would I ask you that?" Grady took a deep breath, hoping to settle her stomach and find some steady ground when the whole world tilted and swirled. She would never doubt Blaise's word as to who had fathered her child, and even if she'd wanted to, she couldn't. She recalled the first time she'd seen Taylor in the pizza shop. How she'd thought Taylor looked familiar and at the time had assumed that was because she looked like Blaise. And she did. But there was something else, in the angle of her jaw, the tilt of her chin, the shape of her face—some hint of familiarity that she realized now was Gavin. "Of course you're sure."

"That's not what your brother said." Blaise grimaced. "I'm sorry. I'm not going to talk about him—about this. Please, would you move so I can leave."

"He knows?"

"He knew I was pregnant." Blaise huffed, a look of disdain—aimed at herself, Grady thought—crossing her face. "I'm not sure what I thought to accomplish by telling him. We were practically strangers."

"You can't mean he—"

"Oh no. The only one responsible is me. He was a friend of my roommate's boyfriend. I never saw him except when we'd all go to parties—he was so busy at the hospital, and I was a college student." She shook her head. "But he paid attention to me, and I believed it was more than flirtation. Obviously, *he* didn't."

"What happened?" Grady said softly. Blaise hardly seemed to know she was talking, and she didn't want her to stop. She needed to hear, to understand. She couldn't make sense of any of it. How could Gavin know he had a daughter? *She* didn't know—no one in her family knew—and if he'd known there was a child, why hadn't he mentioned Blaise or—God—married her? That thought staggered her. She did the math—she would have still been at home, about ready to head off to college when Taylor was conceived. Astute enough to pick up on something this major disturbing the mask of familial tranquility. Gavin would have been finishing his fellowship. And he would have been engaged to Audrey then. No way could Blaise have known that.

"Old story." Blaise sighed. "I believed what I needed—wanted—to believe, and one night—well, the rest should be obvious."

"It's an old story because at some point in our lives, we all do things in the moment that we'd like to change."

"I wouldn't change the fact that I have Taylor," Blaise said.

"Of course not."

"I'm leaving now, Grady. If you care for me at all," Blaise said, "you won't tell your brother about her. Please, for her sake if not mine."

"But you just said you told him," Grady protested. "If he knows—"

"He doesn't know there is a child, only that I was pregnant. As far as he knows, there was no child."

"You told him you weren't going to go through with the pregnancy?" Grady made no judgment—Blaise had been, what, nineteen, twenty? No matter what age, she had every right to decide her own future.

"No," Blaise said coolly as she sidestepped Grady, who still hadn't moved completely out of the doorway. "*He* told *me* I should terminate the pregnancy. To be precise, that he had no interest, even if it was his, in anything to do with a mistaken consequence of a casual encounter. So as far as he knows, Taylor does not exist."

The punch of disbelief hit Grady like a fist in the solar plexus. She'd walked in Gavin's footprints her whole life, and for most of it, she'd been proud to do so. Right now, she was ashamed. When Blaise slipped past her, she didn't call her back, didn't have the strength to push her into revealing any more of the story that so obviously hurt her. The sound of the front door closing left her weak and unsteady, and she sagged against the wall, slowly sinking down until her arms dangled over her bent knees and her head tilted against the wall.

An hour ago she'd thought her life had finally settled onto a path she hadn't even known she'd needed, into a future she hadn't known she wanted. A future she did want, desperately. She wanted Blaise, and yes, Taylor, to be part of that journey.

And now?

Blaise had a past with her brother Grady could barely comprehend, but one thing was clear. Blaise didn't want Gavin to know anything about Taylor, and Grady was a threat to the secret she'd kept all these years.

❖

Blaise slowed on the porch just long enough to slide into her shoes, then hurried down the stairs and toward the corner. She needed to get away from Grady's apartment, away from Grady. And how was she going to do that, when they not only worked in the same hospital but interacted almost daily in the ER? Not to mention the likelihood of running into her almost everywhere—on the street, at a friend's, at local events. She couldn't very well pretend she didn't know her, not after today.

She couldn't think about this morning now. She couldn't. Not if she wanted to keep her life from careening off the careful course she'd plotted.

All right then. If she couldn't physically distance herself from Grady, she would have to close all the other doors that might let her back into her life. The door that had opened into her heart. Into her body. Into her dreams. All the doors Grady had swung wide with effortless ease. Methodically, she began closing them, and with each resounding thud, her heart ached a little more.

When she reached the corner of her street, she turned in the opposite direction, not even realizing she had until she'd gone several blocks. But of course, there was only one place she could go to avoid the screaming silence of her empty house and the memories, old and new, crowding in on her.

She rapped on the screen door. "Abby?"

A moment later, Abby appeared in a T-shirt and sweatpants,

barefoot, with a book in her hand and one finger holding the place. "Hey. I didn't think I'd see you."

"I probably should have texted—"

"Why? Blake's at school and Flann's in the OR. We're the ones with the day off. Come on in." She pulled the door open to let Blaise enter. "I was just thinking about—what's wrong?"

"Nothing." Blaise slipped by her, keeping her head down so Abby wouldn't see her face. "I just need some company."

"Well, that's okay for starters." Abby slid an arm around Blaise's waist and walked her back toward the kitchen. "Have you eaten today?"

Blaise shook her head.

"Okay. That's the first order of business, then. Sit." She guided Blaise to a stool and put water on for tea. "You look nice, by the way. Those don't look like out-for-a-walk clothes."

"I wasn't planning on going for a walk. I just ended up here—a horse returning to the barn out of habit." Suspecting she sounded just a little bit crazy—she certainly felt that way—she waved a hand. "Never mind me."

"Mm-hmm." Abby opened the fridge and piled food on the counter. "We're in between breakfast and lunch, so how about soup and salad?"

"I don't think I can eat."

"No, you probably don't think so, but you need to."

"Yes, all right." Knowing better than to argue with Abby, and too exhausted in mind and spirit to protest anyhow, Blaise folded her hands on the island separating the prep area from the rest of the kitchen. For the first few years after Taylor'd been born, she'd worried what might happen if Gavin somehow took an interest in her, although she couldn't imagine why he would. He barely knew Blaise, after all, and probably never gave her another thought after their last brief conversation. But Gavin's family was powerful and wealthy, and she had no idea what they might say or do or want when they discovered—if they discovered—Gavin had a child.

But he didn't. Taylor was no child of his, whether he'd sired her or not. Taylor was *her* child. And she'd vowed before she was even born she would raise her without the specter of a distant, powerful family that might want something from her they didn't deserve. If and when Taylor had wanted to know about her birth circumstances, she would have told her. But that was a far cry from announcing Taylor's existence to a family a world away in more ways than one.

Abby slid the tea in a blue ceramic mug with a bright yellow chicken adorning it over to her. "Here. Drink some of that."

Blaise wrapped her hands around the mug, wondering why she was so cold. It wasn't cold out, was it?

Abby came around and sat beside her. "Something's happened. You need to tell me what it is."

Blaze swallowed. Stared at her tea. "I can't."

"Did you see Grady after work this morning?"

Blaise nodded. "I just came from her apartment."

"Did Grady do something?"

Blaise started to shake her head, then caught herself. She'd had enough of pushing the truth aside, even if the truth, contrary to all the songs, would never set her free. "Oh, she did. She brought out a side of myself I'd never seen before. Unleashed something in me," she said with a bitter laugh, "that I'd thought was gone years ago."

"And that was scary?" Abby murmured.

"No," Blaise said, hearing the flatness in her own voice. "Not scary. Amazing. Liberating."

"Then something else must've happened. Did she hurt you in some way?"

Blaise met Abby's gaze. "No. I was the one who did the hurting."

Abby squeezed her arm. "You're going to have some soup, and then you're going to tell me how."

Today seemed to be a day for confessions, or maybe she just didn't have the strength to rebuild her defenses fast enough. Leaving Grady after what they'd shared, after the awakening she experienced on every level with her—because of her—had shattered her.

She told Abby, and as she spoke, Abby shifted closer and wrapped an arm around her. When she finished, her head rested against Abby's shoulder. Abby smelled like a comforting blend of chamomile and roses, and right now, her warmth was exactly what Blaise craved.

"I didn't handle things very well when I found out," Blaise murmured. "None of this is Grady's fault."

"Nor is it yours," Abby said. "Do you really want to stop seeing her, Blaise?"

"I could hardly ask her to keep this a secret if we were together."

She hadn't answered Abby's question, and Abby, friend that she was, didn't ask again.

CHAPTER TWENTY-FOUR

Grady didn't turn from her open locker when the hall door opened and closed and footsteps approached behind her. She shucked her scrub shirt and reached for her running shirt. The surgeons' locker room was coed and adjoined the rest of the OR locker room through an open archway. She hadn't really paid much attention to the little bit of solitude the separate changing areas afforded until she'd taken to avoiding Blaise. Now she appreciated it. The last thing she wanted was to make small talk with Blaise in front of an audience or pretend she didn't notice—or care—when she was half undressed.

"How'd the case go?" Flann asked.

The tension in Grady's shoulders eased. Flann. A friend. Really, the only one she had in her new life, and when she thought back over the last ten years, maybe the only one then too. She probably needed one right about now, but she wasn't sure where to start—or what she could say that wouldn't jeopardize Blaise's privacy. And trust. The last two weeks had been some of the darkest she could recall. Fortunately, there was always work to be done, and work had always been her go-to solace. Since she didn't care much for drinking her troubles away and didn't use casual sex as a panacea for fatigue or loneliness, she'd started haunting the ER whenever she knew Blaise wasn't there. The other surgeons were easy about sharing the workload, especially since there was always plenty to go around. Usually on the night shift, or late afternoons when the ORs were running full tilt, having another surgeon to pick up an emergency case was always welcome. When she was working, lost in the landscape of flesh and blood with the dictate to heal, she didn't have to think about the hollow ache in her chest that never went away, a space Blaise had filled with hope and promise, or the sadness when she thought of her brother—the one person she'd always admired and wanted to emulate. Now she faced the harsh truth that she didn't know Gavin, and she never would have wanted to follow in his footsteps, family legacy be damned.

But she was here now—in a life she had chosen, against all the arguments from her father to the contrary. Because Flann Rivers had shown her a different picture of what her future could be. Just like Blaise.

"I haven't seen a perforated ulcer in a long time," Grady said as nonchalantly as she could. "Another one of those diseases the medical guys have found a way to fix that doesn't require us anymore. Gastric surgery used to be a staple, and now, we're lucky when we get one."

"Well, he was lucky you were around," Flann said, opening her locker, "and that you got him up to the OR so fast. Perfs can be nasty."

"He should be fine. Not much contamination. I did a Roux-en-Y bypass. He'll have to make a little adjustment with his diet, and he's got to take his meds." Grady exchanged her scrub pants for running tights. "Hopefully he will."

"I suspect his wife will see to that," Flann said.

"It always helps when family's on your side." Grady couldn't keep the bitterness from her voice. Every time anything reminded her of her family, she thought of Gavin. And Blaise. Blaise had to make a go of it alone, as near as she could figure out, with a young child and probably not much in the way of means. What had Blaise said? She'd gone to school part-time to finish her nursing degree while Taylor was a toddler. Blaise had to scrape by while the father of her child had more money than he knew what to do with. Like Grady. Like the family that should have been looking after her, helping. She was embarrassed. More than embarrassed, ashamed. Of Gavin, of what her family represented.

"I get the feeling," Flann said quietly, "you're not exactly happy here. If this job's not what you were thinking it would be—"

Grady stopped what she was doing and met Flann's direct gaze. "No, you're wrong about that." She scanned the locker room and through into the adjoining staff area to be sure they were alone. "It's exactly what I wanted."

"Nowhere in your contract does it say you need to work twenty-four hours a day, Grady."

"Must be in yours, then," Grady said lightly. No one, with the possible exception of Flann's sister Harper, spent more time in the hospital. Abby Remy was a close second.

"I get restless," Flann said, a soft smile that Grady rarely saw crossing her face. "When I do, Abby sends me off to make rounds or check the board in the ER for anything waiting in the wings for a surgical consult."

"Smart woman."

"More than I deserve," Flann muttered. "I'm not going to tell you how to balance your work and the rest of your life, but if there's a problem, you'll let me know."

Grady blew out a breath. "I appreciate your concern. I'm fine."

"Right," Flann said, clapping Grady on the shoulder. "All right then. See you at M and M later today."

"Right, thanks, Chief."

Flann laughed, grabbed her lab coat, and strode out.

Grady sat to lace up her running shoes. She had an hour free, so she'd run. Running was about the only other thing that kept her from thinking too much. The rhythm of her feet pounding the pavement, the breath coursing in and out of her chest, the air rushing over her sweat-slick skin, brought her the only peace she experienced since those few minutes when she'd awakened with Blaise in her arms, Blaise's hand curled between her breasts, and Blaise's head on her shoulder. So supremely *right*. The sweetness of the memory, the intensity of every second they'd shared, left her reeling with loss.

She hurried from the locker room, took the stairs down to the exit two at a time, and ran.

❖

"Hey," Flann said, checking the hall to see if they were alone before kissing Abby on the cheek. "How's your morning?"

Abby cupped Flann's cheek and brushed her thumb over the corner of Flann's mouth. "Steady, but nothing for you, Tiger."

"Well, there's always hope."

Abby laughed. "Join me for coffee?"

"Sure."

Flann followed her down the hall to the break room, leaning against the counter as Abby poured them what looked to be fresh coffee, for which she gave fervent thanks.

"Something bothering you?" Abby asked over her shoulder.

"Not really," she said.

"Not really but maybe?" Abby said.

"I talked to Grady." Flann sighed. "She's not talking."

Abby turned slowly, held out a cup of coffee. "I thought we agreed we wouldn't interfere."

"I didn't reveal any confidences, especially since I don't know any. You suggested I keep an eye on her, and I am." Flann sipped the coffee. Something involving Grady had Abby stressed out, but she'd refused to discuss specifics, saying only Grady might be having a tough time. Whatever the hell that meant. Although she could guess. Grady was too solid to be having problems with work, and she'd just said she was happy at the Rivers. So—personal. And if Abby knew about it, then the choices were limited. She'd seen Abby's best friend Blaise Richelieu with Grady at the bakery, and talking at the game, and at the party at the Homestead. And casually chatting in the ER quite a few times after that. But not recently. Rocket science this wasn't.

Abby rubbed the bridge of her nose. "I'm sorry. It's just, I can't really tell you anything, and—"

"And Blaise is your best friend, and best friends trump spouses sometimes."

"That's pretty smart of you. I'm not going to ask how you came to the conclusion Blaise is involved, but I appreciate you understanding."

"As long as nothing's going on that will impair Grady's ability to do her job, I'm happy to stay on the sidelines."

"Does a broken heart count?" Abby asked quietly.

"Sometimes it can." Flann set her cup on the counter, cupped Abby's chin, and kissed her, slowly and tenderly. "I'm not sure I could manage without you."

Abby threaded her arms around Flann's waist. "Well then, there's one thing you do not need to worry about. Because you will never have to."

Flann held her close for second, as tightly as she could, and stepped back before they had an audience. "Grady is okay. *Okay* meaning she's working too much, probably eating like crap, and running her ass off trying to pretend she's not hurting. So if you've got a solution to it, I think you should get moving on it."

"Unfortunately, I don't."

"I'll keep an eye on her," Flann said.

"I love you," Abby said. "Now I have to get back to work, and so do you."

"Just one more kiss," Flann murmured.

Laughing, Abby complied.

❖

Blaise finally forced her legs to move and backed away down the hall. She'd almost walked in on Flann and Abby, and they wouldn't have minded, but when she'd heard Grady's name, an invisible wall had crashed down in front of her, halting her in her tracks. The rest of Flann's words burned through her as if written in fire.

She's working too much, probably eating like crap, and running her ass off trying to pretend she's not hurting.

Flann could have been talking about her. Add to it, tired beyond exhaustion but unable to sleep, weary in heart and soul, and ineffably sad. She'd tried running, which only freed her mind of all the mundane responsibilities that usually occupied her and left her thinking of Grady. Grady moved her in the way she'd always dreamed of being moved, touched her in the ways she'd always fantasized about being touched, and listened and laughed and made her laugh. And then she'd not only lost her, she'd hurt her. Hurt her with a truth that wasn't Grady's to own, an obligation that wasn't hers to shoulder, but Grady would want to all the same. Because that's the kind of woman she was.

Gavin—and Grady—McClure came from an old, super-rich line of doctors, politicians, and philanthropists who'd endowed universities, established international charities, and held high political office. An illegitimate child born to the heir apparent would be enough of a scandal to make a splash. She would not subject her daughter to that, and she refused to pull Grady any deeper into a drama not of her making. They were both far, far too important to her.

Grady would heal and move on, and she would go on as she had before Grady seduced her—in the best possible way—into a glimpse of what love looked like.

CHAPTER TWENTY-FIVE

Another week of slow torture passed for Grady, another seven nights of broken sleep, long runs, and losing efforts at not thinking about Blaise. She thought a lot about Gavin, though, about what he deserved to know, what he ought to be held accountable for. Twice she'd started to text him, and twice she'd stopped. He was her brother, no matter they had different mothers, but in this story—*Blaise's* story—he was just a man. One who had turned his back on what was right and honorable. She wasn't walking in Gavin's footsteps now, and never would again. Now she traveled her own path, one Blaise had helped her find.

When she popped into the cafeteria a little after ten on a Thursday night to grab a bite after a case, she caught sight of Blaise at a corner table, eating alone. She didn't think about what was smart, or right, or foolish. All she saw was Blaise.

She crossed to her like a ship navigating a stormy sea by the light of a distant bright beacon. "Can I sit down?"

Blaze looked up, her eyes shadowed with fatigue or something far more bruising. Her smile was wistful. "Of course."

Grady dropped into a chair. Tired as she was, her heart lifted. "How are you?"

"Honestly?" Blaise said.

Grady chuckled. "I don't think you know how to be anything but."

"Oh, you'd be surprised." Blaise grimaced. "If I'd been more honest with myself about the attractions I'd started feeling in high school, I might not have so easily succumbed to the flattery your brother sent my way. And after learning what I've kept buried all these years, I should think you'd be the last person to consider me trustworthy."

"Failing to disclose your personal business is not a lie, and neither is needing some growing time to understand who you are," Grady said. "You're entitled to your privacy. So is Taylor."

"Thank you for that." Blaise sighed. "I wondered how you'd feel when you had a chance to think about it. If you'd feel like I'd cheated your brother out of something. Denied your family something." She hesitated. "Cheated you."

"You didn't cheat me out of anything. I said the time with you was a gift, and I meant it." Grady swallowed hard. "I'd say that Gavin was the one who did that when he turned his back on you and Taylor."

"It was a long time ago, Grady, and both of us made mistakes. I try not to think very much about him. And for the most part, I'm happy."

"For the most part?"

Blaise was too tired to pretend, and she couldn't lie to Grady. Wouldn't lie to her. "I love my daughter more than my life, but I'm a woman too, and sometimes I've been lonely."

"I understand."

"I know, you always seem to understand," Blaise said softly.

Grady could have said she was lonely too, and that she missed her. She wanted to—so much so just sitting beside her hurt. But not sitting beside her hurt far more. More importantly, Blaise was hurting, and Grady railed against her own powerlessness.

"There's something I want you to know," Grady said, offering the only thing she could.

Blaise stiffened. She probably expected Grady to ask her to pretend the past didn't matter, so they could both ignore Gavin's ghost threatening Blaise's peace of mind and Taylor's security. Grady would never put Blaise or Taylor in that position, no matter how much it hurt to walk away.

Grady rested her hand on Blaise's, a tiny bit of comfort warming her when Blaise didn't pull away. "I want you to know that Gavin will never hear about Taylor from me. If and when he does, it will be because you've told Taylor about him, and she wants to reach out. She deserves to make that choice—when and if she needs to."

"Thank you," Blaise said. "I've struggled with what and when to tell her since she was born, and the best I've come up with is to let her decide at her own pace."

"I think that's exactly right," Grady said, even though the words sealed her own fate. She couldn't have any future with Blaise if Taylor didn't know her true relationship to her.

"And what about you?" Blaise turned her hand and ran her thumb over the top of Grady's hand. "She's your niece."

"Maybe someday I'll have a chance to know her better." Grady smiled. "She seems like a great young woman, and I'm not at all surprised considering who her mother is."

"I can't take the credit for that," Blaise said. "All I've ever tried to do is let her be herself. And know I would always love her."

"And that's everything." Grady went on carefully, "There's something else. You know my circumstances—I am a lot more than comfortable financially. I want to help with the cost of Taylor's education."

"Grady," Blaise said, looking away on a long, tremulous breath. "I can't."

"No obligations, Blaise. Taylor never needs to know. No one ever will." She leaned closer. "This is the *least* Gavin should have done for her—for you. Taylor deserves this. Please, let me do this."

"I'll—I'll think about it," Blaise finally said. "I don't want Taylor to lose out because of my fears, or pride. But you don't have to make up for your brother, Grady. Ever."

"I'm not trying to. She's family."

"Stop," Blaise murmured, "you'll make me cry."

"Don't," Grady whispered. "I'm not strong enough not to kiss you if you do."

"I'm not strong enough to say no." Blaise closed her eyes, and Grady slipped away while she could still make herself go.

❖

Sometimes running at night, when the shadows closed in, cocooning her in silence, Grady found peace. City streets hadn't offered much of that, but in this village, with almost all the businesses except the bar at the far end of town closed by the time she was ready to leave the hospital, and everyone asleep, she'd found what she needed. Not tonight, though. Tonight she ran from the hospital down the mountainside into the empty streets, need and frustration roiling in the pit of her stomach. Adrenaline fueled equal parts temper and despair, and heightened the twitchy edginess in her muscles. She'd never been completely free to choose her own destiny—she'd been expected to follow in Gavin's footsteps, who'd followed in her father's, who'd followed in his, and back generations. She loved medicine, so she hadn't minded all that much. She minded now. She minded very much that she could not change her circumstances when it mattered most. She wanted Blaise. Dreamed of her, desired her, longed for her, and ached in her absence. She'd seen her need echoed in Blaise's eyes. She'd felt it in Blaise's body when they'd made love. How many times in her life would she find someone who touched her like that?

The answer was obvious. She'd been lucky to find it once and would be a fool to think she would again.

Frustrated, powerless, helpless, she ran. Her pace picked up, but still she couldn't find the rhythm. She ran past the turnoff to her street, to the end of town and back again, circling, finally coming up Blaise's street for the simple, pathetic need to see the porch where she'd sat with Blaise, sipping wine in the darkness, sharing bits of herself and teasing little pieces of Blaise from the very deep well of her secrets.

And the kiss. The kiss that haunted her and remade her. She slowed, half a block away, and the silence and the stillness settled inside her chest, bringing certainty and assurance at last. She wouldn't give up. If she had to wait until Taylor left home for college, until she was older and strong enough in her own right to weather whatever fallout her relationship to the McClures might bring, if anything at all, she would. Peace stole through her chest, and as if the wind had felt the rightness of it too, the porch swing swayed a little, to and fro. Grady saw herself there again, sitting beside Blaise as Blaise gently rocked the swing.

Grady slowed further, eyeing the swaying swing. The breeze was faint, not enough to provoke that much motion, but the swing was empty. The shadows on the porch were alive, though, shifting pools of inky black melting and reforming the closer Grady approached. As she trod cautiously up the walk, the shadows coalesced into the shape of a man outside the front window, his arm reaching toward the front door latch.

"Hey!" Grady bounded up the steps. "What are you—"

Pain shot through her face. Her feet flew out from under her and she sailed backward, landing with a teeth-jarring thud on the front stairs. The porch light flicked on, and Taylor's voice cut through the fog in Grady's pain-addled brain.

"Who's out there?"

Somehow Grady got her legs to work and staggered up as Billy Riley grabbed Taylor's arm and tried to shove inside the house with her.

"Hold it!" Grady lowered her shoulder and rushed Billy. He was six inches taller and probably a hundred pounds heavier, but she hit him at an angle just above the hips, using every bit of power in her thighs and her center mass to plow into his soft flank. The blow knocked him off balance, and as he stumbled away, he crashed into the railing and tumbled over into the yard along with a good portion of the spindles and rails.

"Get in the house and call the police," Grady yelled.

Taylor, bless her, didn't argue and the door slammed. Grady leaned an arm on the remaining bit of railing and peered over the splintered banister into the yard. Billy sprawled on his back, whimpering. Not going anywhere.

Grady rubbed her forearm over her face, noted absently the streaks of blood as she went back down the front stairs to the side yard, and knelt beside him.

"Don't move," she said. "What hurts?"

"My fucking arm," he groaned.

She ignored the stench of alcohol. Wasn't the first time and wouldn't be the last time she dealt with an injured drunk. In the light coming out from the front room, she could make out his rolling eyes, glazed more from alcohol and likely drugs than injury.

"Can you feel your arms and legs?"

"You hit me," he muttered, moving all extremities except the injured one he cradled against his chest.

"Stay put. Help is on the way." Grady straightened. The broken arm, if that's what it was, looked like his worst injury. Sirens sounded, coming closer fast, and she rose, put her hands in front of her, and stayed in the light. Two uniformed officers trotted up the walk, Maglites directed at her.

"Police," the male officer said. "We got a call there was an attempted break-in and someone was hurt."

"I'm Grady McClure, a doctor at the Rivers. This guy was lurking on the porch and tried to push inside when the occupant opened the door."

The woman officer shone her light on Billy and made a disgusted sound. "Riley, jeez. I didn't think you'd come up with anything dumber than your last stunt, but you managed."

"I think he's got a broken arm," Grady added, lowering her hands.

"I'll call the EMTs," the male cop said. "You look like you took a hit there too, Doc."

She grimaced. The left side of her face was sore, and considering the blood, she probably had a laceration. "I'm okay."

"Perkins," he said to the female officer, "you stay here with this idiot until the EMTs arrive. I'll call for backup and run the doc over to the ER to get looked over."

"Hey, Tom," Taylor said from the porch, "I'm coming too."

"Sure," he said. "You can tell me what happened when we get there."

Grady said to Tom, "Maybe you should let the ER know we're coming, and that Taylor is okay. Her mom is working tonight."

"Yep." Tom headed for the patrol car and Grady followed. Taylor caught up with her on the front walk.

"You okay?" Grady asked quietly.

"Yeah," she said, although her voice shook. "You really nailed him."

"Lucky hit."

"Lucky for me," Taylor said softly.

Grady wanted to put her arm around her, but held back. To Taylor, she was practically a stranger.

❖

"Blaise?" Abby said from the door of the utility room where Blaise had spent the last half hour cataloging supplies.

"Need me?" Blaise said, punching the next to last number on her inventory list into her tablet.

"Everything's okay," Abby said, "but Tom Kincaid is bringing Taylor over here right now. She's *not* hurt."

Blaise carefully set the tablet aside. Her stomach pitched and rolled. She breathed in slowly to steady herself. "You're sure she's not hurt."

"She's fine. It sounds like Billy Riley was trying to get into your house."

"That son of a bitch," Blaise said. "Where is she?"

"They should be here any minute."

Abby stepped aside as Blaise flew past and raced down the hall toward the ER entrance. Halfway there, Taylor vaulted through the door, saw her, and ran into her arms. Blaise clutched her, running her hands over her hair, down her back, and up her arms. She stepped away an inch, all the distance she could bear. "You're not hurt?"

"I'm okay, Mom, but Grady's hurt."

Looking past Taylor to the ER entrance, Blaise gasped. Sean

entered, pushing a pale, disgruntled looking Grady in a wheelchair, a blood-soaked gauze taped to her left temple.

Heart skittering with worry and fear, Blaise said, "God, what happened?"

"Billy Riley, that dickhead," Taylor spat, "was on our porch, looking in the *window*, and when I opened the door, he tried to get in." Her voice broke, and Blaise pulled her back into her arms again.

"It's all right, honey. It's okay. He will never do that again. No one will ever do that."

Abby appeared next to them. "Blaise, why don't I take Taylor back to the break room and get her something to drink."

"Yes, okay, thanks," Blaise said as she watched Sean take Grady into a treatment room.

"I think you should relieve Sean," Abby added. "Vic Perkins is bringing Billy Riley in. Sean or Glenn can take him." Abby threaded her arm around Taylor's waist. "Come on, honey."

"Taylor," Blaise said. "I won't be long, okay?"

"It's okay, Mom." Taylor already looked more settled. "I'm good. And Grady was awesome."

Her daughter gave her a ghost of a smile, and Blaise's heart settled. She kissed her on the forehead and hurried toward the treatment room.

"Sean," Blaise said as she pulled back the curtain and slipped inside, "I can take care of Dr. McClure. Vic Perkins is bringing in another one."

If Sean was surprised, he didn't show it. "Sure."

Grady sat propped up on the stretcher. "How's Taylor?"

"She's okay. With Abby right now." Blaise adjusted the light and pulled on sterile gloves. "Let me see what we've got."

Grady picked at the tape holding the gauze in place. "Got a mirror?"

"Stop playing doctor for a minute. You're the patient now," Blaise murmured, gently swabbing the dried blood around Grady's left eye. She focused on evaluating the wound to calm the sick feeling in her stomach. She would *not* let herself think about what could have happened to Taylor, or Grady, now. "You've got a five-centimeter laceration just above your left eyebrow. The direction is favorable, and it probably won't be noticeable once it's healed."

"He must've caught me just right. Shear forces. Lucky hit."

Blaise meant to smile, but her lips trembled. "Oh God, Grady. You could have been hurt so much worse."

"Hey," Grady said, reaching for Blaise's hand. "I wasn't. It stings a fair amount, but it's not a big deal. I didn't lose consciousness. A little bit of a headache. That's it. How's Taylor?"

"I believe you're her new hero." She trembled as the adrenaline surge abated. "He was trying to get in the *house?*"

"He was drunk," Grady said disgustedly, "and nosing around, looking in the windows, and when he went for the door, I called him off. Taylor heard us, and when she opened the door, he tried to get inside."

"I never worried about her being alone at night. She's smart, and in this town, everyone feels safe at night." Blaise took a steadying breath. Later. She could be terrified later. "What were you doing there?"

"Running. I just…happened by." Grady lifted Blaise's hand and brushed a kiss over her knuckles. "Neither you nor Taylor is at fault here. The door was locked. She's sixteen years old. Plenty old enough to be home at night alone. This is all on Billy Riley."

"I want to kill him," Blaise seethed.

"Get in line," Grady said darkly.

"We need to take care of you," Blaise said, gathering her wits and remembering what she was supposed to be doing.

Grady shrugged. "Just put some Steri-Strips on it."

Flann twitched the curtain aside. "How about you let me decide that, champ."

Taylor stood right beside her, and Grady was still holding Blaise's hand. She let go, and Blaise stepped back an inch or two.

Grady frowned at Flann. "Oh, for crying out loud. What are you doing here?"

"Didn't have anything else to do."

"Abby called you," Grady muttered.

"News travels fast around here," Flann said, rolling up the sleeves on her rumpled plaid shirt.

"I've noticed." Grady tilted her head toward Taylor. "How you doing?"

Taylor moved over to the side of the stretcher. "I'm good. I forgot to say thanks."

"Believe me, it was my pleasure." Grady grinned, and Taylor rewarded her with a smile that lit up her eyes. She looked a little pale and shaky, though, and Grady tamped down the desire to toss Billy Riley over another railing. "You handled that just right, by the way."

Taylor's smile grew. "I wish I could have knocked him on his ass the way you did."

"College rugby—you ought to think about it."

"Ah, maybe we should talk about that first," Blaise chimed in, a hint of laughter in her voice.

Taylor huffed. "Mom, Margie and Blake are on the way over here. Can I stay at Blake's tonight?"

"Of course."

Taylor hesitated. "Um, maybe you could come over later too?"

Blaise brushed a strand of hair from Taylor's forehead. "Can I pick the TV show?"

"We'll negotiate."

"Deal."

Flann said, "Let's get the hero here fixed up, Blaise, and you can get out of here."

"I still have half a shift left," Blaise said.

"Abby says you're covered."

Taylor said, "Thanks again, Grady."

"You're welcome." Grady eyed Flann. "It's nothing."

"Uh-huh." Flann pulled on gloves, examined the wound, and shrugged. "You'll have a pretty little scar above that eyebrow that you can tell lies about in the future. And you'll need some stitches."

Blaise said, "I'll get the suture tray. Three-oh chromic, six-oh nylon?"

"Sounds like a good choice," Flann said, breaking out the sterile drapes and setting them around Grady's shoulder and head. When Blaise stepped out, Flann said more quietly, "You all right?"

"Yeah, just hurts like a son of a bitch. And I feel like an ass for getting clocked. The guy was drunk. I'm surprised he could even focus."

"If he'd gotten into the house…" Flann blew out a breath. "*He* needs an ass kicking."

"He's going to get a legal one this time," Grady said.

"I'm not all that happy to hear that, but he earned it." Flann injected some local around the wound edges. "This won't take long. Then you're off call for thirty-six. And don't even try arguing."

"You'll make sure Blaise gets out of here when you finish?" Grady said softly. "She's more shook than she lets on."

Flann regarded her contemplatively. "So it's that way, is it?"

Grady blanked her features. "I just thought she ought to be with Taylor tonight."

"What about you?"

"Just get me stitched up. I'll be fine."

"Sure you will," Flann said, and set to work.

CHAPTER TWENTY-SIX

A bby followed Blaise into the locker room. "How you doing?" Blaise yanked open her locker, grabbed her backpack, and slammed the door. "I am furious. I want to strangle that boy."

Abby leaned against the lockers and folded her arms. "Don't blame you."

Blaise's anger suddenly drained away, leaving her shaky. She plopped down on the bench. "I keep thinking what might have happened if he'd gotten inside the house."

"He didn't."

Blaise rubbed her face. "It's one of many nightmares that I try not to have, every time she's out of my sight."

"I know exactly what you mean. But you have raised a smart child." Abby huffed. "Not a child anymore—none of them. She did exactly the right thing. From what little bits I heard her telling Margie and Blake, Grady stopped Billy from getting into the house. Taylor didn't hesitate when Grady told her to close the door and call the police."

"What if Grady hadn't been there?" Blaise said quietly.

"Then Taylor would've heard Billy before he got inside, and called the police. But he didn't get inside, and she's fine."

"I'm glad she went to your place. I'm going over there now." Blaise sighed. "I probably need the company more than Taylor right now."

"Don't you believe it. Now, how are you, really?"

Blaze shuddered. "I'm...terrible. I'm over being frightened about Taylor, but I'm not over Grady."

"No," Abby said quietly, "I don't imagine you are. What are you going to do about it?"

"I'm not sure." Blaise looked up at Abby. "But I don't know if I can stand to lose her."

"Go be with your daughter," Abby said. "You'll figure this out. Listen to what your heart tells you, about Taylor *and* about Grady."

Blaze grabbed her backpack. "What if my heart can't choose?"

Abby hugged her. "Then that's your answer."

"You're asking me to take a leap of faith," Blaise said.

"Isn't that what love is all about?"

Look before you leap, her mother often admonished. Another warning that life was not to be trusted. No one was. Disappointment was inevitable.

A leap of faith. Not blind, but believing.

Blaise thought about trust and love and faith all the way to Abby's. She'd lost her trust and abandoned her dreams in the last seventeen years, but having Taylor had kept love alive in her life. And in her heart. Maybe Abby was right. Maybe she just needed to listen.

When she got to Abby's, Taylor opened the door before she had a chance to knock, as if she'd been waiting for her.

"Hey." Taylor held the door wide and Blaise followed her in. Blake, Margie, Tim, and Dave lounged around in front of the TV surrounded by the remains of sodas, chips, and cookies.

"Hi," Blaise said. "What are we watching?"

"*Sex Education*," Blake said.

"At three o'clock in the morning?"

"Mom," Taylor said with her verbal eye roll, "it's a TV show, not a documentary."

"Oh. Right. Can parents watch?"

"Sure," a couple of the kids answered simultaneously.

"Great. I'll be back after I grab a shower." She hefted her backpack and headed toward the downstairs bathroom. Taylor followed her to the door.

Blaise took her into her arms and hugged her. "I'm so glad you're okay."

Taylor stepped back, an unusually serious expression on her face. "So, Mom…"

Blaise dropped her backpack on the counter. "What is it?"

"Do we need to talk about Grady?"

Blaise's heart pounded, and she squelched the automatic denial. Taylor regarded her steadily. "Let's go make some coffee. I think we do."

❖

Blaise left a note asking Abby to text her if Taylor needed anything and slipped out Abby's front door just as the sun came up. The kids were all asleep and Abby wouldn't be off shift for another hour or so. Flann was either doing a case or had decided to catch some sleep in an on-call room before morning rounds. Just as well. She didn't really want to be there when they got home. She loved Abby dearly, but the only person she wanted to talk to was Grady.

She hurried through town, dimly aware of the traffic, mostly pickup trucks heading to the café or the corner convenience store for coffee and pastries before work, but every ounce of her energy focused on getting to Grady's apartment. She hadn't even stopped to have coffee, but her nerves jangled with something similar to a caffeine high all the same. Her body barreled ahead while her mind was blank. She had no idea what she was going to say, but she knew *something* must be said. The pressure in her chest, the ache around her heart, and the distant thrill of excitement fueled her steps. She hadn't texted or called. Grady might not even be home. Like Flann, she could be asleep in one of the on-call rooms. If Grady wasn't there, she'd simply have to find her.

She had to.

She rapped on the door, holding her breath. An interminably long minute passed before Grady filled the doorway, her hair tousled and damp as if she'd just finished a shower, looking casually gorgeous in a T-shirt with a hole just below the neck and faded navy blue sweatpants. And barefoot. Blaise's throat went dry. How had she never noticed how sexy a barefoot woman just out of the shower could be?

"I'm sorry, I know it's early, but—"

Grady reached out, grabbed her hand, and pulled her inside.

"Is Taylor—" Grady began.

"I had to talk to you," Blaise finished.

"I wanted to talk to you too." Grady smiled, the ghost of her usual confident, sexy one. This one was a little sad, and Blaise couldn't bear it.

"Taylor is fine," Blaise said hurriedly. "I'm the one who's a mess."

Grady's brows drew down. "What do you mean? What happened?"

Blaise cupped Grady's cheek and brushed her thumb over her mouth. "You happened. You happened to me."

"That's what *I* wanted to tell *you*. I can't walk away, Blaise. I want…" Grady grimaced and ran a hand through her wet hair. "I'll wait. Until Taylor goes to school, until she's ready to hear about Gavin. But I'm not giving up on us. I know you feel it. We've got something, Blaise. Something that matters."

"I know." Blaise kissed her. Just a brush of lips, just enough to ease the terror of almost losing her. "But I don't want to wait. I want you, Grady. God. So much."

Grady's eyes widened and something dark and hungry passed through them. "Blaise," she murmured, "I want you. I've been going crazy trying to stay away from you. But I don't think I can do casual with you."

"That's very good," Blaise said, moving closer still. Her breasts brushed Grady's and flame burst deep inside. "Because I don't want casual."

"Then what do you wan—"

"You. I want you." Blaise kissed her again and poured every bit of her longing into it. She needed to feel her, to taste her, before she could think. Before she could put her heart into words, before she could take another breath.

Grady's arms came around her, and she groaned, backing Blaise gently against the front door as she answered Blaise's kiss with one of her own, a deep, demanding sweep of fierce need and desire. Grady was everywhere, pressed to Blaise's body, one leg between hers, her hand sweeping up Blaise's side to the curve of her breast. When Grady cupped her breast through the thin cotton of her shirt, Blaise closed her eyes and arched her neck—offering, inviting, demanding. Grady kissed along the line of her jaw and down her throat until she buried her face in the hollow at the base of Blaise's neck.

"I've missed you," Grady sighed.

Blaise stroked her fingers through Grady's hair and caressed the back of her neck. "Endlessly. I've missed you endlessly."

Grady slowly straightened. "What are we doing, Blaise?"

"I hope we're beginning because, Grady, I'm in love with you."

"What about Taylor?" Grady refused to give in to the elation welling in her chest. She might have the strength to wait, but she didn't have the strength to be disappointed, to be so close and have everything she wanted snatched away. "I can't go halfway with you. I need you too much."

"I would never ask you to. I couldn't bear it if I didn't have all of you." Blaise linked her hands behind Grady's neck. "Taylor knows who you are."

"You told her?" Grady's eyes widened. "But—"

"She asked." Blaise laughed. "To be precise, she wanted to know if you and I were a thing. I said it was complicated and she gave me her look, the one that says I'm being dense."

"Your daughter is scarily like you, in all the good ways," Grady whispered, hope welling at last.

"She was waiting for me to trust her—I could see it in her eyes. Like I've been asking her to trust me since she was a little girl." Blaise shook her head. "I said her birth father was your brother."

Grady framed Blaise's face in both hands. "You took a chance for me."

"No, I trust you." Blaise kissed her. She couldn't stop, would never stop. "I couldn't tell her that I was falling in love with you and *not* tell her who you were. And Taylor deserves to know who you are. A wonderful, strong, caring, selfless woman. And the one I want in my life."

"You forgot sexy."

Blaise laughed. "I didn't forget for a second, but my daughter doesn't need to be thinking about that in reference to anyone."

"You also forgot the *only* one you want," Grady murmured.

"Oh no," Blaise said softly. "I didn't. I never will."

"I want to be yours," Grady whispered. "I want you to be mine."

"I am."

"Tell me that again when we're in bed." Grady laced her fingers through Blaise's and led her down the hallway, stopping just outside her bedroom door. "Do you need to be anywhere this morning? The rest of the day? Once I touch you, I may never stop."

Blaise grasped the hem of her shirt, drew it up over her head, and dropped it on the floor. She was naked beneath, and Grady forgot to breathe. Blaise laughed, a slightly wild edge to her voice. "Take as long as you like. Take whatever you want."

Grady gripped her shoulders, spun her a quarter turn, and kissed her backward into her bedroom and over to the bed. On the way, Blaise grasped Grady's T-shirt and tugged it up. When her hands found Grady's breasts, Grady groaned.

"I love your body," Blaise whispered, bending her head as she lifted Grady's breast to her mouth.

Grady staggered, her thighs turned to jelly. "Blaise. Bed. Now."

Laughing, Blaise tugged on the tie to Grady's sweatpants. And then Grady was naked and fumbling with Blaise's pants.

"I'll get them." Blaise shed the rest of her clothes as Grady pushed the covers aside and tugged Blaise down.

"I need you," Grady said, "so much."

Blaise gripped her hand, brought it to her breast. "I'm here. Right here."

Leaning above her, Grady kissed her while she explored the slope of her breast, the curve of her abdomen, the wings of her hips. When she stroked between her thighs, Blaise arched with a purr that became a growl and gripped her wrist, guiding her hand between her legs.

"Inside," Blaise gasped. "I need you inside."

Eyes closed, Grady rested her forehead against Blaise's shoulder and filled her, breathless with wonder and aching with the need to claim her, to find her way home. As much as she needed that with every beat of her heart, she needed to go slow. To show Blaise with every deep thrust how much she needed her, how much she wanted her. How much she loved her.

"Deeper, Grady. I need you everywhere." Blaise canted her hips, urging Grady to the pace she wanted. Grady followed every lift and fall, forgetting to breathe, forgetting everything except Blaise. When Blaise gripped her shoulders and rose to meet her, a beautiful arch of grace and power, Grady's soul soared. Then Blaise was coming, her cry of release sealing Grady's fate.

"God," Grady whispered, "Blaise. You're so beautiful."

Blaise's arms came around her, and she tugged Grady down full-length against her.

"You make me feel more than beautiful. You make me *feel*, Grady, so much."

"I love you," Grady said.

"Everything is going to be all right." Blaise fisted a hand in Grady's hair and pulled her head back until their eyes met. "I have never been surer of anything in my life. As long as you love me, we will all be all right."

"Always," Grady said. "I swear."

"As do I. And now," she said, pushing on Grady's shoulder until Grady obediently rolled over onto her back, "let me show you."

Blaise kissed her until she lost her breath again, and before she could catch a full breath, Blaise kissed her way down the center of her chest, to the inside of her thigh, and in between, until sight and sound disappeared and all that remained was pleasure. And Blaise.

CHAPTER TWENTY-SEVEN

A t seven p.m., Grady climbed the front steps to Blaise's porch. The splintered railing hadn't been repaired yet, but someone had swept away the bits and pieces. Though it wasn't yet dark, it would be by the time the football game ended around ten, and the overhead porch light was already on to mark the way home. Grady knocked on the door, anticipation and uncharacteristic uncertainty rippling through her. Tonight was her first outing with Blaise in public—the first time she'd seen Taylor since she'd found out about Gavin, and that Grady was related. Life looked very different than it had before Blaise had appeared at her door and reset all her dreams and desires with a kiss and a promise. The bleak emptiness that cloaked her future when she'd thought she'd lost Blaise disappeared. She loved, and was loved.

The inside door opened, and for a fleeting instant she couldn't help seeing Billy Riley looming in the dark, but tonight the light—inside and out—chased the shadows from the night.

Taylor stood framed in the door. "Hi. My mom isn't ready yet."

"Okay, I can wait out here."

Taylor came out and closed the door. Grady sat on one end of the porch swing, and Taylor took the end opposite her.

Taylor toed it into motion. As it gently swung, she said, "So, you know my mom told me, right?"

"Yes."

Taylor drew one leg up onto the seat, keeping the easy rocking going with her other foot. The night was forecast to get cold later, and she'd dressed for it in jeans, a pale green cardigan, and white tennis shoes. Her hair was down, and she looked an awful lot how Grady imagined a young Blaise must've looked.

Taylor added, "Do you care that I'm not interested in knowing anything about your brother?"

"No," Grady said instantly. "If you ever do, and there's something I can tell you, I'll try."

"Do you think it's weird that we're related?"

Grady grinned. "I think it's kind of cool. I figure you'll want to get to know me a little better before, you know, you decide how you feel about it."

Taylor tipped her head and rested her chin on her knee, studying Grady. "I think we have the same chin."

Grady took a long breath. "So do I."

"*That* is really weird."

"It is kinda. You have a good eye."

"I really love math."

Grady laughed. "Okay."

"I also like to sketch."

"That's probably why you have a good eye," Grady said.

"I've been considering astrophysics or maybe aeronautics."

"That works for the math."

"I was also thinking plastic surgery might be cool."

"Surgery?" Grady said.

"He's a doctor too, isn't he?"

"Yes. Pretty much everybody in my family."

"That's not why."

Grady nodded. "I was thinking it was more because of your mom."

"You know she's amazing, right?"

Just a hint of heat there. Grady liked her all the more for it. "I know that. I think she's the most amazing woman I've ever met."

Eye roll. Grady grinned.

"She says it's serious," Taylor said.

"Between her and me? Yes. It is." Grady wanted to ask Taylor how she felt about it, but this was Taylor's conversation, so she waited.

"I'm planning on calling you Grady, no matter what."

"Well, that works, because I was planning on calling you Taylor."

Taylor grinned at her. "Okay. We understand each other."

"We do. And if your mother didn't tell you, then I will. No one will know about you from me. Someday if you want me to make introductions, you can tell me."

Taylor shrugged. "I don't really see why I'd want to."

Grady didn't either, but things could change, and the only person's opinion that mattered was Taylor's. "Well, just so you know."

Taylor stood. "Okay. So we're all good."

"We are." Grady looked past Taylor as the front door opened and Blaise came out, the most beautiful smile breaking over her face when she glanced at the two of them. "It is all definitely good."

"Ready for the game?" Blaise crossed the porch and kissed Grady quickly.

"Hi. Yes. You look great."

"You too," Blaise said softly.

"So," Taylor said as they walked over to the football field, "it would be really good if you guys could, you know, keep down the PDA so I'm not totally humiliated."

Blaise laughed, a light, happy sound, and wrapped her arm around Grady's waist. "No promises there."

"Yeah," Taylor said as she sent Blaise a smile, "that's what I thought."

A pickup truck slowed down opposite them, and Margie called out the window, "Hey, Taylor, you want a ride? We're picking up Tim on the way."

"Yes!" Taylor sprinted toward the truck, calling over her shoulder, "I'll text you about later, Mom."

"Have fun," Blaise said.

"You too," Taylor yelled as the pickup pulled away.

Blaise leaned a little closer into Grady. "Everything okay?"

"Everything's perfect."

"It is," Blaise said, hauling her close for another very public display of affection. "It is all that, and then some."

About the Author

Radclyffe has written over sixty romance and romantic intrigue novels as well as a paranormal romance series, The Midnight Hunters, as L.L. Raand.

She is a three-time Lambda Literary Award winner in romance and erotica and received the Dr. James Duggins Outstanding Mid-Career Novelist Award by the Lambda Literary Foundation. A member of the Saints and Sinners Literary Hall of Fame, she is also an RWA/FF&P Prism Award winner for *Secrets in the Stone*, an RWA FTHRW Lories and RWA HODRW winner for *Firestorm*, an RWA Bean Pot winner for *Crossroads*, an RWA Laurel Wreath winner for *Blood Hunt*, and a Book Buyers Best award winner for *Price of Honor* and *Secret Hearts*. She is also a featured author in the 2015 documentary film *Love Between the Covers*, from Blueberry Hill Productions. In 2019 she was recognized as a "Trailblazer of Romance" by the Romance Writers of America.

In 2004 she founded Bold Strokes Books, one of the world's largest independent LGBTQ publishing companies, and is the current president and publisher.

Find her at facebook.com/Radclyffe.BSB, follow her on Twitter @RadclyffeBSB, and visit her website at Radfic.com.

Books Available From Bold Strokes Books

Forging a Desire Line by Mary P. Burns. When Charley's ex-wife, Tricia, is diagnosed with inoperable cancer, the private duty nurse Tricia hires turns out to be the handsome and aloof Joanna, who ignites something inside Charley she isn't ready to face. (978-1-63555-665-0)

Journey to Cash by Ashley Bartlett. Cash Braddock thought everything was great, but it looks like her history is about to become her right now. Which is a real bummer. (978-1-63555-464-9)

Love on the Night Shift by Radclyffe. Between ruling the night shift in the ER at the Rivers and raising her teenage daughter, Blaise Richilieu has all the drama she needs in her life, until a dashing young attending appears on the scene and relentlessly pursues her. (978-1-63555-668-1)

Olivia's Awakening by Ronica Black. When the daring and dangerously gorgeous Eve Monroe is hired to get Olivia Savage into shape, a fierce passion ignites, causing both to question everything they've ever known about love. (978-1-63555-613-1)

The Duchess and the Dreamer by Jenny Frame. Clementine Fitzroy has lost her faith and love of life. Can dreamer Evan Fox make her believe in life and dream again? (978-1-63555-601-8)

The Road Home by Erin Zak. Hollywood actress Gwendolyn Carter is about to discover that losing someone you love sometimes means gaining someone to fall for. (978-1-63555-633-9)

Waiting for You by Elle Spencer. When passionate past-life lovers meet again in the present day, one remembers it vividly and the other isn't so sure. (978-1-63555-635-3)

While My Heart Beats by Erin McKenzie. Can a love born amidst the horrors of the Great War survive? (978-1-63555-589-9)

Face the Music by Ali Vali. Sweet music is the last thing that happens when Nashville music producer Mason Liner and daughter of country royalty Victoria Roddy are thrown together in an effort to save country star Sophie Roddy's career. (978-1-63555-532-5)

Flavor of the Month by Georgia Beers. What happens when baker Charlie and chef Emma realize their differing paths have led them right back to each other? (978-1-63555-616-2)

Mending Fences by Angie Williams. Rancher Bobbie Del Rey and veterinarian Grace Hammond are about to discover if heartbreaks of the past can ever truly be mended. (978-1-63555-708-4)

Silk and Leather: Lesbian Erotica with an Edge, edited by Victoria Villaseñor. This collection of stories by award-winning authors offers fantasies as soft as silk and tough as leather. The only question is: How far will you go to make your deepest desires come true? (978-1-63555-587-5)

The Last Place You Look by Aurora Rey. Dumped by her wife and looking for anything but love, Julia Pierce retreats to her hometown only to rediscover high school friend Taylor Winslow, who's secretly crushed on her for years. (978-1-63555-574-5)

The Mortician's Daughter by Nan Higgins. A singer on the verge of stardom discovers she must give up her dreams to live a life in service to ghosts. (978-1-63555-594-3)

The Real Thing by Laney Webber. When passion flares between actress Virginia Green and masseuse Allison McDonald, can they be sure it's the real thing? (978-1-63555-478-6)

What the Heart Remembers Most by M. Ullrich. For college sweethearts Jax Levine and Gretchen Mills, could an accident be the second chance neither knew they wanted? (978-1-63555-401-4)

White Horse Point by Andrews & Austin. Mystery writer Taylor James finds herself falling for the mysterious woman on White Horse Point who lives alone, protecting a secret she can't share about a murderer who walks among them. (978-1-63555-695-7)

Femme Tales by Anne Shade. Six women find themselves in their own real-life fairy tales when true love finds them in the most unexpected ways. (978-1-63555-657-5)